25 ALIVE

Meet The Women's Murder Club

EXCLUSIVE PROFILES **by Our Crime Desk**

LINDSAY BOXER

A homicide detective in the San Francisco Police Department, juggling the worst murder cases with the challenges of being a first-time mother. Her loving husband Joe, daughter Julie and loyal border-collie Martha give her a reason to protect the city. She didn't have the easiest start to life, with an absent father and an ill mother, but she didn't shy away from a difficult and demanding career. With the help of her friends, Lindsay makes it her mission to solve the toughest cases.

CLAIRE WASHBURN

Chief Medical Examiner for San Francisco and one of Lindsay's oldest friends. Wise, confident and viciously funny, she can be relied on to help whatever the problem. She virtually runs the Office of the Coroner for her overbearing, credit-stealing boss, but rarely complains. Happily married with children, her personal life is relatively calm in comparison to her professional life.

CINDY THOMAS

An up-and-coming journalist who's always looking for the next big story. She'll go the extra mile, risking life and limb to get her scoop. Sometimes she prefers to grill her friends over cocktails for a juicy secret, but, luckily for them, she's totally trustworthy (most of the time...). She somehow found the time to publish a book between solving cases, writing articles for the *San Francisco Chronicle* and keeping together her relationship with Lindsay's partner, Rich Conklin.

> "When your job is murder, you need **friends you can count on**"

YUKI CASTELLANO

One of the best lawyers in the city, she's desperate to make her mark. Ambitious, intelligent and passionate, she'll fight for what's right, always defending the underdog even if it means standing in the way of those she loves. Often this includes her husband – who is also Lindsay's boss – Lt. Jackson Brady.

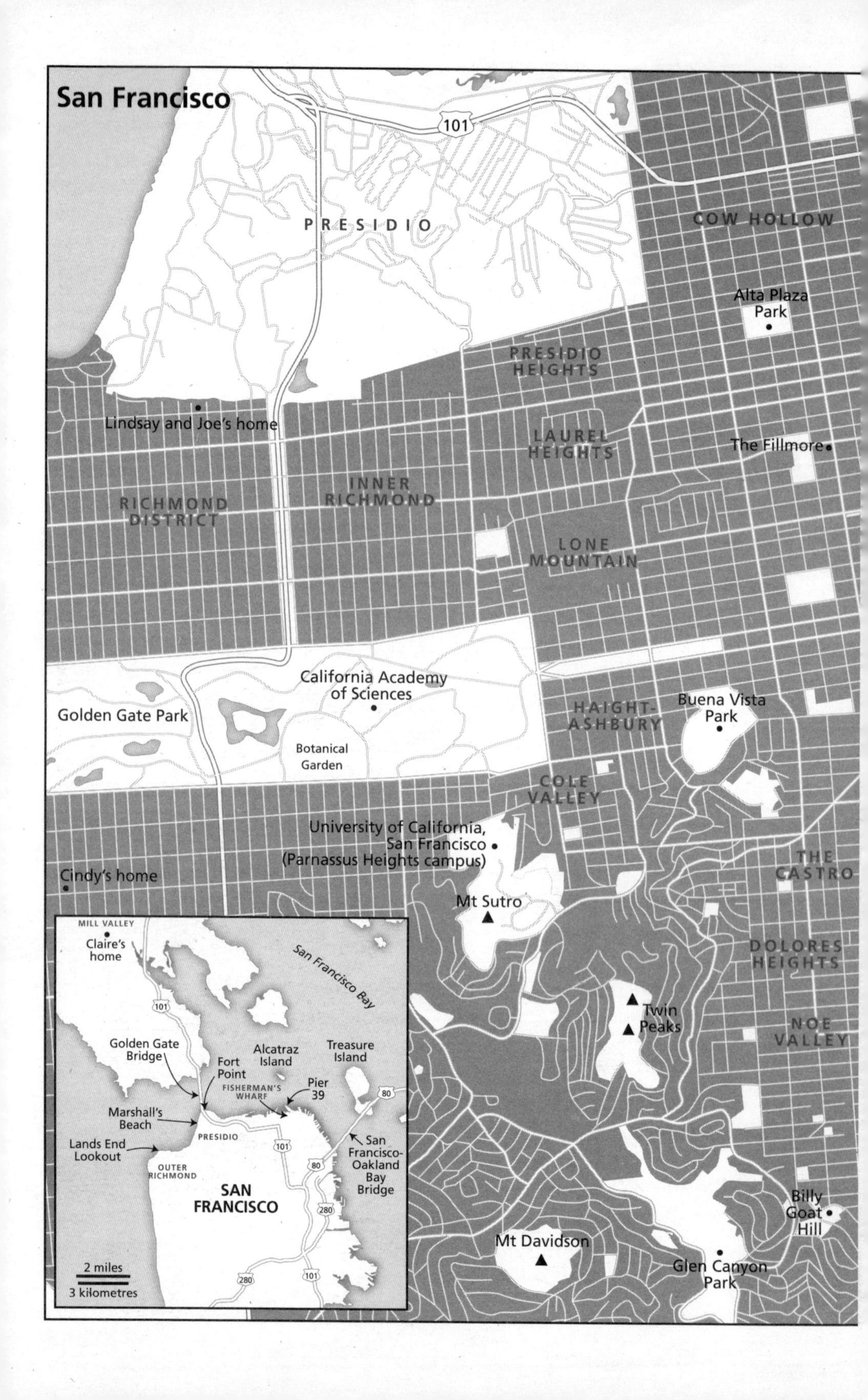
San Francisco
101
PRESIDIO
COW HOLLOW
Alta Plaza Park
PRESIDIO HEIGHTS
Lindsay and Joe's home
LAUREL HEIGHTS
The Fillmore
INNER RICHMOND
RICHMOND DISTRICT
LONE MOUNTAIN
California Academy of Sciences
Golden Gate Park
HAIGHT-ASHBURY
Buena Vista Park
Botanical Garden
COLE VALLEY
University of California, San Francisco (Parnassus Heights campus)
THE CASTRO
Cindy's home
Mt Sutro
DOLORES HEIGHTS
Twin Peaks
NOE VALLEY
Billy Goat Hill
Mt Davidson
Glen Canyon Park
MILL VALLEY
Claire's home
San Francisco Bay
101
Golden Gate Bridge
Alcatraz Island
Treasure Island
Fort Point
FISHERMAN'S WHARF
Pier 39
80
Marshall's Beach
PRESIDIO
Lands End Lookout
San Francisco-Oakland Bay Bridge
OUTER RICHMOND
SAN FRANCISCO
280
2 miles
3 kilometres

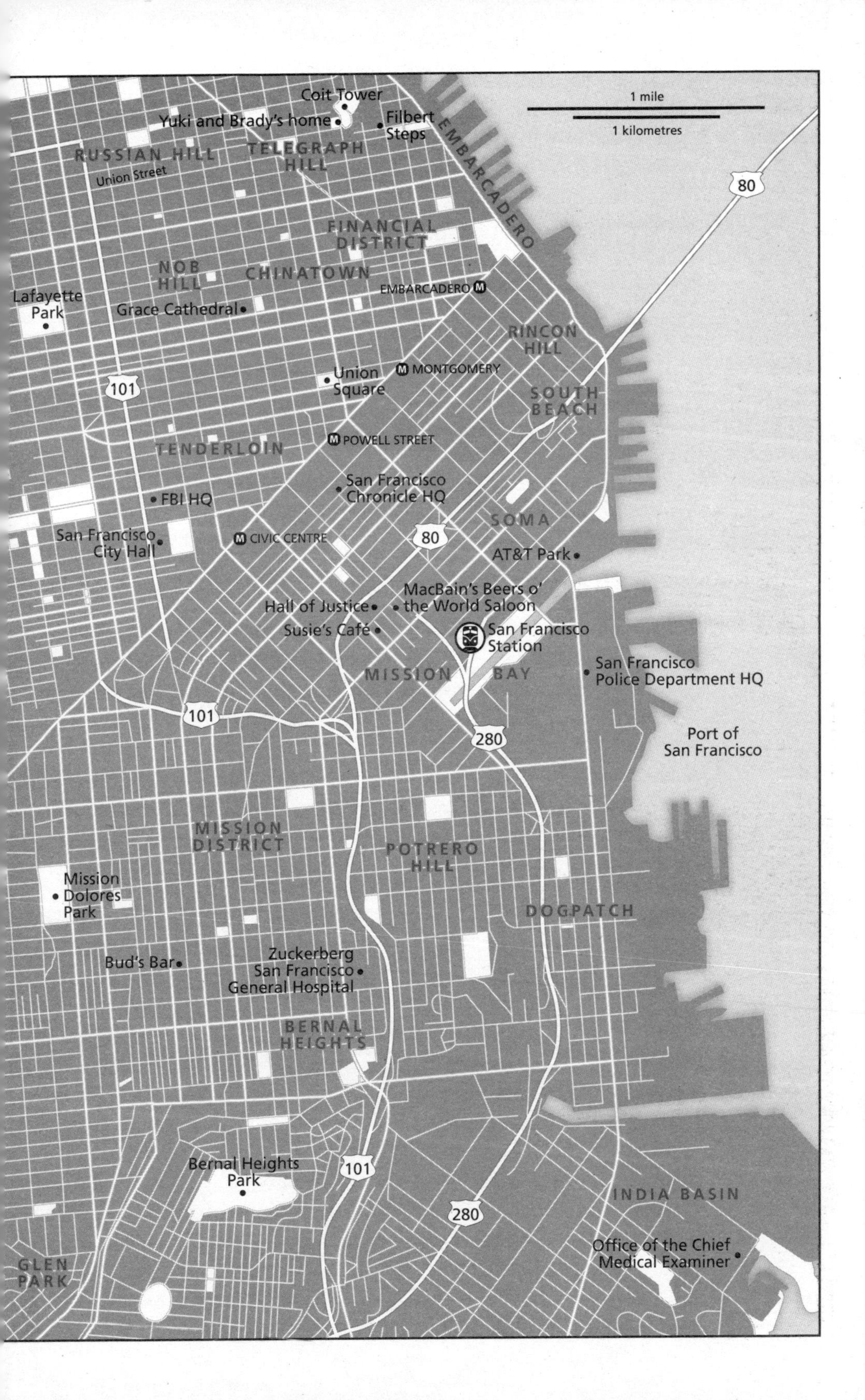
1 mile
1 kilometres
Coit Tower
Yuki and Brady's home
Filbert Steps
EMBARCADERO
RUSSIAN HILL
TELEGRAPH HILL
Union Street
80
FINANCIAL DISTRICT
NOB HILL
CHINATOWN
EMBARCADERO
Lafayette Park
Grace Cathedral
RINCON HILL
Union Square
MONTGOMERY
101
SOUTH BEACH
TENDERLOIN
POWELL STREET
San Francisco Chronicle HQ
FBI HQ
SOMA
San Francisco City Hall
CIVIC CENTRE
80
AT&T Park
MacBain's Beers o' the World Saloon
Hall of Justice
Susie's Café
San Francisco Station
MISSION BAY
San Francisco Police Department HQ
101
280
Port of San Francisco
MISSION DISTRICT
POTRERO HILL
Mission Dolores Park
DOGPATCH
Bud's Bar
Zuckerberg San Francisco General Hospital
BERNAL HEIGHTS
Bernal Heights Park
101
280
INDIA BASIN
Office of the Chief Medical Examiner
GLEN PARK

A list of titles by James Patterson appears
at the back of this book

JAMES PATTERSON
& MAXINE PAETRO

25 ALIVE

C
CENTURY

CENTURY

UK | USA | Canada | Ireland | Australia
India | New Zealand | South Africa

Century is part of the Penguin Random House group of companies
whose addresses can be found at global.penguinrandomhouse.com

Penguin Random House UK,
One Embassy Gardens, 8 Viaduct Gardens, London SW11 7BW

penguin.co.uk
global.penguinrandomhouse.com

First published 2025
001

Set in 12.5/17pt Janson MT Std
Typeset by Jouve (UK), Milton Keynes
Printed and bound in Great Britain by Clays Ltd, Elcograf S.p.A.

The authorised representative in the EEA is Penguin Random House Ireland,
Morrison Chambers, 32 Nassau Street, Dublin D02 YH68

A CIP catalogue record for this book is available from the British Library

ISBN: 978–1–529–92298–1 (hardback)
ISBN: 978–1–529–92300–1 (trade paperback)

Penguin Random House is committed to a sustainable future for our business, our readers and our planet. This book is made from Forest Stewardship Council® certified paper.

This book is dedicated with our thanks to our readers, the unofficial members of the Women's Murder Club.

25
ALIVE

PROLOGUE

ONE

JUST AFTER SIX that morning, Warren Jacobi, a sixty-year-old retired homicide lieutenant and former chief of police, parked his Ford F-150 within walking distance of one of the eastern entrances to Golden Gate Park.

Jacobi was edgy in the best possible way, amped up, excited, feelings he hadn't had in years. Today was the day. After weeks of planning and tracking, within the next hour, he would bring down a killer.

He was a big man, 240 pounds, but he'd stayed in shape. This morning, he wore his bird-watching gear, camouflage pants, and a matching sweater under his tac vest. Binoculars hung from a strap around his neck, and his weapon was wedged against the small of his back by the waistband of his pants.

Jacobi entered the park, keeping to the tree shadows, looking for a merciless killer who delighted in outfoxing the police. Jacobi had to do this alone, and he could—but he was still haunted by the bureaucratic bull crap that had forced him into early retirement. He hadn't been able to shake the humiliation. Bottom line, he would not, could not, close out his life's work by leaving this psychotic predator at large.

Jacobi quickly slipped into a narrow pocket of rampant vegetation, a cleft in the living walls of dense vines and saplings. Inside this natural bivouac, he was virtually invisible but had partial views of the path looping around the Lily Pond below and back up to the street.

Years ago, he'd been walking the park when he saw a man acting suspiciously near the Lily Pond. When a teenage girl's dead body was pulled from the pond later that day, Jacobi knew what he'd witnessed—and what he'd failed to do earlier. He'd been too far away, and it had happened too quickly, for him to even make an ID.

Parting branches and peering around a clump of trees now, Jacobi saw a great blue heron swoop down between the treetops and veer toward the pond. Through the zoom lens in his phone, Jacobi followed the large heron's flight path, then took pictures of the bird with its dark crown and long gray plumes on its breast. Below the heron, at the edge of the pond, Jacobi spotted his subject wearing a dark windbreaker, jeans, and a dark-colored baseball cap. The killer took a gun from his pocket and threw a shot at the bird. The bird veered away at the sound, and the shooter tossed the gun into the water. There was a splash, and then he turned on the path and slowly began to retrace his steps uphill.

Jacobi waited impatiently. He didn't have the authority to perform an arrest, but the former detective had zip ties in his vest pocket. Jacobi planned to surprise the guy as he walked past his hidey-hole and bodycheck him to the ground. Then, once he'd immobilized the SOB, he'd call Chief of Police Charles Clapper to let him know that he had a wanted killer secured and ready for roasting.

TWO

WARREN JACOBI PATTED his vest's breast pocket and pulled out a tangle of zip ties, accidentally snagging the rest of the pocket's contents at the same time. *Never mind.* He shut off his phone's flash and took a few shots of the killer climbing the path. Then Jacobi paused to review the photos he'd just taken.

As he'd expected, the light from the faint sunrise behind him had been just bright enough to define plumage on a big freaking bird, but not so bright as to positively ID the killer. Jacobi slipped the phone into his vest's side pocket—and that's when he felt the crushing grip of a hand between his neck and right shoulder. A voice in his ear said, "You think I haven't seen you tailing me? Don't turn around."

He almost recognized that voice. *Who?*

"Okay, okay. You got me." Jacobi didn't dare resist capture with his back turned. He was tensing his muscles, reaching his right hand around toward the gun in his waistband. But before he touched the grip, he felt a searing pain in his lower right side.

Again and again while he was on his knees, then again and again, dropping him face down on the ground.

Jacobi turned his head to see his attacker, then cried out, "*No!*"

He closed his eyes as what felt like a saw ripped through the right side of his neck. His scream was cut short. As he wheezed out his last breath, Warren Jacobi was no longer in the present.

A soft breeze blew across his face, illuminated images strung together in a bright, lightning-like flash. Jacobi saw himself gathering his family into his arms. Putting a hand on his beloved Muriel's cheek and kissing her. Entering a crime scene in a deep black night with Lindsay Boxer, his ride-or-die former partner. A brilliant sunset lighting up the bay, followed by drinks after work with old friends, his comrades in arms.

He didn't want to die, not like this. He'd called the chief and told him who had cut him down—hadn't he?

But then it didn't matter.

He was gone.

PART ONE

CHAPTER 1

THE WINDOW BLINDS were half open, slashing the morning light to ribbons and flinging them into my face. *Am I late for work?* My phone was on the nightstand, and I picked it up to read the time. *No.* I had just over an hour to eat, dress, play.

I turned to hug my husband, but he wasn't there. Lying beside me in the bed was Julie, our five-year-old little girl, clutching her plush stuffed cow she'd named Mrs. Mooey Milkington.

"Hey," I said, hugging her, "you're not Joe."

"Nope," she said, laughing at me.

"Is he making breakfast?"

"No, Mommy. He had to go out."

"Out where?" I asked her.

"He took the car," she said.

Yes, I love her with all my heart, but this complicated daughter of ours is smart as well as so damned cute, she gets away with maddening behavior—all the time.

"Julie, this is what we cops call 'pulling teeth.' Just tell me where Dad went and why. Please."

"Huh? What does 'pulling teeth' mean?"

"'Pulling teeth' means someone is saying as little as possible about what they know, so the other person must really work hard to get their little girl to tell."

"Ohhhhh," she said. "So, you want me to say that Daddy took Martha to the vet and he'll bring breakfast home after?"

Talk of my elderly border collie, Martha, and her veterinarian in the same sentence turned my heart into a fist. I've known Martha longer than I've known Joe. I'd adopted her from a dog rescue, and it had been love at first sight for both of us. Lately, I'd been consciously ignoring signs of her aging, of her mortality.

I was scared, but I had to ask.

"Why did Daddy take her to the vet, Julie?"

"I'm not pulling your teeth, Mommy. Daddy didn't say why. He just picked Martha up and said he was taking her down to the car."

"Okay. That sounds . . . I'm sorry."

"Sorry for what?" Julie asked me.

"For—*grrrrr*—snapping at you. Okay, we've got to get dressed and eat something, then I'm taking you to the school bus."

"I don't know what to wear," Julie said, bouncing out of bed and running for her room.

CHAPTER 2

I KNEW WHAT to wear. Pushing worry for Martha into the back of my mind, I stripped the dry cleaner's bag from one of my half dozen pairs of blue trousers. I did the same with a blue striped men's tailored shirt, and once dressed, stepped into my regulation brown lace-up shoes.

I called Joe's phone. No answer. Fear was back, morphing into panic. I pressed Redial again. I got his regular upbeat outgoing voicemail message.

I was in the bedroom brushing tangles out of my hair when I heard the front door open and Julie call out, "Dadddddddyyyyy!"

Joe was home, thank God. But Martha wasn't with him. I came into the kitchen and saw he was scowling as he set a bag of pastries down on the kitchen counter.

"Hon? What's wrong with Martha?" I asked.

He said, "Don't know. She just seemed . . . lethargic. Doc's going to run some tests on her."

I sucked in a breath and Joe came over to give me a big

hug. "Tests are good. Martha is having a CAT scan . . . I'll call Dr. Clayton later."

Julie reached her arms around her father's waist and said, "Dogs get CAT scans?"

Joe was beginning to explain when my phone buzzed.

The text from Claire was brief and urgent.

Call me.

I tapped my phone right away and Claire picked up mid-ring.

"Linds. There's been a murder. You should come before we move . . . the body." She yelled away from the phone, "Hey. Step back." Claire Washburn, San Francisco medical examiner and my BFF, sounded rattled. She came back on the line and told me she was on the path by the Lily Pond in Golden Gate Park, and that I should hurry. *What the hell?*

"On my way," I told her. Now that Joe was back home, he could handle getting Julie off to school.

I took my Glock from our gun safe, shrugged on my shoulder holster, and slid the weapon into place. As I was hanging the chain with my badge over my head, Joe called out that he'd brought crullers and had put the coffee on. I called back that I was needed at work.

"Please call me as soon as you know something about our good dog," I said as I hurried into the kitchen to say good-bye before leaving.

"The tech won't be in until this afternoon," Joe pointed out.

I nodded. I kissed my husband, then stooped to kiss our little girl on each cheek, checking for tears shed over Martha. None yet. I squeezed Julie's shoulders, and she hugged me hard around my neck. I murmured that Martha would be home soon, then stood up and kissed Joe again. I felt two pairs of eyes on me as I made for the door.

I fled down the stairs to the street.

CHAPTER 3

I PHONED MY boss, Jackson Brady, from the car to let him know that Claire had called me to a murder scene at Golden Gate Park. "She wants me to see the body in situ in the park, ASAP."

Brady said, "Check in with me when you get there. I don't know squat about this homicide."

I copied that and strapped in. I took a quick detour on my way to the park, stopping at the car pool in front of the Hall of Justice just long enough to exchange my blue Explorer for a squad car. I translated Claire's urgency as Code 3, meaning all lights, sirens, and maximum speed.

The street that accessed the park's Lily Pond was blocked by three squad cars, and both the Forensics unit and the coroner's van. I pulled up to the curb, disembarked, and followed a spur of pavement to a parking area that was cordoned off with yellow barrier tape—a warning to joggers and curiosity seekers to stay the hell out.

I badged a uniform named Maggie Cannon. She held up

the tape and gave me a warning look, like I was headed toward a five-car pileup. I didn't question her, just ducked under the tape and kept going. I found Claire standing with four uniformed officers inside a smaller taped-off perimeter within the larger one. Even from a dozen paces, I could see that the victim was lying face down in a pool of blood.

"Who's in charge?" I asked.

"I just spoke to Brady," said Claire. "You're it."

I knew two of the uniforms protecting the scene: sergeants Nardone and Einhorn. I texted Brady to give him an update and gloved up.

Einhorn handed me a pair of booties, and Nardone said, "Lean on me," which I did as I slipped the booties over my shoes.

I entered the smaller perimeter and looked at Claire. She shook her head and said of the victim, "I just can't believe this. It's . . . it's so *bad* . . . " Her voice cracked.

I didn't understand what she'd said. "Are you okay, Claire?"

She didn't answer me, just looked down at the dead man, whose face was turned away from me. I could see that he had bled profusely from wounds in his lower back, and from a ragged tear halfway around his neck and face. The only other things I could really determine from where I stood was that he was a gray-haired white man dressed in camouflage pants, a matching sweater, a tactical vest, and rubber-soled shoes. A CSI flag was next to a pair of binoculars lying just outside the tape, half hidden in the shrubbery. *Was this guy a bird-watcher?*

Claire's primary investigator, Sage Dugan, had stooped beside the body and was taking photos. Since Claire seemed unresponsive, I asked Dugan, "Did he have a camera?"

"If he had one, it's gone," she said. "Just a cell phone. And the binoculars are not the photographic kind."

"Any sign of the murder weapon?"

The CSI held out a plastic evidence bag with a knife inside. It was a KA-BAR and it was made for killing. The blade was sturdy, good for jabbing and slashing. The handle was equal in length to the blade, rounded for a firm grip and designed for bludgeoning.

I remembered that there'd been some holdups in this neighborhood. A masked robber, or a pair of them, had stolen expensive camera gear—thousand-dollar cameras with German lenses—but nothing more violent had been reported than shouts of "Don't make me hurt you! Hand over the camera!"

"We've got his wallet?" I asked.

Claire spoke up. "No wallet. Had some loose cash and credit cards, and an ID in his vest pocket. He's carrying, too, but the gun is still in his waistband." She paused, then said, "Linds. This is going to hurt."

I don't know the victim—do I? Something was trying to break through the smoke screen obscuring much of my working memory.

Claire called my name, and I turned to her.

"What is it, Claire? Who is the victim?"

She sputtered, then said, "It's Warren Jacobi. He was ... killed."

CHAPTER 4

I STARED AT the dead man, but I didn't believe what Claire had told me. I said, "This can't be Jacobi. He . . . He . . . He's retired."

"I'm so, so sorry, Linds," said Claire.

She put her arms around me. Her sobs released mine, and Claire and I both cried into the other's shoulder until, somehow, I finally accepted the unimaginable.

When we let go, Claire asked, "Can you handle this?"

"No. But I have to."

Another tidal wave of disbelief and grief washed over me. I loved Jacobi. He'd been my first partner in the Homicide squad. Everything I hadn't learned in the Academy, he'd taught me by example at crime scenes or explained to me inside a patrol car. We'd bonded early, and our deep friendship had continued before and after he cut loose from his job, his career, his reason for being.

And now Warren Jacobi was dead, lying curled up at my feet. I leaned down and put my hand on his shoulder.

"I'm so sorry this happened to you, my dear friend," I said, looking into my former partner's face. "You have good friends working to find out who did this to you. And that person who did this will damn well pay. I hope that you know I'm here."

I smoothed his hair and kept my hand on his forehead. I couldn't be sure if it was true or my imagination, but I thought he still felt warm. Everyone around me was quiet. I took another moment to pray, and when I said, "Amen," the little group echoed that solemn word.

Then I inspected Jacobi's injuries, snapping photos with my phone. My vision was blurred by tears, but from what I could see of the degree and angles of his wounds, Jacobi hadn't seen the attack coming. He hadn't even pulled his piece. From what Claire had told me so far, this assault didn't sound like a robbery.

But then why? What had been the killer's motive? Had it been a personal beef? Someone who'd hated Jacobi? Or was my old friend a victim of circumstance?

I turned and asked Claire, "What do we know?"

CHAPTER 5

CLAIRE CLEARED HER throat, then ran the facts.

"Time of death, approximately two, two and a half hours ago, so, say 6 something a.m. The killer surprised him from behind and knew how to use a blade."

Einhorn said, "Plus a matchbook we found in the ferns over there."

"Let me see."

CSI Dugan opened her kit and held up a small, clear plastic evidence bag containing a matchbook with JULIO's printed on the cover. I recognized the design. It matched the look of the sign belonging to a dark hole of a bar on Valencia Street at the edge of the Mission District. I'd driven past it but never been inside.

"Don't know if it belonged to the victim or it's been there for days. But either way, it's interesting," Dugan said. "Look at the writing inside."

I managed to open the matchbook without removing it from the evidence bag and saw that someone had used a ballpoint pen to inscribe a message in block lettering on the inside cover. I could just make out the words: I SAID. YOU DEAD.

What? What the hell does that mean?

I handed the bagged matchbook back to Dugan and addressed the people around me. "'I said. You dead.' We're assuming this was left here by the killer. Is the killer bragging? Fulfilling a prophecy? Has anyone heard this statement before?"

There were no ideas at that moment, but we were just getting started.

I edged out of the scene to let the CSIs and the Forensics unit do their work as ME's team raised the tape, hefted Jacobi's body onto a gurney, and rolled it toward the van.

I walked like a zombie to my squad car. I turned it on, released the brake, backed up, then headed east on Nancy Pelosi Drive and toward the Hall of Justice.

At a stoplight, my mind was flooded with fresh images of Jacobi's lifeless, bloodied body, the horrible sight of his head half sawn off by a strong hand with a killing knife. Tears spilled and I didn't try to stop them. Warren Jacobi had been a great cop as well as my mentor, partner, and friend to the end.

That made his murder personal.

CHAPTER 6

WHEN I REACHED the Hall of Justice, I took the stairs three flights up from the lobby to the Homicide squad room. I yanked open the wood-framed glass outer door, bumped the hinged gate with my hip, and entered our small bullpen, a study in its many shades of gray. The day shift was filling the room with the crackle and buzz of conversation. Telephones rang at every desk.

Our front desk guard dog, Robert Nussbaum, was at his station.

I asked, "Is Brady in?"

"And good morning to you, Sarge."

"Too late for that, Bob. But thanks."

He pointed down the center aisle to the glass-walled office at the far end of the squad room. Jackson Brady was visible, leaning back in his chair with his phone to his ear. I waved to Richie Conklin and Sonia Alvarez as I rounded the turn, then started down the aisle. I nodded to Wang and Michaels, narrowly missed bumping into Samuels, and kept going.

The glass door to Brady's office was closed, but I could also see Assistant District Attorney Yuki Castellano, Brady's wife and my dear friend, sitting inside on a side chair, wearing a smart, gray, grown-up pin-striped suit and three-inch heels.

"Hey," I said to Brenda Fregosi, Brady's assistant. "I like your hair."

Two long blond braids hung down her back.

"Thanks, Lindsay. Can I do something for you?"

"I have to see the lieutenant. How long before he's free?"

She shrugged. "I never know."

That's when Brady hung up his phone. Yuki got to her feet, spoke to him briefly, then leaned down and kissed him good-bye. Our paths met in the doorway, and she gripped my hand.

"Oh God, oh God," said Yuki. "Brady just told me about Jacobi. I cannot believe it. Why would anyone kill him?"

"Not a clue," I said. "Really. I never expected anything like this. He should have had another twenty-five years."

"At least. Call me when you can," Yuki said.

Brady keyed his intercom and asked Brenda to hold his calls.

Then he waved me into his office.

CHAPTER 7

CINDY THOMAS WAS at her desk at 8 a.m.

The petite, curly-haired blonde wearing a rhinestone-studded hair band and loose-fitting clothes looked nothing like what she was—a tenacious investigative reporter, twice-published bestselling true-crime author, and leading writer on the *San Francisco Chronicle*'s crime beat.

Cindy's coffee mug was beside her right hand, her police scanner crackled on the windowsill, and her laptop was open. She was completely absorbed in her reading: the editorial page of a New York tabloid called the *City News Flash.* The top letter to the editor took up most of the screen—and it was making her sick.

The headline above the letter read, NEWS FLASH. "I SAID. YOU DEAD."

The text read, "NOT a joke. I just stumbled upon the blood-soaked body of corrupt former San Francisco Homicide cop Warren Jacobi inside Golden Gate Park."

That sentence raised the hairs on the back of Cindy's neck.

What kind of crap is this? Warren Jacobi was not *corrupt and he was* not *dead.* She reread the letter, which claimed to be a first-person account of a passerby who had just come across Jacobi's dead body, wrote it up, and sent it to the *Flash.* The second graf described the clothing Jacobi had been wearing as "a bird-watching outfit" and said that he'd been "knifed to death." It went on to say that a matchbook with the message "I said. You dead" had been left nearby.

The author was "Anonymous," and nowhere did the writer say that the crime or the victim's name had been verified by law enforcement. But the last time Cindy spoke to Jacobi, he *had* told her that he was photographing birds, recording their signature songs. Bird-watching was his new hobby.

Oh, my God. Cindy clapped her hands over her eyes. This could not be true. No newspaper, not even a rag like the *Flash,* would print anything about a murder without a statement from the police. But there was no such confirmation. Nothing from Chief Clapper or Lieutenant Brady. She'd tried reaching her cop husband, but her call had gone straight to Richie's voicemail. Had she missed a mention of it on the scanner? No. This crime hadn't happened. No freaking way.

Cindy dropped her hands from her eyes and printed out the nightmare from the *City News Flash* letters to the editor.

Beyond her desk was a large window in her wall that looked out onto the newsroom. Her coworkers were all on deadline, working hard and fast on their columns and assignments. There were shouts across the floor to "Look at this," the voices penetrating the glass.

She took the printout from the printer tray and read it again. The bombshell was time-stamped 9:15 a.m., East Coast time, today, so 6:15 a.m. local. A little less than two hours ago. If true, the writer had emailed his or her findings to that infamous New York City tabloid in the time it took a second hand to sweep around a clock's dial.

Why had Anonymous sent this letter to the *Flash*? To take credit? To win a bet? To get revenge? To get published? One thing was sure: Whoever wrote and sent that smut to the *Flash* knew something that she did not.

CHAPTER 8

CINDY'S PHONE BUZZED with an incoming call. She grabbed it, hoping it was Richie calling her back. But no. It was a reporter from the *Examiner* who had also read the letter in the *Flash* and was asking her for a comment.

"I have nothing, Sarah. Just what you have."

"How about a quote about how you miss him or something?"

"Take care, Sarah. I've gotta go."

There was a tap on Cindy's wall. She saw Phil Balshi standing outside her office. He signaled that he wanted to come in, and didn't wait for an okay.

Once inside, he said, "Something big just broke. Warren Jacobi was found dead this morning."

"It's a rumor," Cindy said.

"Oh. I see. No corroboration from SFPD?"

"Right, Phil, it's *gossip* until or if Clapper verifies this. Sit on it, okay?"

As Balshi returned to his desk, Cindy sent a text to Jacobi.

She hoped he'd answer, then after they laughed, they'd track down the bastard who'd made up this garbage. When Jacobi didn't reply immediately, Cindy stared out the window into the city room for ten minutes, then texted him again. There was still no reply, so she tried her good friend Lindsay, Richie's SFPD partner. No answer from her, either. She tried her husband again, typing *URGENT* in all caps. And when she *still* got no reply, she phoned Frank Barto at the SFPD.

Barto's job was to keep the police blotter, an ongoing, constantly updated record of all incidents phoned in by police officers, citizens filing complaints, and witnesses reporting crimes.

He picked up on the second ring and said, "Make this quick, Cindy. I'm taking incoming."

Cindy said, "Frank, d'you have a murder in Golden Gate Park?"

Barto told Cindy, "Uhhh. Can't say. A call came into dispatch a few hours ago about a potential victim in the park," he said. "I notified Sergeant Nardone. This is between us, Cindy. Do not quote me."

Cindy pressed Barto for more details, but he dug in his heels and claimed not to have the victim's name. "And even if I did, I wouldn't share it with you."

"Frank. Just tell me this. Was he or she with the SFPD?"

"I don't know. Maybe." Cindy's stomach dropped as Barto continued. "Remember, Cindy. Leave me out of this. I like my job."

"Thanks, Frank. Don't worry. You've told me nothing."

"Use your wiles," Barto said. "I'm hanging up."

Barto had given her an unquotable hint, but it was verification enough for her. Jacobi was dead.

Cindy spun her chair around so that she was no longer facing her window onto the newsroom. Then she bent over and cried into her hands.

CHAPTER 9

BRADY SAID, "TERRIBLE news about Jacobi, Lindsay. I'm so sorry."

I nodded, thanked him, and pulled out the chair across from my boss. I propped my feet against the front of his desk and leaned my chair onto its hind legs. The chair creaked. Brady moved piles of papers out of my way. I wanted to be present, but my mind was swamped with too many images. This had been my office once, and it had also been Jacobi's. Brady slid a pack of tissues toward me and I leaned forward again to take it.

"Jacobi's murder is job one," he said.

I nodded and took my hand back so I could pat my eyes dry with the tissues.

Brady said, "Talk to me."

I told Brady about Jacobi's gruesome death, my assessment that he had been unaware of his killer coming up behind him, and that "Jacobi was carrying a piece in his waistband, but he didn't pull it."

Brady made notes as I talked, broke a pencil or two, and looked sadder than I'd ever seen him.

"You have pictures?"

I opened my phone's picture library, found the photos of Jacobi's dead body, and handed the phone over to Brady, saying, "See here. He was stabbed multiple times. And this slash across his neck . . . "

"His carotid," said Brady. He gave a deep sigh. "That . . . That took him out fast."

Brady swore as he scrolled through the horrific images and then he had questions. Did I know any Jacobi haters? Why was Jacobi wearing a bird-watcher's outfit? Did I have any ideas that could shed light on the motive for his murder?

I answered, "I don't know." "I have no idea." "I don't frickin' know."

Brady said, "So, Boxer. We have nothing to go on."

"We have one measly clue. Maybe. CSIs found a matchbook nearby from a bar called Julio's. It's a hole-in-the-wall on Valencia Street. I've never been inside."

I took back my phone and showed Brady pictures of the matchbook and read aloud the "I said. You dead" inscription inside.

"If that's from the killer, he's a narcissistic psycho," Brady said.

I could only nod. "The matchbook is at the lab. I'll have Alvarez and Conklin check out Julio's as soon as the bar opens."

My phone pinged with a text. I glanced at the message and typed, *BRB.* Then I said to Brady, "Claire's doing Jacobi's postmortem now. She told me you said this case is mine. Right?"

I was prepared for a flat no, Brady changing his mind and deciding that I was too close to the victim.

But he surprised me, saying, "You and Conklin take the lead on Jacobi. I'll put Cappy and Chi on this, too. They'll report to you, Boxer. Grab up a task force and I'll head it."

I needed no convincing. I returned the side chair to its upright position and was preparing to leave Brady's office when his phone rang.

He picked up and held up a finger to me, meaning *Wait.* He said into the phone, "Say again, Gene."

As he asked his caller for details, I worked out who Brady was talking with. It had to be Crime Scene Unit director Eugene Hallows. While I wondered what was being said, Brady grabbed his yellow pad and a pencil and quickly wrote down what looked like an address.

He said, "I've got it, Gene." Then he pounded the receiver down on the console hook and said to me, "That was Hallows. He says there's another dead body near the park."

"No! Where? Who?"

"A woman was killed in her apartment, a couple blocks from the park. Hallows is on his way over there. Get that task force together, Boxer. I want to brief Clapper before the close of day."

CHAPTER 10

CINDY PRESSED HER desk phone hard to her ear and waited impatiently as it rang and rang. Where was Richie? Why wasn't he picking up? Did he know about Jacobi?

Finally, her husband answered, "Conklin."

"Hey," she said. "It's me. I just read—"

"Cin, I'm working. Can I call you later?"

"This is important. And it'll just take a second."

"I'm timing you."

"Okay, so a New York tabloid, the *City News Flash,* carried an anonymous letter about a murder in Golden Gate Park. Said the victim is Warren Jacobi. Our Jacobi. The story was posted online this morning."

Cindy hoped that Richie would either deny the so-called news of Jacobi's death or say, *I'll get back to you.* She heard unintelligible muffled voices in the background over Rich's phone. Wherever he was, he wasn't alone.

"Rich? Did you hear me?" she pressed. She had a feeling Rich was going to be a dead end. That's how cops, even those married to crime reporters, behaved. Admittedly a good thing, even if not good for her.

"I'm going to have to make some sketchy promises," Cindy muttered to herself.

"Cin, put your mouth next to the little holes."

Cindy adjusted the phone and said, "Sorry, can you hear me now? Rich, I have to ask you something—"

"About Jacobi," he said. "Lindsay and I are working on it. It's horrible. And now this."

So it was true. But what was "now this" about? "This what?"

"I'll call you later. Okay?"

"I just want to say one more thing."

"I'm listening. Make it quick."

"Whoever wrote this letter and sent it to the *City News Flash*. In New York! And used Jacobi's name! Whoever wrote the letter quoted the 'I said. You dead' written inside the cover of a matchbook and used Jacobi's name. That information could have only come from the killer or a leak—"

"A leak?" Conklin barked. "What are you saying?"

"This anonymous letter in the *Flash* was dated this morning at 9:15 a.m., 6:15 *our time.* That's inside news that could have been sent by the—"

Rich raised his voice and said to Cindy, "What are you saying?" Then, "Oh, God. I hear you. I'll call Brady."

"It's going to *blow up,* Rich. I've already been called by the *Examiner* looking for a quote. It'll be twenty-four-hour news *starting now*... If Brady has contacts in New York—"

"I'll move as fast as possible, Cindy. Brady's in a meeting with Clapper. You talk to Tyler," he said, meaning Cindy's boss, Henry Tyler, the *Chronicle*'s publisher. "We need some time before this story breaks."

"Richie. It's *already* out," Cindy said loudly to the dead phone line. *Damn it.* She clicked off the phone, then grabbed the printout of the letter in this morning's *City News Flash* and ran for Tyler's office.

CHAPTER 11

HENRY TYLER WAS editor-in-chief and publisher of the great *San Francisco Chronicle,* and he and Cindy had a special relationship. Years ago, she'd been instrumental in locating his kidnapped five-year-old daughter and getting her home. He'd thought of Cindy as a family member ever since.

As Cindy crossed the teeming newsroom and struck out for Tyler's corner office, she reminded herself not to box Tyler in. If he gave her the go-ahead, she would write the story. If not, she would try him again, later.

Cindy knocked on the chief's door.

Tyler called out, "Come innnnn." Then the boss said, "Hey, Cindy. I have three minutes."

"I only need one."

"Okay. Shoot."

Cindy laid down what she was now thinking of as "a psycho-killer's self-promotional ad" on Tyler's desk. She picked up a pencil and drew an arrow to the headline on the letter sent to a New York tabloid, then put the page in front of Tyler.

"Did you see this?" Cindy said.

Tyler pushed his glasses up so they were closer to his eyes as he read. "What the hell?"

"I need a green light," she said.

"Jacobi? Warren Jacobi was murdered? Is this true?"

Cindy lowered her head. "I'm 99 percent sure, but—"

"Get 100 percent, Cindy. Call your husband."

"I already did. He can't talk to me about this. I also confirmed it with my source on the police blotter. Sort of. He would only confirm that a call came in about a possible crime in that area. He wouldn't tell me the victim's name."

Tyler said, "Call Lieutenant Brady. If he won't help, I'll call Chief Clapper. Call your friend Dr. Washburn. If you can get a reliable source on record, you've got your green light. I want to see your copy an hour before you submit it to edit."

Cindy said, "Thanks, Henry." As she left Tyler's office, she was already composing her lede.

CHAPTER 12

I STOOD SURVEYING Frances Robinson's murder scene, the second one I'd attended this morning.

I was still shocked from seeing Jacobi's dead body two hours ago and now this. According to the time-of-death estimates, Robinson's murder had occurred sometime *before* Jacobi was killed.

Her top-floor condo had a glorious north-facing view of Golden Gate Park, and was only two blocks away from where Jacobi had been found at the Lily Pond. I didn't have to be psychic to feel that these two murders were connected. But the how, who, and why were opaque.

There were three evidence markers near the foyer. Only three. Robinson's killer was a pro. Maybe CSU would find trace evidence, but from where I stood, her killer had left nothing behind but a dead woman and a pool of blood.

I was here with Rich Conklin and Cappy McNeil. We all wore booties and gloves, and CSI had plugged in 360-degree high-intensity scene lights to better see every inch of the murder scene. Two other CSIs sketched and photographed the room. Conklin walked to the mantel over the fireplace and bagged a framed photo of the victim while Cappy and I checked out the other rooms, again.

I asked Cappy for his thoughts. Cappy is a first-rate homicide inspector of long standing. He likes to say he's of the "beat" generation. Not of the 1960s, but because he walked a beat in the '90s. Cappy knows every confidential informant and cop over the age of forty in San Francisco. He was once partnered up with Warren Jacobi.

Cappy took off his cap, slapped it against his thigh, and said, "This might be something. I called Fran Robinson's sister, Natalie Cook. She told me that Fran used to be married to a jerk named Paul Robinson for around four years. You know who I mean? The fat-cat real estate developer?"

"I know his name."

Cappy continued: "The sister told me that Paul Robinson was a serial womanizer. A real dog. Natalie said Frances reached the point of no return a couple of years ago and sued the bum for divorce."

Conklin walked up as Cappy was talking. "I remember reading about that," he said. "After the divorce he moved to Maine, I think."

"Natalie also told me that Fran is a well-known author. I looked her up," Cappy said. "She was an author of forty-three romance novels, bestsellers all."

I typed that note into my phone and then searched the closets and cabinets in the bedroom, looking for an idea, a connection to Jacobi, a lead of any kind. Nothing popped.

Back in the living room, Conklin and I frisked a few hundred books. We found no dog-ears, no bookmarks, no underlined text, and no notes to or from Mr. Robinson. Conklin took a call as I walked over to Fran Robinson's office area. It was as tidy as an operating room.

CHAPTER 13

FRANCES ROBINSON'S LAPTOP was open and angled so that it faced the desk chair. I lightly tapped her computer touch pad to wake the screen and turned the computer around, wondering what she'd last been working on.

There was only a single page open on the screen, and blank but for four words centered and typed in twenty-point boldface type.

I SAID. YOU DEAD.

Conklin came over and stood behind my right shoulder. "Jesus. This again."

"Here's our connection to Jacobi. Right?"

I called out to CSI Dale Culver. "Dale. I need you over here. Get a shot of the screen."

I pulled out my phone and snapped a photo of the four enigmatic words myself.

That line had to be behind the killer's motive, but how so and what did it mean?

Our crew of homicide cops came together in the center of the living room, exchanged comments and theories. We were all in agreement that the smartly furnished condo looked like a spread in *Architectural Digest.* It hadn't been rifled or tossed, and there were no signs that anything had been stolen from Frances Robinson—except for her life, of course.

Sometime in the last few hours, a killer had delivered one bullet to her brain and another to her chest.

I pictured how the murder might have gone down.

The shooter rings Fran Robinson's doorbell. Does she know him? Was it her ex-husband? Maybe the killer was wearing a uniform. Did he present himself as a cop? Or a utility worker? Was the killer a woman? An avid romance fan gone wild?

Fran opens her door. *Hello?*

Bang-bang.

The killer steps over the body, careful not to bloody the soles of his shoes. He walks across the hardwood floor to Fran's desk. Wearing gloves, he opens the laptop, calls up a blank page, and types, "I SAID. YOU DEAD." Then the killer moves on.

The sky is still black and moonless when Robinson's killer leaves by the building's service door without drawing attention to himself. Then he beats it over to Golden Gate Park, where he assassinates Warren Jacobi.

Were my old friend and Frances Robinson random victims of a spree killer? Or did they have a connection?

And if so, what was it?

CHAPTER 14

YUKI CASTELLANO GATHERED up her silk scarf and shoulder bag from the passenger seat of her car. She was reaching across the console for her computer case when a knock on the driver's side door startled her. She whipped around to see Nick Gaines, her friend and second chair of choice, but this was the first time in ten years that he'd ever met her in the All Day Parking lot.

Gaines said, "Hey there, Yuki."

She said, "Well, Nick. This is a first. What's up?"

He hooked a thumb over his shoulder toward the Hall of Justice across the street, the huge gray granite building that housed the DA's office, a half dozen courtrooms, administration, motorcycle police, a jail, and the Southern Division of the SFPD. A mob was circling the sidewalk outside the Hall's front entrance, carrying signs and chanting as they marched.

Gaines held out his hand, saying, "I'll drop off your keys. Be right back."

He took Yuki's car keys to Kenny, the key keeper in the

kiosk, then returned to the car. "Kenny says he's got money on you for the win."

Yuki turned and waved at Kenny. Gaines handed her the ticket and a hand up and out of the driver's seat.

Yuki was shading her eyes from the sun when she saw what Gaines had been pointing to across Bryant Street's four wide lanes. "Nicky. Am I reading that right? 'Dario Innocent. Cops Guilty.' "

"You know Dario has a fan base," said Nick. "He can sing and he's got some dance moves. Ever see him dance? A couple of years ago he was on *America's Got Dancers*."

"Huh. I just know him as an unconvicted serial killer," Yuki said.

Esteban Dario Garza, known simply as Dario, was a handsome and wealthy twenty-three-year-old on trial for the murder of a single victim—but Yuki was certain there had been many others. Over the past three years, seven young women had been found killed by different methods—some were shot, others were stabbed, bludgeoned, or strangled to death—but all of the women had last been seen at dance clubs, their dead bodies later found wrapped in sheets in shallow graves and left in nearly identical poses, with their hands clasped over their breasts. In each case, Dario had been seen at the same clubs, but nothing more significant tied the victims to him, and neither the San Francisco crime lab nor the local FBI field office had been able to locate any definitive evidence. And so Yuki was not prosecuting Dario for the deaths of these young women.

She was prosecuting Dario for murdering someone who'd *talked* about him killing these women.

And for that murder, there'd been a witness.

"Don't worry," Nick said. "I've been working out. You're safe with me."

Yuki laughed as Gaines, a slight young man with a neat blond haircut and wearing a khaki suit, flexed his arm in a parody of a macho man.

While they waited to cross the street, she told him the mob wasn't what she was worried about. "I'm worried about Dario. I'll be the one dancing once he's in prison for life."

Brave talk, Yuki thought, again reading the words DARIO INNOCENT painted in shocking red paint on protestors' poster boards. But convicting Dario of capital murder was going to be like running in quicksand during a hurricane. Complicating matters was that Dario, remanded to a holding cell in the sixth-floor jail for the last two months, had let word get around that if he was found guilty, there would be blood to pay. A lot of it. And none of it would be his. This was widely interpreted as: If Dario was convicted, his father, a ruthless cartel boss, would have a bloody party.

During one of Yuki's depositions, Dario had confirmed the future bloodletting to her face and even told her to "spread the word."

She had said, "A fine idea," and then arranged to have police and security assigned to the stairways, elevators, and the entire second floor while court was in session.

As the morning rush whizzed by on Bryant Street, Yuki thought about Dario, the good-looking monster who'd taunted her in meetings with his lawyer. She mentally ticked off the killings she couldn't even charge him with, but she had a good case against him starting today.

The light changed and she only knew it because Gaines said, "Hey. Yuki. Let's go."

"If we don't put this guy away . . . " Yuki muttered as the two of them crossed the street.

"Stop doing that," Gaines said. "We've got him. Got him good. He's going away forever."

"From your lips, pard."

Gaines put his hand on Yuki's back and steered her across the street and over the curb to the sidewalk. That's when the protestors and press closed in around them, pushing microphones and cell phones up to Yuki's face.

"Look," someone shouted. "It's her!"

"ADA Castellano, I'm Seth Carter from the *Seattle Times*—"

"Ms. Castellano, I'm Marcia Briggs, *Boston Globe.* Is it true that Dario maintains that this trial is a joke? That he was arrested under false—"

"Yuki, Sarah Cole from the *Examiner.* I have it on good authority that Dario's friends and family are going to war with you—"

Before Yuki and Gaines could charge through the gaggle, six uniformed cops appeared. They grouped around Yuki and Nick and escorted them up the stairs to the Hall.

CHAPTER 15

THE ELECTRIC CLOCK on the eastern wall of courtroom 2A read 9:34, about a half hour before go time. Yuki and Nick Gaines sat at the prosecution table, Yuki mentally rehearsing the first lines of her opening statement while Gaines scrolled through emails on his phone.

She and Nick had tried dozens of cases in 2A, as they had inside each of the five other identical oak-paneled courtrooms along the second-floor corridor. Yuki usually felt like these courtrooms were extensions of the DA's office suite at the far end of the floor. But now, as she silently went over her opening statement, she felt less like she was in familiar territory and more like a young girl in a smart, gray, grown-up pin-stripe suit and three-inch heels about to be tried for imposter syndrome.

Yuki straightened her lapels again and scrolled through the notes on her phone, doing her best to steady herself for what the media was calling "The made-for-feature-film face-off between the law and the lawless." Yuki understood that, win or lose, she would be known for the Dario verdict.

And her mentor and superior, District Attorney Leonard Parisi, recently returned from medical leave after a heart attack, was still projecting onto her his doubts about the odds of winning this case.

Which was not helpful.

DA Parisi was known around the Hall as Red Dog for his grizzled red hair, his 3XL size, and his ferocity at trial. He had acquired an impressive record of wins during his career. He was a damned good prosecutor, and Yuki owed him a lot. Still, his recent heart attack was not his first. This one was "massive." Yet even after being discharged from the hospital, he had been coming into the office regularly and refused to stay at home.

Yuki took her briefcase from the table and placed it on the floor beside a table leg, glancing across the aisle at Dario's defense attorney, Jon Credendino.

Jon Credendino was a "bomb" from Los Angeles. He was tall. Photogenic. A Harvard Law graduate. And after thirty years spent defending the worst of humankind, he no longer needed the attention of the fourth estate. He didn't need the money, either. So why was Credendino representing the suspected killer Dario Garza?

Why? He was doing it for the challenge. For the glory of getting another high-profile client off without jail time.

Credendino looked unworried. He and his second chair, Donna Villanova, were chatting and softly laughing together. Then they both half turned and smiled at her.

Yuki wished she felt as blasé as Credendino looked. She shot the defense a fake smile of her own and turned away.

Gaines texted her without looking up: *He's scared of us. Terrified.*

Yuki side-kicked his leg, making him laugh. Well, if Credendino expected to destroy her case, he was going to have to work hard to discredit the prosecution's star witness.

The courtroom had filled with spectators. As Yuki glanced at the clock and saw it was now ten, Judge Martin Orlofsky entered the courtroom through the door behind the bench. The bailiff walked to the front of the courtroom and called out, "All rise."

All did.

Judge Orlofsky was a boyish-looking forty-five-year-old with rumpled brown hair, rimless glasses, and a Wounded Warrior pin on the collar of his robe. He was new to the criminal court division. Yuki had never tried a case before Orlofsky and knew little about him except his reputation for being lenient and compassionate. Not qualities she would have wished for under these circumstances—at all.

Once Orlofsky was seated at the bench, the bailiff swore in the jurors and directed them to sit also. Then the judge introduced himself to the jury, as well as Credendino and Villanova, the counsels for the defense, and Yuki and Nick for the State.

Yuki gripped the edge of her chair. Only one person was missing.

Where was Dario?

CHAPTER 16

THE PRESS AND the public, now seated in the gallery, shifted and stirred when the courtroom's side door opened. Necks craned as two court officers escorted Esteban Dario Garza through the doorway and to his place at the defense table.

Dario was trim, and wore his dark hair slicked back. His blue suit, white dress shirt, and casually knotted indigo-striped tie were expensive looking, and despite an uncool accessory—a pair of iron shackles around his ankles—he wore an air of invincibility that looked like the real thing.

Yuki observed all of this as Dario hobbled across the well of the courtroom. He shook hands with his attorneys, grinned when he got a double handgrip from Credendino, and took his seat beside his counsel. But he wasn't through making his entrance. Yuki noted that when Dario flashed his perfect smile at the jurors, three of them smiled back.

Nick was studying his phone as if it held the secret to eternal life. Gaines abhorred Dario. Couldn't stand that the public viewed him as some kind of celebrity. Dario was not only a feature at nightclubs; he also had bragged to the press that his family gave back to their neighborhoods in Mexico and the United States.

Of course, Dario looked nothing like the killer the State had to prove he was. What Yuki knew was that Dario was the ultimate monster, a serial killer so good at extinguishing innocent life that he had left no trace of his crimes, not on him or on his victims. Only one of his alleged kills had been observed by a still-living witness. That witness was currently housed in a hotel room under a false name. Said witness had lost about ten pounds since he'd agreed to testify against Dario. He could still back out at the last moment due to sheer terror. The man was lucky to be alive and knew it.

"Thought should be given," Yuki had earlier told Credendino and Judge Orlofsky, "to sequestering the jury."

That suggestion was still under consideration.

Now, as Judge Orlofsky banged his gavel, Yuki's mouth went dry. No matter how many times she tried a killer, she felt the enormity of her responsibility. Her nerves knotted up until she spoke. And then the feeling passed.

Orlofsky said, "Ms. Castellano. Are you ready with your opening statement?"

"Yes, Your Honor."

Yuki got to her feet, stepped out to the center of the well, the space between the judge's bench and the lawyer's tables, and faced the jury.

CHAPTER 17

THE "I SAID. You dead" task force met in an empty corner office at the far end of the fourth-floor corridor. Cappy, Chi, Conklin, Alvarez, and I sat on opposite sides of a long table, leaving the desk chair at its head for Brady. The tension in the room was palpable. We were all shocked and anguished over the death of our friend and former colleague Warren Jacobi. And there was more.

This so-called war room was the largest office in the Homicide department and the most depressing. It had a history overrun with ghosts caused by disgraced former lieutenant Ted Swanson, who'd gone to prison but left his stink behind at SFPD Southern Division. It was a stink no amount of scrubbing or air freshener could remove, and from which the Southern Division still hadn't fully recovered.

But his old office was huge, so now we used it as a conference room.

The circumstances surrounding Jacobi's so-called retirement had been due unequivocally to Swanson's actions.

Swanson had been devious but smart and persuasive, and he'd headed up a squad of a dozen cops assigned to Robbery and Narcotics—then he'd redefined the term "corruption" by turning the cops reporting to him into thieves and killers, inveigling his department into a get-rich scheme by targeting a drug dealer who'd been doing big business in San Francisco.

For a couple of years, Swanson Inc. had robbed this drug boss of multiple millions, inevitably leading to a shootout between his people and ours, the bloodiest wholesale murder ever known within our Homicide department.

Warren Jacobi had been in the dark about Swanson's drug business. Still, as Swanson's boss, my good friend had to take the fall for internal and public relations reasons.

Knowing how Swanson's detestable criminal behavior had affected Jacobi's life, career, and legacy, sitting here bothered me now more than ever.

CHAPTER 18

JACKSON BRADY ENTERED the war room, took his seat, and tapped the table with his pencil, calling us to order.

He said, "Ya'll know what happened to our old friend Warren Jacobi, who led this department for years. It's sickening to have to post his morgue photo, but here it is. Shots from the scene are on the way."

Nobody spoke as Brady taped the picture to the grubby wall. The shot of Jacobi's half-draped body, his gruesomely slashed neck and face, his blank eyes, left us all speechless.

It hurt to see Jacobi's photo up there next to the photos of Frances Robinson. One of her crime scene photos showed her lying face up, legs bent, on the marble floor of her foyer, blood pooled around her head and torso. There was a look of surprise on her face. She was open-mouthed, with a bullet hole in her forehead. Another photo showed Robinson's draped body on a stainless-steel table awaiting autopsy. She'd been cleaned up but looked pitifully, painfully dead.

Brady retook his seat and went on.

"Clapper called the New York City chief of police. He wanted to know the source of that letter to the editor about Jacobi's death that ran in the *New York Flash*, but according to the *Flash*'s editor-in-chief, it came via email from a temporary or 'burner' address."

Brady stated that no one had any idea who had authored the mysterious letter to the *New York Flash*. But it had since been picked up by social media. Maybe we'd get a tip. Maybe.

Brady moved on to assignments. "Boxer is point on Jacobi and Robinson. But we all need to work together on both murders. As you know, they are connected by the two 'I said. You dead' notes left at the scenes. Or a version of that. And by their relative proximity in time and location.

"I'm available day or night," Brady said. "Call me."

Once the organizational part of the meeting was over, we discussed what we didn't have. No prints, no DNA, no witnesses. We were at square one, but we had a damn good team and, between us, decades of homicide investigation experience with contacts across the greater San Francisco Bay Area and beyond.

Brady said, "Cappy. You have anything?"

Cappy stood, tucked in his shirt with his thumbs, and said, "Chi and I canvassed Robinson's building for three hours. So far, we haven't found any other connections to Jacobi beyond the proximity and the notes left at the scenes. So, what else did they have in common?"

I said, "They were both in their sixties. Neither one

married. Robinson was divorced. Jacobi had a long-term live-in girlfriend. Muriel Roth. Muriel is retired from her acting job in daytime TV—"

Brady cut me off. "I'll notify Muriel. And she needs twenty-four-hour protection. Who do you like for that?"

Cappy named three uniforms in our division and two each in Northern and Central. Brady took notes, then said, "I'll call their COs. Cappy, as soon as I get names, you assign them as needed. Are we good?"

Cappy nodded. "Let me know when it's a go."

Brady said to Chi, "Your thoughts?"

"We've sent Robinson's computer and phone to the lab. They may get lucky and find something on them," Chi said. "But we had our best people on both crime scenes and it's clear this killer isn't sloppy. He picks up after himself. I'm hoping the perp will show up on surveillance footage from Robinson's building. We're still looking at the last twenty-four hours and working back hour by hour."

Conklin said, "People who knew Robinson said that she was quiet. Friendly. That she didn't socialize much or at all. Neighbors figured she was too busy writing. Nothing suspicious about or around her. We're talking to her agent and lawyer today and going back to her friends to see if there's any crossover with the lieutenant."

Brady said, "Good," pushed back his chair, stood up, and said to all of us, "Dig hard into their social lives. Conklin. See if Cindy can find out anything from her coworkers."

To me, he said, "Boxer, I want a written report by end of day, every day. Email is fine. Thank you."

The desk chair Brady had been sitting in spun as he got up abruptly and left the room.

I said, "Let's go."

We stood and slapped hands across the table. It was bravado, but still, we all meant it. I touched Jacobi's morgue shot on my way out of the room.

CHAPTER 19

YUKI GREETED THE jurors, who were giving her their full attention. Her job with the opening statement was to tell the jury about slick and stealthy Dario Garza.

Yuki had spoken to potential jurors during voir dire, and despite the horror of the recent crime with which Dario was charged, these jurors had been willing to serve.

She began. "Ladies and gentlemen of the jury, the defendant, Mr. Esteban Dario Garza, has been charged with the murder of a college friend whose name was Miguel Hernandez.

"Like the defendant, Mr. Hernandez was twenty-three years old and a graduate of UC Berkeley. He had plans to become a graphic designer and art director after he finished his apprenticeship with a respected advertising agency that had offered him a job.

"But his plans were not to be."

Yuki continued her opening statement to the court. "Come back with me in time to a mild evening last year in mid-June. Mr. Garza was in the driver's seat of his lightly used, secondhand BMW sedan. Mr. Hernandez, a schoolmate and good friend, was in the passenger seat beside him, and a third, somewhat more recent friend sat in the back seat, smoking a cigarette. This friend, age twenty-two at that time, has told us that he was enjoying the motion of the car, the soft night air, and the conversation of his two friends in the front seat whose voices carried back to him."

Yuki knew but could not say that shortly before the defendant started up his car that night he'd come under scrutiny by homicide investigators from all three divisions of the SFPD, who had, over the previous three years, investigated the remains of seven young women found in shallow graves. All seven had disappeared after partying in the same clubs Dario attended. Homicide investigators theorized that Dario used clubbing as an opportunity to pick up a woman he didn't know and reduce her lifetime to the remaining hours of that night.

But a new variable entered the equation for Dario that night in June last year. Yuki had to get the presentation of the current case exactly right or have it thrown out because of her prejudicing the jury.

She put her hands into her jacket pockets and walked from one end of the jury box to the other. And then, having given the jurors time to wonder what Yuki had to tell them about the murder of his friend in the passenger seat of his car, she stood at the halfway point outside the jury box and resumed her opening remarks.

"Mr. Dario Garza, the defendant, is charged with the death of Miguel Hernandez. His brutal murder witnessed by the friend in the back seat. In pretrial proceedings, the court has determined that due to 'special circumstances,' the name and face of that third man who was riding in the back seat of the defendant's car will not be revealed. He will testify over closed-circuit television wearing a facial covering so that he is not identifiable. This is for his safety.

"When law enforcement met this third man, he was wearing a cap with a feline logo on the front of it. So we will refer to him as El Gato."

CHAPTER 20

YUKI COLLECTED HER thoughts, then continued her opening.

"Here is what El Gato told the district attorney. That night in the car, Dario was bragging to Miguel about what a good life he was having, specifying all the girls he could have and had had, that he had all the money he wanted or needed, and that he'd had more fun than was humanly possible due to his 'social activities.'

"According to El Gato, Miguel turned to him in the back seat and said, 'You know what he means by "social activities"? You ever seen a snuff film? A lot of people don't think they're real. But they are. I'm telling you. That's what Dario here does for fun.'

"Again according to El Gato, Miguel said that he enjoyed hearing these stories, and during that drive through the city, Miguel told Dario that he had a connection in LA who was a producer interested in making a movie like *Get Shorty,* starring a Chili Palmer–like character, possibly Dario himself.

"Instead of being flattered, El Gato said Dario was angry. He wasn't pleased to hear that Miguel was sharing his business. El Gato said that Dario told Miguel, 'What I was talking about, Miguel, that was privileged information.' Then Miguel said, 'Dario, you know you'd love a movie about you.' "

Yuki tucked a strand of hair behind her ear and said to the jurors, "Ladies and gentlemen, Miguel was twenty-three years old with a good job and a better future. He'd heard many of Dario's wild stories, but at heart Miguel thought Dario's stories were all made up.

"But El Gato told us that he became alarmed when Miguel and Dario began talking about killing people. When Dario pulled his car over on a deserted side street near Harbor Road, he asked Miguel to come with him, to look under the hood and to listen for a little ping in the engine that was bugging him. Miguel was not suspicious, El Gato said. He seemed happy to help."

Yuki said to the jurors, "Imagine, ladies and gentlemen, we're in Dario's BMW sedan. It's dark on that night last June. Picture Miguel with his head under the hood of Dario's car, listening for a ping in the engine. El Gato gets out of the car to get some fresh air, and to his shock, he sees Dario now has a pistol in his hand. He observes Dario Garza walk up behind Miguel Hernandez and shoot him through the back of the head."

Dario jumped to his feet and yelled across the courtroom. *"Lies. Those are damn lies!"*

At this interruption, Judge Orlofsky immediately employed his gavel and admonished the defense counsel to control his client. Orlofsky then looked directly at the defendant and stated, "Mr. Garza, if there are any further outbursts, you will be removed from the courtroom."

Counselor Jon Credendino put a hand on Dario's arm. Yuki watched as Dario yanked his arm from his attorney's grasp and sat down.

She turned back to the jurors and began again.

"According to our eyewitness, Dario dragged Miguel's body toward the open trunk of his car, calling out to El Gato to give him some help. But El Gato feared for his own life. As Dario bent over, struggling with Miguel's body, El Gato snapped four quick photos before bolting from the scene."

Counselor Jon Credendino, Dario's defense attorney, called out, "Objection, Your Honor. Every word of the State's opening is hearsay and highly prejudicial. We move that it be stricken from the record and the jury be instructed to ignore Ms. Castellano's storytelling."

Judge Orlofsky said, "Motion denied. You'll have an opportunity to make your case and to question the prosecution's witnesses."

Yuki said, "Your Honor, the People will enter these four photos into evidence. And we will prove each of these statements with evidence and the underlying testimony of our witnesses."

Yuki heard Red Dog's warning inside her head. *He'll never testify because someone who knows El Gato's identity will sell the information to Dario's family. El Gato will be a dead cat.*

Judge Orlofsky spoke again. "Ms. Castellano. Do you wish to continue?"

CHAPTER 21

YUKI TURNED BACK to the jury and headed into the final stretch of her opening statement.

She told the jurors and the court that the People's eyewitness would testify to the murder of Miguel Hernandez by Dario Garza's hand, and that evidence would show Dario wrestled Miguel's body into the trunk of his car and then drove a short distance to an open construction site.

"Workers at the construction site will testify to finding Miguel Hernandez's headless body the following morning, in a pit of concrete rubble, beside a bloody chain saw.

"Shortly after disposing of his victim, Dario drove with Miguel's severed head to *this very building,* where he placed it at the top of the front steps to the Hall of Justice. He also took the murder weapon, a .22 caliber Smith & Wesson handgun, and jammed it muzzle first into Miguel Hernandez's mouth.

"As his ghoulish coup de grâce, Dario found a parking ticket on the sidewalk or a windshield, dated the evening of the murder, and wrote on that ticket. Then he rolled up his handwritten note and screwed it into the dead man's ear."

Yuki took a photograph from her jacket pocket. She held it up and read from it.

"Here's the note. 'To those who ask: Why? Because Miguel had a big mouth.' "

Yuki returned the photo to her pocket and continued.

"Naturally, the severed head was examined in situ by our crime-scene experts, then brought to our lab.

"The gun left in Miguel Hernandez's mouth is unregistered but has been positively identified as the murder weapon.

"After killing and decapitating Miguel, Dario created an alibi. He went to three dance clubs in succession that evening. He made sure to show his face, to be seen dancing, drinking, and partying until closing time at the last club, Hvar.

"While Dario was attempting to cover his tracks, El Gato was speaking to Sergeant Ronald Whitecliff, the night-shift commander in charge for the SFPD. Sergeant Whitecliff videoed his interview with El Gato and immediately arranged for his disappearance into protective custody.

"Since Miguel Hernandez's murder, for his safety, we've given our eyewitness a new identity and a well-guarded place to live.

"El Gato's photographs of Dario Garza manhandling Miguel Hernandez's dead body have been entered into evidence and will prove beyond any doubt that Dario is a killer, guilty of Miguel's murder. And more."

Yuki thanked the jurors for their attention. As she turned to walk back to the counsel table, she shot a look toward the defense table.

Dario smiled at Yuki and, making a gun with the fingers of his right hand, placed his forefinger to his temple, squeezed an imaginary trigger, and smiled.

Just then there was a loud boom, like an explosion. Like a *bomb had gone off right outside the courtroom.*

CHAPTER 22

THE SOUND INSIDE courtroom 2A was one loud discordant scream as everyone, including the judge and court officers, dove under something: chairs, tables, even the judge's bench. Once the turmoil died down and silence returned, court officers Louis Menges and Brad Fleishman, who had been in the corridor, rushed in through the courtroom's double doors, yelling, "It's safe. You can come out."

Yuki pulled herself out from under the counsel table. The court officers were panting but uninjured.

"Everything is all right," Menges shouted. "But the corridor is full of smoke."

"It was just a smoke bomb, Your Honor," Fleishman told Judge Orlofsky. "I spotted a small cardboard box under a bench between courtrooms 2A and 4A. I was five feet away and heading over to pick it up when it went off. Looks like someone put together a combo of a flash-bang and a smoke grenade. Gave off fifteen seconds of sound and fury. Still, I've called the bomb squad to take a close look and do a sweep of the floor, other rooms, and so on."

The Honorable Judge Orlofsky took charge, speaking to the court officers and the bailiff. "Court officers, please return the defendant to his cell on the sixth floor. Bailiff, please clear the courtroom. People in the gallery, please exit through the double doors behind you and go home. Members of the press, use good judgment. It was a smoke bomb. A scare tactic, but not harmful."

Orlofsky instructed the jurors to return to the jury room.

He added, "As before, do not discuss the case. I'll be with you shortly."

Nick Gaines dusted himself off and called out to Menges, "Did you see who left the box?"

Menges said, "No, but we're getting the surveillance footage."

Yuki asked, "Did you look inside the box?"

Menges said, "Yes. Hang on."

He left the room and came back with a plain cardboard box, about a foot square. He put it in the middle of the room and held up the remnants of a grenade. "This is a flash-bang. Police use them for riot control, or to create a diversion, and they operate on a delay timer."

Orlofsky yelled angrily, "Why don't you let the bomb squad do that?"

Too late. Menges had opened the box and upended it. A small flurry of colored cards, like index cards, fell out.

Menges called out, "Your Honor, it's just colored cards."

Fleishman picked up a few, looked them over, and said,

"Judge. There are names and addresses on the cards. Should I bring them to you?"

Judge Orlofsky said, "Leave them for the bomb squad. Attorneys, please come to my chambers."

CHAPTER 23

THE JUDGE'S CHAMBERS were furnished in impersonal secondhand decor. There were no wall hangings or personal objects on his desk. Lights were on. Curtains were closed.

Yuki and Gaines sat opposite Jon Credendino and Donna Villanova, his second chair, at Judge Orlofsky's conference table. The judge took a seat at the head. The court reporter took a chair behind and to the right of the judge.

"We're off the record," said the judge. "I will not permit anyone to intimidate this court. Nor will I let anyone further interfere with the continuation of this trial to its completion. However, a new secure site for this trial is required. I'd like us to discuss where and when to best continue."

There was a knock on the door leading from the judge's chambers to the corridor, and Orlofsky opened it. It was Ben Bukowski, the head of security.

"Your Honor," Bukowski said. "We've cleared everyone from the floor except for those of you here in your chambers. The bomb squad is coming through with detection equipment, and hounds are going through every courtroom and the full length of the corridor. Given the smoke in the hallway, it does appear to have been a smoke bomb."

"Good. Please keep me apprised."

Bukowski also handed over a loose pile of the colored index cards that had been inside the carton with the smoke bomb, now cleared by the bomb squad.

We watched as Judge Orlofsky put on latex gloves and laid the cards out in front of him on the table.

"Okay," he said. "Here's the only red one, and it bears my name and address. These blue cards are all addressed to counsel by name and with your addresses. The yellow cards have the numbers of the jurors, one through twelve, plus six alternates. No names, but there are addresses."

He flipped the cards over, looking angry and determined. He said to the group at the table, "They all say this: 'If Dario Garza is put on trial, the judge and the prosecutors will die. The jurors will die.'

"None of us, not the officers of the court or legal counsel, can stay with the jurors, but we can get law enforcement to safeguard our homes. Does anyone have another idea?"

No one did.

Orlofsky said to Credendino, "Dario stays in our jail. The trial will be delayed until further notice. I'll set up meetings with the mayor, the chief of police, and the DA."

As the meeting ended, the judge let the participants out into the corridor. Yuki called Brady to fill him in, then walked with Nick Gaines down to the crowded street.

CHAPTER 24

SONIA ALVAREZ WAS in the pod when Conklin and I returned to our desks. She was bent over her keyboard, typing fast, when I edged behind her to get to my desk.

"Hey, you guys," she said. "I'm typing up my notes. Richie, are we still going to check out Julio's, the bar the matchbook came from, after work?"

"Yes," Rich said. "Dress like it's a date."

"Sure," she said. "How's this?" She was wearing black leggings, an off-white turtleneck, and a plaid blazer. "I'll put on some lipstick."

He said, "Fine," and I cracked my first smile of the day. Before she came to us, Alvarez had worked as an undercover narc in Vegas for a couple of years. She'd earned her homicide chops when she and I brought in a serial killer, who'd shot a hostage in front of our eyes inside a basement room in a Vegas hotel.

Since then, she, Conklin, and I had bonded into a three-person team working from our "pod" with its million-dollar view of the bullpen and close access to the front desk and the break room.

I knew better than most that cases could be open for months or years or never solved. But this one would damn well be solved. I pictured a sunflower blooming in our lifeless case. I thought of it as hope.

"Bring backup to Julio's," I said to Rich.

"Will do," Conklin said.

I emailed my own notes and research to Conklin and Alvarez and copied Brady. I was out of steam and out of ideas, so I said good-bye to my partners, wished them luck, and told them I'd keep my phone on and fully charged. Then I got the hell out of there. I had an unbreakable appointment in twenty minutes. And I didn't want to be late.

CHAPTER 25

I CALLED DR. SIDNEY Greene from my car and told him that I was on my way. I parked my blue Explorer across the street from his two-story white stucco office building, rang the bell, and, after the answering buzz, took the stairs and opened the door to his outer office. The reception room was empty, but the door to the therapist's office was wide open.

Greene called out to me from his brown leather-covered recliner, "Come in, Lindsay. Shut the door behind you."

My hands were shaky, but I closed the door and sat in the armchair across from Dr. Greene. The first time I met Greene was after I'd shot an armed twenty-three-year-old male who'd killed two people with his assault weapon and was about to fire on Brady and me. I'd put the guy down before he could. It was a good shoot or maybe a great one, but I'd been put on administrative leave as per protocol.

The review board had sent me to see Dr. Sidney Greene. It's not like I'd had a choice. It was see Dr. Greene or leave the force. But I liked Greene and hadn't resisted, since he'd held my job in his hands. He was a middle-aged man with spectacles in his shirt pocket, a clean-shaven, unlined face, and a nice smile.

I was seeing him now because I feared having a breakdown.

"Talk to me," Dr. Greene said.

I gave him a snapshot of my day: waking up to the news that my aged dog was sick, my fears that Martha would die, and then being called to an early morning homicide only to learn when I arrived at the scene that the dead man was a person I'd respected and loved for the whole of my career. Now I was in charge of finding his killer.

The images of Jacobi's death scene were vivid in my mind as I told my good doctor how long it had taken me to fully absorb the reality that the dead man really was my dear friend and former partner. That his wounds had been violent, devastating. And that didn't even begin to include what must have been his fear and fury.

I admitted that I'd cried a lot already today, and still had miles of tears left for Jacobi.

"I'm so sorry, Lindsay," Greene said. "I'm very, very sorry."

CHAPTER 26

DR. GREENE SAID, "LINDSAY, I've said this before. You have many of the signs of post-traumatic stress disorder. Look, PTSD is common enough among homicide cops."

"So, if that's true, what now?"

He said, "Talk therapy is recommended. But so are antidepressants. Have you ever been on SSRIs before?"

"No. Prozac, right? I've never taken it."

"Lindsay," said Dr. Greene, "have you given any more thought to what we've talked about before? Maybe transferring to a different job or putting in for early retirement?"

I imagined working behind a desk in the booking department. No solving homicides for me. I imagined resigning from my job entirely. It wasn't the first time I'd thought of this. I pictured myself sitting in my cozy Mom's chair at home after doing the breakfast dishes and taking my daughter to the bus, then watching daytime TV and later picking Julie up from school—but that wasn't me. That was the death of me.

"Dr. Greene. I'm not ready to quit Homicide. I have a killer to find right now. I would be more miserable if I were sidelined. How about we resume regular sessions but put off the discussion about medications off for a while, until I can . . . ”

“Until you can what, Lindsay?”

“Until I can make a decision about whether they’ll help or hinder me to be the person I am.”

He looked at me with compassion. “Sure. Of course we can give it some more time. But you know talk therapy is not an absolute cure for grief, night terrors, the shakes.”

I thought about the sleepless nights, the rocky rubble of fear I might have to climb over on my way to the next murder scene.

I nodded.

“But I need a promise from you,” he said. “If your depression gets worse . . . ”

“I’ll tell you and I’ll ask for a leave of absence.”

“And you should tell Joe.”

“That I have PTSD?”

“Yes.”

I said I’d think about it, stood up, and, to my surprise, Dr. Greene stood up, too. He stepped forward and put his hand on my shoulder. I heard him say, “Breathe, Lindsay.”

I did it without breaking into tears.

Dr. Greene patted my back. He told me again that he was sorry about Jacobi, and to please call if I needed him.

I said I would. I found my car and pointed it toward home.

CHAPTER 27

IT WAS 6 p.m. by the time I picked up three orders of yat gaw mein on my way home to Lake Street. I rang the doorbell of our "ever-lovin'" nanny, friend, and across-the-hall neighbor, Mrs. Gloria Rose. She buzzed me in and, as always, welcomed me with a hug. She took the bag of dinner and whispered, "Julie's been crying about Martha, Lindsay. Quite a bit."

My little girl ran across Mrs. Rose's living room and grabbed me around the waist. I picked her up and took her to Gloria's blue sofa with a sweeping view of the street and held her while she cried into my shoulder.

Her cries went in and out of words. I felt my own tears welling up, but I forced them down as I tried to comfort her.

"Jules, Martha is warm and safe."

"You don't know."

"Yes, I do. Because I've been to the doctor's office before and saw the room for sleep-over pets."

"You didn't see her."

Julie was looking up at me with her blue eyes, her dark curls a tangled mess, tears trickling down her cheeks. Martha was a huge part of my life, but in many ways she was now closest to Julie. She played with Julie, slept next to her, and had been her friend since before Julie was old enough to understand what a dog, or a friend, was.

I said, "Julie, Dr. Clayton is a very good veterinarian. I know she will care for Martha like she's her very own. The office is probably closed now, but Dad may have spoken to her earlier. If not, I'll call the nurse later."

I hadn't heard from Joe all day and had been too busy—and too shocked about Warren Jacobi's murder—to reach out to him myself. I knew he was working late tonight. We'd have to catch up on news later.

Julie broke down crying, and I hugged and rocked her, and Mrs. Rose brought over my phone from where I'd left it on the counter. I called Dr. Clayton's number and listened intently as it rang. I hung up and tried again.

"They're not near the phone, Julie. I bet it's feeding time. I'll call back in a little while, okay?"

I grabbed a tissue and wiped Julie's face until we were in shape to go to the table, where Gloria had laid out dinner. We slurped down the noodle soup and read our fortunes, all of which were off point.

Mine: "You will see something amazing today." Thank you, person in the fortune cookie factory.

Julie's: "Everyone is the architect of his own fortune."

She asked me, "What does that mean?"

I knew but couldn't explain to a sad little girl. I said, "I don't know, honey. I'll try the vet again."

I pressed the buttons until a phone recording asked me to leave my name and number. I left them and clicked off.

Mrs. Rose spoke to Julie for me.

"The nurse is working, darling. She's feeding all the dogs and cats and changing litter boxes and giving medicine. I know how hard this is, but we'll hear from the doctor as soon as—"

A ring-back call from the vet's number interrupted Gloria's explanation.

"Mrs. Molinari? Hi, this is Margaret, one of Dr. Clayton's vet techs. I just checked in on Martha. She seems the same as when I came on shift. I'll call the doctor if there's any change, and yes, I'm sure she'll call you in the morning."

Julie and I went to our place by seven. It sure felt empty without Martha's barking and tail wagging. I called Joe but only got his voicemail. "I'm not in. Please leave your number . . . "

I put Julie to bed and read her to sleep. Just as I snuck out, closing her door behind me, a text came in from Conklin: *Alvarez and I are at Julio's. No one recognizes Jacobi's picture. It's just "Nope," "Nah," "Never saw him in my life." That goes for the bartender, too.*

I texted back, *Thanks. You two sign out. See you tomorrow.*

I fell asleep in my chair, and when I awoke some hours later, Joe was in his pajama pants, turning off the TV and the lights. He took me to bed and asked me, "How are you doing, Linds?"

I put my arms around him and cried while telling him about Jacobi. He tried to soothe me like I had comforted Julie earlier, but I was too pent up with sadness over Jacobi and fear of the inevitable with my old dog.

"Sleep, Lindsay. I've got you."

Feeling like a little kid, I turned my fears over to Joe and cried some more. When I woke up, it was morning, and he was still holding me in his arms.

CHAPTER 28

WHEN I GOT to my desk the next morning, I texted Muriel Roth, Warren Jacobi's partner, and she called me right back.

"Any news, Lindsay?" she asked me. "Did you get the guy?"

My heart rolled over when she asked me that. I wished I had something promising to tell her, but I only had the same lame comments to offer, the ones we say when we're at minus square one.

"We have nothing yet, Muriel, but we will find the SOB. Warren's case is open until we nail his killer."

She said, "I still can't believe that he's gone. Warren and I were planning a trip to LA this weekend. And we had just started looking into taking a big trip—like a month or more in Europe," she continued. "Warren probably didn't tell you, but he'd recently had quite a windfall. He got a million-dollar settlement."

I wonder what that was about? I didn't press, and she didn't offer any further explanation.

I didn't have any response other than to promise Muriel

again that we were still investigating. I needed to go through Jacobi's phone, and knowing him, I suspected he would've saved any potentially useful evidence. I asked, "Do you know if Warren backed up his phone to a computer or to the cloud?"

"Gosh, he mainly put photos and things on external drives that he kept in his sock drawer. You want them? Do you think there could be something useful on them?"

"Let me take you to lunch today, Muriel. Tell me where and when, and bring the external photo drives."

CHAPTER 29

MURIEL WAS WAITING for me inside a woodsy café that was hung with baskets of spider plants and stands of foliage acting as curtains at the windows. Jacobi's beloved partner stood to greet me with a hug. The former TV actress's features were drawn with grief, but she was still lovely when she gave me a sad smile. We sat at a sturdy table with stocky wooden chairs, our knees nearly touching, and ordered cold casseroles of black beans, kale, cheese, and rice, with a drink order of pale Chablis that smelled like roses.

"How are you holding up?" I asked.

Muriel said, "The worst was last night when I went to bed alone, and this morning when I woke up alone. Warren and I used to hold hands until we fell asleep."

I thought of my relationship with Joe, and the worry I always felt when he was away. My expression must have changed because Muriel was calling my name, and I only responded the third time she said, "Lindsay."

"Slide a little closer, Lindsay. I'll be your photo tour guide."

I'd checked out Jacobi's iPhone from evidence, and now I placed it on the table and Muriel pulled her chair around, so we sat side by side. I pulled on gloves and removed it from the evidence bag, then fixed my eyes on the screen as Muriel gave me the log-in code, and we went through Jacobi's photo library together.

"That's the great blue heron," she said, pointing. I poked the thumbnail to enlarge it. "Have you ever seen this bird in flight?"

"Warren never mentioned bird-watching to me."

"Ah," she said. "Well, I'll let you in on the secret, Lindsay. He enjoyed the bird-watching, but it was a cover. He did it mainly for show. He was actually going to Golden Gate Park to look for a man he suspected of killing a teenage girl in the park years ago. Warren saw him drag her body into the Lily Pond. And then the guy disappeared into the shadows. He was never identified or caught, and Warren was the only witness."

"Tell me more."

"Well. He told me it was on a night when he was taking a walk through the park to work off his dinner. It was pretty dark, and he said that it happened fast—like, in seconds—but Warren was sure he saw a guy manhandling a girl's dead body, tossing her into the pond. He was too far away to make any kind of ID on the guy. He reported it, and the girl's body was recovered a few hours later, but she had no ID and was probably homeless. I think it was attributed to a suicide."

Muriel shrugged. That was all she knew.

I asked, "So, Warren kept returning to the Lily Pond, and eventually he saw a guy there he thought might be the murderer? Thought the guy might've come to relive his crime all this time later?"

"Warren didn't know why, but this one guy kept showing up there. And this case still woke him up at night. He wanted to do something about it."

Muriel and I then went back to the photo gallery. I saw tranquil wildlife pictures of birds flying, pecking tree trunks, and feeding baby birds. But I was thinking like a cop.

If Jacobi was watching for a killer, maybe the killer knew he was being watched. Did Jacobi take a picture of him? Maybe there's a better picture on one of his hard drives.

Muriel rummaged in her handbag and pulled out three external drives held together with a rubber band. She pushed the packet over to me, and I plugged one drive after the other into my tablet. As we reviewed the digital images, I did see a few pictures of a man in the park near the Lily Pond. He was lanky, looked to be of average height, wearing tattered jeans, work gloves, and a dark sweatshirt with the hood pulled up. The hood did its job of obscuring the man's face beyond any chance of identification. And if that wasn't enough of a handicap, Jacobi's images were underexposed and unfocused.

Still, Jacobi had taken several pictures of this person. Was this the same man Jacobi assumed had killed a homeless teen-aged girl? Or was he just a guy who liked the park in the early hours? Was he a serial killer? Or was this the man who'd sunk a KA-BAR into Jacobi's kidney, then encircled his neck with the blade? Had he left messages inside matchbook covers, spelling out, "I said. You dead"?

Who the hell is he?

I had to find out, to complete the circle, to close this open case in Jacobi's name.

CHAPTER 30

TWO DAYS AFTER Frances Robinson was shot and Warren Jacobi was knifed to death, and we were still nowhere. It made me sick. I'd organized my schedule, my to-do list, but from the moment I arrived at the Hall, it became a running-in-place kind of day.

It was just before eight in the morning when I met with sergeants Nardone and Einhorn in the war room. They had been the first officers on Jacobi's scene, and I needed to review their work for the record. I didn't care if it pissed them off. I read over their notes and grilled them with elementary questions, but they took it well, telling me that they'd canvassed the park after I'd left, and that Einhorn had filmed the area around where Jacobi's body had been found. Nothing new had been uncovered after the matchbook was found.

Cappy and Chi were next up.

They'd been the first officers at Robinson's apartment, and Chi's notes were precise. Although we had all of the forensic data, including more in-depth information on Robinson, we still had less than nothing. I'd seen the photos of Frances Robinson's body where she'd fallen, before she'd been trundled off to the morgue. Chi handed over a printout of his notes with his impressions, and I would file them in the Robinson murder book.

In both cases, all procedures had been followed properly, all paperwork had been completed, and both bodies had been fully autopsied. The cause of death—both homicide—had been filed with the coroner, and the bodies had both been released for burial.

Results? Nothing we hadn't already known.

I thought about my last session with Dr. Greene. I knew I had to separate my feelings from Jacobi's death so that I could work on these horrible, pointless crimes, but my emotions were sloshing around inside my head, threatening to break free.

For now, they stayed under wraps.

Leaving the war room with my notes and the photos that had been taped to the wall, I went to the well-lit break room, which had a good-sized table. I made small stacks of materials: notes from the medical examiner (Claire), notes from the CSU (Hallows), notes from the first responders (Nardone/Einhorn and Cappy/Chi), plus my own scribbles. Everything gathered in the interest of compiling two murder books.

One for Jacobi, the other for Robinson, both binders would be updated as long as the cases were open.

It was a sad but necessary process, and as I worked, colleagues came through the break room to ask how I was doing and if I needed any help. "Thanks. I'm fine." Several of my coworkers ate their lunches over the sink without complaint while I used the table, and I thanked Officer Lemke for making more coffee.

At one o'clock, Brenda Fregosi joined me and we sorted through a million go-nowhere leads from the tip line. It was a six-hour job that we compressed into three hours, but all we got for our efforts were condolences, rants about crime in San Francisco, and other iffy remarks that couldn't be called leads.

There had been one legitimate sighting of Jacobi watching birds. A pair of joggers had seen him engrossed in his phone. The couple ran past him, and no words were exchanged. Another jogger thought she had heard a shot. But she hadn't seen anyone with a gun.

I heard a distant echo of Jacobi's voice telling me to take it easy. *Tomorrow's another day, Boxer.*

Once I closed the murder books, Brenda took them to Brady for his contributions and review. I wrote a summary of the day's work and the no-progress report on the "I said. You dead" homicides, then, after I stared at a photo of Julie with her arms around Martha, I emailed today's anorexic case update to Brady.

CHAPTER 31

AT HALF PAST six, I drove to Julio's on the off chance that today's bar staff would have useful information. The bartender's name was Bressia Cruz. She looked to be just above legal age, dressed in a short skirt and a tight blouse, with hair falling in waves to her shoulders. The bar was starting to fill, but she agreed to answer questions as long as I made it fast. I gave her the day and date of the homicides and asked her if she had been working the night before those murders.

"Yes, ma'am. I started bartending at six p.m. and left at four in the morning." She spoke with a slight accent.

Claire had estimated Jacobi's time of death at just after six in the morning. I showed Bressia photos of Jacobi when he was alive, and she said, emphatically, "I never seen this man."

She was absolutely sure.

I said, "He was killed in Golden Gate Park, and this matchbook was found near his body." I showed her an image of the matchbook. "It came from here. See 'Julio's' on the cover?"

She nodded and said, "Sure. We have millions of these. We give them away."

I said, "Ever seen anything like this?" I showed her a photo of the writing inside the critical matchbook.

Bressia peered at the images as I scrutinized her expression. She read the message out loud. " 'I said. You dead.' What does it mean?" she asked me.

"Two people are dead. Seems like this is the killer's way of taking credit and saying, 'I did it,' without signing his name. Please call me if you hear or learn anything, okay?"

I gave her my card and a twenty-dollar bill, which she slipped into her skirt pocket.

She wished me a good weekend.

"You too," I said. I put my hand up to my ear as if it were a phone and raised my eyebrows. The universal sign for *Call me?*

She was smiling at me when I walked out the door.

CHAPTER 32

ONCE BACK IN my car, I mentally put Julio's in my rearview mirror and home in my headlights. That's when my phone rang from its spot on the dash mount. Just before I jumped a curb as I turned left onto California Street, I pushed the talk button.

I said "Cin—" but she was already talking over me on speakerphone.

"I've got something good, Linds. Dug up by your own dear Girl Reporter."

I slowed for the light at Divisadero and said, "I'm overdue for good news, Cindy. Please don't make me beg."

She laughed and said, "Can you meet me at Grumpy Lynn's tomorrow morning at eight? I have exhibits. I have a theory—and half a plan."

"Cindy, Yuki asked me to help her settle down some freaked-out jurors first thing tomorrow before they—"

"Do not worry," said Cindy. "Coffee only. We'll be there for twenty minutes, tops, I swear."

"Can you give me a clue?"

"Tomorrow. Let's say seven thirty at Lynn's."

We agreed.

CHAPTER 33

THE STICKY REMAINS of the day clung to me as I locked up my car on the street. I looked up toward our apartment's windows and saw that all the lights were on. I imagined Jacobi opening the Explorer's door for me, saying, *There ya go, Boxer.* I silently thanked him and headed for the building's front door.

As I reached our floor, I imagined Martha at home, wagging her tail and dancing on her hind legs like a puppy. And I pictured Julie rolling around and panting with laughter.

I keyed open our apartment's front door with those visions in mind, but they didn't exist in real life. There were no welcoming yaps, no out-of-control laughter from Julie. But Joe was there. He had beaten me home and was stowing the piece he used in his FBI work in the gun cabinet. He took mine, too, put it on a shelf, and locked the door.

"Talk to me, Blondie," he said, hugging and kissing me so that I couldn't talk at all. I loved being manhandled by this particular man.

"You talk first," I said when I was free. "Tell me a joke. Or a shaggy dog story."

He let loose with a long rolling laugh that was rare and welcome. We walked into the main room that squared the corner of our spare but comfortable apartment. I dropped into my Mom's easy chair, and once I'd toed off my shoes, I looked over to Joe, who'd dropped into the chair we called Dad's.

I couldn't put it off another second. "What news of Martha?"

"I got a call from Dr. Clayton," he began.

Our front door swung open and a voice I loved called out, "Anyone home?"

I answered, "Glori-ahh. We're both in here!"

Julie, who never walks when she can run, galloped toward my voice and flung herself across my lap. I had my arms around her when I looked again at Joe, this time with a question in my eyes.

Mrs. Rose read the room, noted the tension, and said, "Well, I'll be going. Call if you need me," and turned back toward the front door.

I got out from under Julie and walked Mrs. Rose to the door. Joe called out, "See you in the morning, Gloria!"

She called back, "I'll be at your door."

Julie yelled out, "Bye!" as I reached our good friend. I hugged Gloria and asked her how she was doing.

"I'm fine, Lindsay. But you. You need some sleep."

"I should be in bed in an hour or less."

"Good. Me too."

We laughed, hugged again, and I locked the door behind her.

When I rejoined the family group, Joe was saying to Julie, "Sweetie, Dr. Clayton must do some surgery on Martha. I know you have questions, a million of them, but we won't know anything else until Martha's doctor has answers."

Julie couldn't take that for an answer.

"What'd she say? What, Daddy? What?"

Joe sighed and after a moment said, "Martha has some little, uh, bumps on her spine."

That sounded to me like tumors. Julie wanted to know what Dad meant, and I wanted to stop her from crying out, but I, too, wanted to know more.

"It's operable," Joe said, looking at me. To Julie, he said, "The doctor's going to remove the bumps and send them to a lab to look at under a microscope. Martha will have to stay with Dr. Clayton for a little while longer to heal."

"No, no, no. Martha is going to be hurt."

"A little bit, but she will be in a nice dreamy sleep during the operation, honey. When she wakes up tomorrow, we'll go see her if the doctor says we can, but we don't want her to bust her stitches. Okay?"

Julie wasn't buying much of this. She protested loudly, skated around the room on her socked feet, and pumped her clenched fists against her hips. Joe caved. He called Dr. Clayton's office and asked the vet tech on duty if we could bring over a toy for Martha.

"We can be there in twenty minutes. Thank you very much." Joe hung up the call and said to me, "I'll take Julie. Okay? Let's see a show of hands."

"Okay, Jules?" I asked my daughter.

She ran into her room and returned seconds later with

Mrs. Mooey Milkington in her arms. Julie told her stuffed toy, “You’re so lucky you get to spend the night with Martha.”

Aw, Jeez. Two full-grown adults and a little girl all snuffling and wiping away tears with our sleeves.

“We’re all a bunch of crybabies,” Julie said.

Joe and I began to laugh.

CHAPTER 34

IT WAS STILL dark when my eyes flew open the next morning. I slipped out of bed and looked in on our kiddo in the room next to ours. She was sleeping on her side, hugging a pillow, and she didn't stir when I opened her door. I dressed quickly and quietly, left Joe a sticky note on the bathroom mirror, and stuck another note on Gloria Rose's door across the hall.

It was half past dawn's early light when I strapped into my Explorer and headed out to meet Cindy, a.k.a. Girl Reporter, at Grumpy Lynn's. What did she have that she couldn't tell me about over the phone or via email? I wanted to hear and see it all, fast, then go to work. I needed the "I said. You dead" clues to pay off—preferably with the name and location of the psycho killer who'd brutally murdered Jacobi.

Cindy and I arrived at Lynn's at the same time. We parked our vehicles nose to rear on the south side of Geary Street. When we were both standing on the pavement, we hugged awkwardly because Cindy's computer bag got between us.

Still, it was so good to see her. I took Cindy's computer bag and we crossed the street to the humble 1950s-style diner, where we always enjoyed indulging in freshly brewed coffee and homemade pastries.

When Cindy pulled open Lynn's door, the bell over it jangled, and I followed her in. Lynn was in the kitchen, but she waved, saying, "Morning, girlies. Sit anywhere you like."

Cindy and I were the only customers so far that morning, so we had the place to ourselves. We took a booth beside the front window, then Lynn came out of the kitchen with a pad in hand. It took less than thirty seconds to order coffee and choose between the chocolate and the caramel-glazed donuts. We ordered one of each.

After Lynn brought us our orders, Cindy unpacked and opened her laptop.

"Another front-page update in the New York tabloid, the *City News Flash*," she said, reading from a story on-screen. "And I quote: 'Sadie Witt, a twenty-year-old college student and the victim of parental abuse, was found shot to death at her home in Nevada. Her father, Herman Witt, is a twice convicted child abuser who was in jail pending a third trial over the latest incident in a pattern of family violence when his daughter was killed. He is not a suspect in Sadie Witt's murder.' "

Cindy went on.

" 'Homicide detective Steven Wilson, of Verne PD, told this paper that a typed note was found in Sadie Witt's pants pocket—' "

I interrupted to say, "Oh my God, oh my God, not 'I said. You dead'?"

"Bingo."

Cindy shoved her laptop to the side of the table and pushed my coffee mug toward me.

"Have some more java, Lindsay. Finish that donut. I'm just asking myself and you: What did these three people have in common besides the notes and being murdered?"

Coffee sloshed over the lip of my mug. Cindy and I mopped it up. We were both thinking about the Witts.

"How much time do we have left?" Cindy asked.

I looked at my phone. "About five minutes, or however long it takes to make the last of these donuts disappear. Cin. Question. Do you think these three murders are the work of one person? Or a gang? Is 'I said. You dead' a thing about to go viral? Does that make sense?"

"I think I'm supposed to say, 'Off the record.'"

I laughed. The other members of the Women's Murder Club—me, Claire, and Yuki—have said "Off the record" to Cindy so many times, it's automatic even if she just asks, "Will you pass the salt?" And she always keeps our secrets. Never spills our beans.

"Do psychotic killers ever make sense?" she asked me.

I said, "Not to normies. Psychotics have their own rules."

Cindy nodded as she thought about this. "I'm catching the commuter flight from San Francisco to Reno in a few hours. I've booked a car to Verne, and I have a meeting with Detective Wilson at the VPD later today. Want to come?"

CHAPTER 35

CINDY SAT IN an extruded plastic chair in Detective Sergeant Steven Wilson's office in the police station in Verne, Nevada. It had been too short notice for Lindsay to join, but Cindy promised to alert her if she found out anything useful. She had her laptop up and running, coffee in a paper cup, and her cell phone on the desk between them.

"No, you can't record this," said the good-looking, forty-something, sun-weathered detective sitting across the desk from her. "Turn it off, Ms. Thomas."

She turned off the recorder on her phone and put the phone in her bag.

"You don't trust me," she said.

"I'm a cop. And I don't want this interview to kill my job. Do not mention my name when you write this up. Deal?"

"It's off the record," she said. "I forgot your name." It was hilarious. Half her working life was "off the record."

"You want to frisk me for a wire, Detective Wilson?" she asked, cocking her head, smiling, showing him she was joking.

"Gladly," he said. "Stand up and put your hands on the wall."

She laughed and so did he. "I'm reaching for my handbag," she said. "But I'm not armed." She pulled out her book on serial killer Evan Burke and put it on the desk. "How do you want me to sign it?"

"You have to ask? 'Dearest Steve, Love and kisses. Thanks for the good time. Always, Cindy.' "

She signed it, "To Steve, With thanks and best wishes, Cindy Thomas," and slid it over to him. He read it, grinned at her, and said, "Okay. Thank you. Now. You understand, I'm willing to kick this around with you because you asked nice and your husband is a cop. But everything I tell you is in the public record. Which you will find out shortly."

"Fine," she said. Even if he was telling her stuff she already knew, as long as he kept talking, Wilson might slip in a detail no one else had. "So, Detective Wilson, tell me about Herman and Sadie Witt."

Wilson pushed his chair back and crossed his arms over his chest.

"Okay. Here's what I know. Sadie's father, Herman, was a bookkeeper at an H&R Block in Reno. Sadie's mother, Anabelle, died when Sadie was twelve. Car crash, or so it says on her death certificate. More bad news for Sadie—Herman was abusive. Her dad was arrested, fined, and released twice while she was in high school. The third time, he punched his daughter in the face, and she nearly lost an eye because he was wearing a big gold ring with a stone. Tiger's eye, if you like that kind of detail. More importantly, the ER doc said Sadie coulda died from loss of blood."

Cindy was taking notes, wishing she could use her voice recorder, but you don't always get what you want. Wilson slugged down his coffee and tossed the empty cup toward his trash can. Then he went on.

He said, "After that last attack, Herman was remanded to the court and sent to lockup pending trial. Sadie threatened a lawsuit of about a hundred grand against Herman, but her father—looking at minimum six years in prison, more if she got a sympathetic jury—went ahead and transferred ownership of the family home to Sadie as compensation."

Cindy said, "But." It was a prompt for Wilson to keep talking.

Wilson said, "So Sadie is missing. Herman is in jail when a neighbor goes looking for Sadie and finds her murdered in her bed. Our ME says she was stabbed with an eight-inch blade a dozen times in the chest. Sadie was small. She had no chance against her killer, who might as well be a ghost. We have nothing on him."

Cindy asked how far they'd gotten in the Sadie Witt investigation.

"We're at square effing one," said Wilson. "No evidence. No witnesses. No nothing."

Cindy said, "So. You've left no stone unturned?"

"Right. We've broken our picks on stones. But we're not giving up." Wilson smiled. "You doubt me?"

"Of course not," she said, while thinking, *Of course I do. People lie to me all the time.* She said, "I have a question, though. Could Herman Witt have hired a hitter?"

"Maybe, but nothing points to a hired gun. No suspicious withdrawals from his bank account. We checked out his phone and internet history. I tracked down his calls and mail both incoming and outgoing from before he was locked up. Herman had no friends of the confidential sort. Well, his anger disorder discouraged friendship. And we got no tips worth a damn."

Cindy said. "What about that note in Sadie's pocket?"

Wilson said, "Right. I wasn't thinking about that. 'I said. You dead.' It made no sense then or now."

"Those same words were left near the bodies of two recent homicides in San Francisco."

"No kidding," said Wilson. "Sounds like you've got a copy-cat. Maybe your killer read about Sadie Witt."

"That's possible," Cindy said. "Anything else you want to tell me off the record?"

He laughed. "Off the record, if your husband nails this killer, call me first."

Cindy said, "Of course." She held up crossed fingers, gave him her card, and caught the afternoon flight back to SFO.

CHAPTER 36

CHIEF OF POLICE Charles Clapper was the respected top police official in San Francisco. This morning, three days after Jacobi's death, Clapper called a task force meeting in the war room. As always, he was smartly dressed and closely shaven, with comb marks in his salt-and-pepper hair. To my mind, he shined like a freshly minted silver coin. At the same time, he looked as though he hadn't slept all week.

I had a crazy hope he was going to tell us that Jacobi's killer had confessed or had been caught, but that wasn't it.

Clapper said, "First, I want to let you know that Warren Jacobi's funeral will be held on Friday—tomorrow. I spoke with Jacobi's partner, Muriel Roth, yesterday. She's lived with him for most of the last ten years or so. Some of you may have met her."

Clapper went on. "As you all know, when a top cop dies, he usually gets a full military-style funeral. A parade from here to the church and then out to Cypress Lawn in Colma. Everyone wears dress blues. Gun salute. Et cetera. And we would like to do that for Warren. However, the degree of pomp in that level of funeral service is up to the deceased's family, and in this case, Jacobi preplanned and left his preference with Muriel and his lawyer, who brought this note to me."

Clapper paused, unfolded a sheet of notepaper.

"Jacobi wrote this:

> "To my family, former coworkers, and dear friends who are also my family, these are my long-considered wishes in the event of my death.
>
> "I don't want a lavish funeral. No parade, no gun salutes, no herd of black cars flying flags making the trip from the Hall to Colma. I'm not that guy. What I'd like is for those who worked, socialized, or shared an elevator with me to please come to St. Mark's for my funeral service. This is the church that I love and where I have been worshipping since I moved near Hayes Valley.
>
> "It gives me great comfort, as I sit on the sofa with my beloved Muriel, to know that when it's my time, my funeral will be overseen by Pastor Casey Elliot at St. Mark's, a beautiful church that is so dear to me. And that you will all be with me in spirit."

Clapper cleared his throat, folded the paper, and returned it to his inside jacket pocket.

"The funeral service begins at 10 a.m. tomorrow. The church holds fewer than five hundred people but standing room is permitted. What's important is to say good-bye to a great cop and a great friend."

CHAPTER 37

TODAY WAS THE day.

Brady had hired limos for the top brass—Chief Clapper, District Attorney Len Parisi, and Mayor Costanza—as well as longtimers like Cappy McNeil, who had known and worked with Warren Jacobi for almost twenty years at the Hall.

I rode comfortably out to St. Mark's Church in Claire's Escalade. She drove and I sat beside her, while Cindy, Conklin, and Yuki took the back seat. I had never seen inside St. Mark's before but was familiar with its redbrick exterior, the spiked towers, and the stained-glass "rose" window. Richie was telling Yuki and Cindy something about its architecture, but I blocked out his voice and concentrated on what I would say when it was my turn to get up to speak during the service.

Claire parked in the church lot and then we all went inside the church Jacobi had loved.

The five of us slid into a pew in the second row. Jacobi's flag-draped coffin rested on a bier at the foot of the altar, and a life-sized photograph of him in his dress-blue uniform rested on an easel behind his casket.

I remembered when that photo was taken. It had been a sunny day at a St. Patrick's Day parade. Someone had taken the photo of Jacobi, surrounded by fellow cops, as a brass band marched down Market Street toward City Hall.

None of us could have imagined that four years later that photo would be facing out over hundreds of mourners who'd come to say good-bye to a dear friend and great leader taken away far too soon.

After about twenty minutes, during which time the church reached capacity, Pastor Casey Elliot climbed a few steps to the pulpit, gently tapped the mic, and began the funeral service by offering a prayer for Warren Jacobi and speaking of our loss. Behind us in the balcony, the organ played, and a choir sang "Amazing Grace." The chords and the voices filled the church and settled around our shoulders like a blessing. I lifted my eyes to the arches and to the stained-glass windows, and as if on cue, a beam of sunlight broke through the colored glass and painted the floor with a wash of blue and gold.

When the last notes trailed off, Pastor Elliot called upon Muriel Roth, Jacobi's love and partner of the last ten years. Muriel rose from where she'd been sitting between her two daughters in the front row.

CHAPTER 38

MURIEL ROTH WAS known to soap opera fans as Mrs. Gregory Laughton on a long-running TV show called *Day by Day.* She carried herself with the poise of an accomplished actress who had been in front of cameras for many years, but also with the warmth and sweetness that was at her core in real life.

Muriel stood with the pastor as he introduced her, then she thanked him and all of us for coming to St. Mark's to celebrate Warren Jacobi's life.

And she spoke of their love, her voice trembling at times, while dabbing at her eyes.

Regaining her composure, Muriel said, "Warren and I met because we were neighbors but also, I think, by divine intervention. What began as comfortable casual meetings grew into caring and affection and friendship, and then so much more. Our friendship became deep love.

"Even though we were not legally married, sitting together

in this church, sharing our faith and our love over the years, we felt married in the eyes of God."

After concluding her eulogy, Muriel stepped down from the dais, walked over to the flag-draped coffin, and placed her hand where Warren's heart would be. She lingered there, looking up at his beaming portrait. Then her knees folded, and her daughters quickly stepped forward to catch her before she dropped to the floor.

Pastor Elliot found me with his eyes.

"Sergeant Boxer, you would like to speak?"

CHAPTER 39

YUKI STOOD UP to let me into the aisle when Pastor Elliot called my name. I was unnerved by the gravity of the day, but when she put her hand on my back, I knew that I was at the right place and time and with Jacobi's friends.

I stood at the altar and began: "I'm Lindsay Boxer. I am so very lucky to have known Warren Jacobi. Since my first week on the force, he was my teacher and my partner—even when I was promoted and he officially reported to me. He was always confident that I had the right skills, and he made sure that I knew it, too. At all times, we had mutual trust and were true friends.

"Our friendship was formed in a patrol car. We talked about why we had become cops, mistakes we had made, and what we were expected to do in our jobs and how that work made us better and stronger people.

"We talked about what it meant to be a good cop. And looking out at all the dark uniforms filling this church, I know that we've all experienced the feeling of being called to this way of life. Your senses become so sharp, they're superpowers. You see things before they happen. You'd step in front of a loaded gun to save a partner, or a bystander, or a victim cornered behind the cleaning supplies in a grocery store.

"But of all the time Jacobi and I spent together, one time that wasn't on the job stands out and will never be forgotten.

"Joe Molinari and I were getting married, and my father wasn't there."

I stopped, steadying myself, wanting to phrase it to just tell the important parts, to not dwell on my father at all.

I said, "I was dressed in my wedding gown. My dear friends, my maids of honor, were all there, too. Joe was in the wings, waiting to join with me in what the future held for us. Though I knew better than to count on my father, I'd still hoped he would show up. He'd told my sister, Cat, that he was coming to the wedding, so I'd assumed he would be there to walk me down the aisle.

"He wasn't.

"Dr. Claire Washburn offered to give me away, but it was Yuki Castellano who came up with the idea to ask Warren Jacobi to stand in for my father. She asked Jacobi to walk me down the aisle, and my God, he did it. He set the pace and put his hand on mine and handed me off to our minister. And Joe and I got married in a gazebo overlooking Half Moon Bay.

"Unlike my actual father, Jacobi was always there. And not only for me but also for every recruit and colleague. He was there for those who'd lost their way because of a bad bust, or a trial that didn't end in a conviction, or any of the many disappointments that arise when a person runs up against something too big to handle alone and needs a good friend, a wise soul. A hero."

I paused and looked over at Muriel. "Jacobi . . . How can I say this? He radiated happiness when he and Muriel fell in love. And seeing how happy that made my dear friend made me radiate happiness, too. Muriel, I'm so, so sorry that we lost him."

I pictured Jacobi's terrible wounds, his bleeding body curled into a fetal tuck by the Lily Pond in Golden Gate Park. I wanted to say, *Muriel, we'll find out who did this, I swear we will.* But even as I was gripped by the impulse, I kept that part to myself. Instead, I said this:

"Joseph Campbell once wrote, 'A hero is someone who has given his or her life to something bigger than oneself.'

"Muriel, Jacobi was a hero. In every way. And our memories of him will live on in all of us who knew him."

CHAPTER 40

AFTER THE CHURCH service, we followed Jacobi's casket to the cemetery, where a few more speeches and prayers were delivered. We were walking toward Claire's car at the end of Cypress Avenue at the conclusion of a wrenching day of tears, eulogies, and long good-byes when an SUV marked SAN FRANCISCO CHRONICLE pulled up alongside us.

The driver buzzed down his window and said to Cindy, "Ms. Thomas? Mr. Tyler asked me to give you a lift back to the newsroom."

Cindy said, "Lindsay, can you come with me? I have business to discuss with you."

Transportation got sorted out in the street. Cindy and I got into the *Chronicle*'s SUV. I'd catch a ride back to the Hall later. She and I and Yuki and Claire made a plan for us all to meet at Susie's Café for dinner tonight.

This day of loss and grief was complicated by a car accident on the freeway. When we cleared the tangle, Claire's

Escalade was only two cars behind us. Cindy and I could count on a good ten minutes of private time ahead of us.

Cindy lowered her voice and said, "Breaking news from Verne, Nevada."

And she got right into what she'd learned from her meeting with homicide detective Steven Wilson about the murder of twenty-year-old Sadie Witt.

Cindy said, "After Herman Witt was arrested and locked up, waiting for sentencing, he had his quarter-million-dollar family home legally transferred to Sadie. No strings attached. Yeah. An act of contrition. But weeks after he'd transferred the deed to Sadie, she was murdered."

"First, I want to say, Cindy, good catch. Based on what you've told me, all three victims came into money, but none of it was taken from them. It's like someone coming into sudden wealth just angers this psycho killer. Does that make sense?"

Cindy said, "So, you think the wealth factor is a blinking red light that somehow attracts this killer?"

"Let's say that's right, Cindy. But how? And why? The killer gets nothing from his killings except a brief moment of infamy—in the media. Is that reason enough?"

Cindy said, "That could be way more than reason enough. He gets attention, big time. I mean, maybe he works in an office, doing spreadsheets, which goes unnoticed. This big idea occurs to him. *I could kill people because I say so.* Now he's building a legacy . . . "

"Okay. I get that," I said. "So, how does he choose his targets? How? People come into windfalls—by inheritance or a big cash settlement in a divorce. Jacobi got a million-dollar settlement. That could explain why he was targeted. The flashing red light theory only works if there's publicity, right? You said the Witt story was in the local paper? On the paper's website?"

Cindy said, "Yes to both. Wilson showed the story to me. But, Linds, unlike the letter in the *New York Flash,* which we thought was probably written by the killer, Sadie Witt's murder was followed and written up by a reporter from the *Verne Morning News* from beginning to end. The details were all there: times, dates, cause and manner of death. Except for whodunit—"

"Right. The paper ran the whole deal."

I said, "So, if I'm getting this right, Sadie Witt was murdered before Jacobi and Robinson."

"Correct. Sadie was first of the three—that we know about."

I finished Cindy's thought in my mind. If the killer wasn't caught, he would kill again.

CHAPTER 41

IT WAS HALF past six when the four of us met at Jackson and Sansome Streets. All that remained of the light outside was a swath of pink near the horizon. But inside, we were drawn to the bright light shining through Susie's picture windows. When we pushed open the restaurant's big glass door and filed into the sunshine-colored Caribbean-style restaurant, it was as if a new day had dawned.

The walls were hung with rustic paintings of Jamaican markets, and the atmosphere was alive with happy talk and the aroma of island cuisine. This was our place, what we thought of as the Women's Murder Club headquarters.

A dozen after-work bar regulars shouted out hellos, as did Fireman, the beefy young bartender who might have a crush on Yuki, remembered everything, and kept it all to himself.

Susie, the owner and creator of this haven, was a tall, athletic blonde with blue eyes and a great smile. She was setting up for the nightly limbo competition but stopped to call out,

"Hey, girlfriends! Your table is waiting, and tonight the beer is on the house."

"Awwww, you don't have to do that," Claire said.

Susie gathered us into a group hug, saying, "Richie called to say you were on the way. I'm so sorry about what happened to your friend."

We returned Susie's hugs, then crossed from the main room into the narrow corridor by the kitchen, leading to the smaller dining room at the back, and the booth we called ours. We slid onto a pair of banquettes, and by the time our usual irrepressible waitress, Lorraine O'Dea, arrived with beer and chips, we were ready to drink. More than ready. I hadn't been this sad since my mother died.

Cindy said, "There's going to be some serious drinking tonight, Lorraine. What do you recommend? Start with margs and then go to the beer? Or chase the beer down with tequila?"

"Don't anyone try to keep me from Margaritaville," Yuki said as if it were a genuine threat. She was the margarita drinker in our crowd.

I gave her a little shove while Cindy shouted, "Permission granted to Yuki for two margaritas. Or three. And that goes for all of us. Okay, Yuki?"

Yuki confirmed Cindy's suggestion with two thumbs up.

CHAPTER 42

"IF YOU'RE *REALLY* asking my advice," Lorraine said to the table, "I suggest you guys work on the drinks and chips and trust me with the dinner menu. Okay?"

I was starving. "We do trust you, Lorraine. Food. Hurry."

I poured each of us a beer, and we raised our frosted mugs of brew.

Claire said, "To Jacobi, with love. May he rest in peace."

I added, "May we find his goddamn killer, forthwith."

Claire reached across the table and squeezed my hand. Soon enough, Lorraine and Maria, her new waitressing understudy, were back with trays of lechon asado and arroz con pollo, a big basket of warm rolls, and sides of salad for all.

Yuki had her phone in her hand, crying as she looked at a photo of herself with Jacobi, when Fireman appeared beside our table and placed a watermelon margarita in front of her. Yuki patted her eyes with a paper napkin, noticed the margarita, lifted it to her mouth, and downed it. She held out the glass and said to Fireman, "Hit me again."

Minutes later, Fireman brought Yuki her second margarita.

She didn't acknowledge the bartender but made the drink disappear with only slightly less lightning speed. Then she slumped against the seat back and wiped away new tears with her hand. I put my left arm around her shoulders.

For a while, the four of us ate and drank in silence, giving all our attention to the food. But memories of Jacobi started creeping back in.

Cindy signaled to Lorraine and pointed at the pitcher, meaning, *More beer.*

Claire asked, "What are you thinking about, Lindsay?"

"Larkin Street," I said.

Claire nodded. Everyone at the table knew about what had happened on Larkin Street, a traffic stop that had almost killed me and Jacobi. Two teens had crashed; the driver was a fifteen-year-old girl without a license. I'd asked her for her learner's permit. She'd put her hand inside her jacket, and instead of a permit, she'd pulled out a gun.

And shot me repeatedly.

My mind went back to that night. The other passenger shot Jacobi, then got out and kicked him in the head.

The bullet in my shoulder had nicked my carotid artery, and my blood was pumping out onto the alley. Jacobi was lying nearby with a couple of rounds in his hip, bleeding heavily from an injury that never completely left him.

I'd managed to return fire. And Jacobi and I had both lived to be with the loves of our lives. It was before Jacobi had handed me off to Joe in marriage. Before he'd met Muriel and left a legacy as a hero cop whose career and life ended too soon.

Yuki, Cindy, and Claire had stories about Jacobi, too. Though theirs didn't involve near-death experiences, all were indelible. Cindy spoke of Jacobi vouching for her at a no-press-allowed crime scene, saving her reputation and maybe her job. Claire remembered losing her medical kit and camera at a murder scene and Jacobi rescuing her from this unfortunate circumstance by finding it under a patrol car.

Yuki said, "I don't think I even told you guys this one. A few years ago, Jacobi and I got stuck in an elevator. For hours. Yeah. And there was no reason that this had to happen. We both could have taken the stairs."

I cracked a grin. "I remember."

"He told you?"

"No. You were missing. Your phone was off. Luckily Jacobi got a call through to maintenance."

"I was late for court. I punished myself for weeks after that. Jacobi and I never mentioned it to each other. It was our secret."

We four spontaneously clasped hands, making a circle around the tabletop. It felt to me as if we were enclosing Warren Jacobi in our arms. Yuki bowed her head and said, "Chief Jacobi, Warren, if you can see and hear us, know that you are loved. If you see my mom—her name is Keiko Castellano—please tell her that I miss her very much, and that I'm doing fine."

I said to the spirit of my old friend, "Wish you were here."

We all said, "Amen."

CHAPTER 43

AFTER SWITCHING FROM beer to coffee and dessert, we settled our dinner tab and prepared to go home and get a good night's sleep. And maybe have good dreams to wash through our sadness.

As we neared the front room, the steel drum band got louder. Rikki sang, "Shake, shake, shake, Señora. Shake it all the time."

We heard the claps of encouragement as the limbo contest began. I didn't recognize the song, but it had a calypso beat, and a thin man was arched backward, knees bent, dancing barefoot under the bamboo pole. The point of the game is to go low enough and to dance as expressively as possible while moving under the pole without knocking it off the supporting brackets. He was directly under it when he breathed a little too deeply and bumped the pole. It fell off the brackets that held it loosely at opposite ends.

The thin man got thunderous approval from the crowd for his efforts . . . and when I looked again, I saw that Claire had joined the line.

Claire calls herself a big girl. That means size 20 or so, and she's past her fiftieth birthday. Not to mention she's got a bum knee.

Well, tonight Claire was *on.*

She was shaking her shoulders, and with bended knees and a horizontal torso, she was shimmying under the limbo pole. Sure, the pole had been reset for her. But I knew *I* couldn't do it.

Yuki, Cindy, and I joined in with the crowd, chanting, "Claire! Claire! Claire!" as she progressed inch by inch under the pole. "Low-er, low-er, low-er!"

When our medical examiner, my boo, had cleared the pole and it had stayed put, the place erupted in applause. She had done the next to impossible, and the front room was egging her on to do it again.

But Claire was leaving on a high note. She bowed to Rikki and his band, waved at the crowd, and pushed Susie's front door open with the rest of our Murder Club following, laughing, hugging her, teasing her about her heretofore hidden talent.

"And that's without practice," she said.

Cindy said, "Where you from, lady? Tobago? Jamaica?"

"San Francisco, California," Claire said, laughing.

I said just loudly enough to be heard: "A star is born."

PART TWO

CHAPTER 44

TIAGO GARZA SAT behind the wheel of an ancient gardener's truck. It was black, with scrapes along the truck's left side, a dented rear fender, and an undercarriage heavy with rust that had crept out and over the wheel wells.

The back held a gas can for the mower and two bags of mulch. Tools bristled from the bed, and the words YARD WORK with a 415 area code and phone number were painted on the driver-side door.

No one looked twice at this truck.

And they didn't look twice at the driver, either. Tiago Garza was scruffy, bent, and he passed for a working man, an easily overlooked handyman. That was the whole idea.

Garza had parked the truck across from the eight attached houses in this pretty, tree-lined residential block. Like the others, number 1848 was a cream-colored Victorian with a peaked roof and a bay window on the first level. Two cars, a Chevy sedan and a Buick, were parked out front, the Buick in the narrow driveway. There were also two police cars partially blocking Garza's view of the front steps. But Garza knew that his target was at home.

Twenty minutes ago, one of the cops had leaned against Garza's truck and asked for his license and registration and an explanation for his presence. It was not the first time he'd been carded, and Garza handed it all over, license, registration, plus a discount card for a local fast-food restaurant. The name on the ID was Luis Perez. The truck, too, was in Perez's name. Perez was long dead and buried in Guadalajara, but his ID lived on.

Garza told the cop in deliberately accented and hesitant English that he was waiting for the homeowners to wake up because he didn't want to "make, uh, loud sounds? Noise? With grass cutter."

English was Garza's native language. He was of Mexican descent but had been born and raised in San Diego, so was able to cross the border at will. Which he did.

The cop had returned Luis Perez's ID, noted the plate number, and returned to his patrol car. Garza moved the truck down the block, but still with a desirable view, then settled back in the driver's seat.

Today was a workday for Garza. Many self-important individuals and families were living in the eight three-story houses across the street, but the owner of number 1848 was the enemy.

Garza pulled his knit cap down over his ears and pulled up the hood on his sweatshirt while watching the target house in his rearview mirror. A ceiling fixture came on, lighting up the second floor. Garza checked his watch: 7:40. The target walked past the window and another light went on. That would be the bathroom.

Garza watched the interior house lights go on and off. Then at 7:55 a.m. the owner of number 1848 left through the front door in a hurry. As he descended the front steps and reached his driveway, Garza could see that the man was dressed in a golf shirt and carrying a nice set of clubs. It pleased Garza to see that number 1848 would be enjoying his last day.

The man was just a stride away from the blue Chevy sedan when a woman called to him from the open second-floor window.

"Hon, can you drop off the dry cleaning on your way out?"

The target called back, "Sorry, Sandy. I'm already running a little late. Call you later. Love you."

The man got into the Chevy, pulled away from the curb, and turned north toward 22nd Street. One of the squad cars pulled out behind him. Taxpayer-funded protection.

Garza noted the time, his target's stated busy day, and the rear guard protecting the important man. Seven minutes later, "Sandy" ran out of the house wearing jeans and an SF SPCA sweatshirt, and carrying a garment bag. She opened the back door of the Buick and hung the bag from a hook above the door. Once she was in the driver's seat, she backed out onto the street. She waved to the cops in the remaining cruiser and drove away, with them on her tail.

CHAPTER 45

GARZA DROVE HIS vehicle at normal speed and took a left turn from 22nd into an alley that ran behind the row houses. He parked two blocks away, near a different row of two-hundred-year-old cupcake houses.

There was no traffic and no one in sight when Garza got out of his truck, unlatched the tailgate, and pulled several items from the bed: a hand rake, pruning shears, and a machete. He put the tools into a canvas bag.

After slinging the strap across his shoulder, Garza walked along the alley behind the row houses, avoiding a swing set, a trampoline, and a shed with a sign on the door reading GIRLS ONLY. Security cameras would pick up a bent, brown-skinned gardener in worn jeans, a hooded sweatshirt showing at the neckline of his blue peacoat, and a knit cap pulled down over his ears.

Garza stopped at the rear door of number 1848.

He listened for shouts, or the barking of dogs. Hearing only a distant sound of someone playing a 1980s hit music station,

Garza removed a chisel from his coat pocket and popped the old lock on the ground level back door. The hinges creaked as he pulled the door open a few inches.

No alarm sounded. Sandy, Garza assumed, had forgotten to double bolt the doors or set the alarm. He stepped inside a dim, dusty utility space. Hefting the bag of tools, he closed the door and was in total darkness.

Within a couple of steps, Garza tripped over something like a metal pipe, the metallic clanking against the concrete floor sending a spear of panic through him as he fell to the ground. But he got his hands out in front of him, breaking his fall, and then he lay still. He listened until he was sure that no warning sounds were coming from inside the house.

Garza's eyes adjusted to the dark. He moved the pipe out of the way and secreted the machete between two side-by-side shelving units. He thought about what the two men in his crew were doing, how his boy was making out, the number of hours until his target came home divided by how long it would take him to drive back to Guadalajara.

Tiago Garza peeled off his coat, tossed it to the floor, and, using it as padding against the cold concrete, settled in for a rest. It would be at least ten hours before his target came home and went through his nightly routine.

CHAPTER 46

ALMOST TWELVE HOURS later, around eight fifteen in the evening, Tiago Garza stood near a vertical heating duct, which carried down the muffled sounds of the couple upstairs talking over dinner. A little later, he heard the clinking of dishes as they cleaned up.

Garza napped. When he woke up, he could just make out the sounds of the laugh track to a late-night talk show coming from the bedroom TV on the second floor.

He waited another hour and ten minutes. It was now after 1 a.m. The house was quiet. Garza stepped out of his hiding place, did some stretches, put his coat back on, and patted his pocket, reassuring himself that the .22 was there. Picking up his machete and keeping his head down, Garza climbed a half dozen steps and opened the door leading into the kitchen and the rest of the house.

The house was in darkness, but he'd been here before. He knew where the chairs, end tables, and entertainment unit were, and how to avoid them. He also knew where the main staircase was. He headed for it and started to climb, then crossed the landing and took the remaining stairs to the second floor. He paused at the half open bedroom door and listened for movement or any sound—but heard nothing.

Garza slipped into the bedroom and stood with his back to the wall. He could see by the light of the clock on the night-stand that two forms were lying on the bed. Taking two steps toward the bed, he pulled out his stolen gun and aimed it at the man gently snoring beside his wife. He fired into the center left of the man's chest, killing him instantly.

Sandy stirred and rolled toward her husband, giving Garza a clear shot of the back of her skull. He fired and her body bucked. She turned over again, this time toward Garza. His shot had landed but hadn't killed her.

She sputtered, "Who are you? What did you do?" Her eyes opened and her left hand flew to the side of her head.

"Sandy. Do what I say," Garza instructed. "Turn over. Put your arms around your husband."

Garza shot her again, this time in the forehead, and gave the husband another shot to the heart for good measure.

Neither of his targets moved. But Garza wasn't finished yet. He rearranged the bodies so that they were lying face down and administered the coups de grâce.

Based on the bedside clock, less than twenty minutes had passed since Garza first stepped into the room. He left the bedroom and walked down the hallway to the bathroom, where he placed his bounty in the bathtub, along with the machete. He removed his hoodie, turned it inside out, and tied it around his waist. Then he washed his face and hands, ran water over the machete, and dried off with a bath towel.

He took the towel, the gun, and his machete with him, and returned to the ground level.

He collected his bag of tools. Then Tiago Garza left the same way he came in.

It was just before noon when, nine and a half hours after leaving number 1848 and crossing the border between San Diego and Tijuana, Garza drove his truck to a prearranged spot outside a junkyard in La Joya, where his friend Juan Carlos Allende greeted him. They exchanged a few words as Juan Carlos opened the gates. Garza drove the truck into the asymmetrical mess of a junkyard, then took out the bag of tools and handed the truck's keys to his friend, along with a folded inch of cash. He tossed the hoodie into the fire that burned in a fifty-five-gallon drum.

Juan Carlos in turn handed Garza the keys to a late-model Honda as well as a cage holding two chickens. Garza got into the car, pulling his wallet with Mexican ID from between the front seats. Twenty minutes later, he was at his house near Tijuana. As he carried the chickens into the backyard, he said to them, "Winner, winner, chicken dinner."

He killed, gutted, and plucked the birds in the yard, then brought the carcasses inside to be thoroughly cleaned.

His wife, Luisa, hugged and kissed him in greeting.

"Sweetheart, please put the birds in the sink," she said in Spanish. She poured two glasses of wine and asked, "How did it go?"

"I don't think there will be a trial anytime soon," Garza told his wife. "It was a good day."

CHAPTER 47

JULIE AND I visited Martha on Sunday morning.

Dr. Clayton's waiting room was full of adorable pets and their owners. Julie was ecstatic. She talked to everyone and everything. Finally, the door to the examination room opened and Dr. Barbara Clayton called us in. Julie and I saw our favorite border collie lying on the table.

"Gentle, okay?" Dr. Clayton cautioned my little girl. "We don't want her to rip her stitches out, right?"

Martha and Julie were so very excited to see each other, and I was part of all that love and reconciliation. Julie and I put our arms around her, ruffled her fur, and cooed at her. And Martha lapped it up. She whined, barked, and wagged her tail, but she couldn't stand up on her hind legs. I saw that her back was shaved and bandaged. My old doggie turned her big brown eyes on me and yipped and kissed me. I interpreted her high-pitched yipping as *Please break me out of here.*

After another minute of hugs and sloppy kisses, Dr. Clayton

gently maneuvered our furry kid back into her cage. Martha became distressed when the cage door was closed, which almost wrecked me and Julie both. Jules was saying, "If Martha stays here, so do I."

I picked up my squirming and tearful daughter and thanked Dr. Clayton, who said, "I should have the labs back tomorrow. I'll call you." It was painful, but we had to leave Martha with our vet for a still unknown number of days.

I was heading out to run some errands and had just dropped Julie off at home with Mrs. Rose when I heard police sirens screaming. They got louder, closing in on me from behind.

I pulled over to the curb so the cruisers could pass—and one of them pulled up in front of the Explorer and stopped, blocking me in.

What was this? I hadn't been speeding. I hadn't gone through a red light. I saw in my rearview mirror that the cop driving the police car had leaped out of it and was coming toward me. I knew that cop very well, but seeing him on the street, striding toward me, froze my brain. Had something happened to Joe? To Yuki?

I got out of my car and met him halfway between our vehicles while trying to read his grim expression.

"Brady. What's wrong?"

"Double homicide," he said. "Boxer, I need you to follow me in your vehicle, okay?"

"Where are we going?" I asked, but Brady was already back in his car and buckled up. He hit the lights and sirens, full bore as I followed him to Divisadero Street, then south.

I stared holes through the windshield and kept tight on Brady's tail. Traffic ahead pulled over to let us pass. The car radio crackled, but I couldn't make out what dispatch was saying over the racket of the sirens.

This was a Code 3, destination unknown.

CHAPTER 48

IT WAS JUST after nine in the morning when Brady and I arrived at the crime scene. I saw a row of fancy Victorian houses in different colors, canting downward at the angle of the street. The block had been cordoned off with crime-scene tape and barriers, a thick blue line of uniformed officers and their squad cars.

I've worked hundreds of murder scenes, but this was more security than I'd seen—ever.

Brady stopped his car at the end of the street near the control center, a small trailer filled with communication gear. I pulled up behind him and hopped out.

Brady pointed to one of the houses and said, "I'll walk through the scene with you, if Hallows says okay. It's the whitish house, second one in from the end," he said. "Number 1848. You'll run point until the scene is released."

I looked up and down the street and saw two medical examiner's vans, three CSU vans, and a herd of patrol cars banking the street. And I saw Yuki, standing outside her car on her phone, no doubt getting warrants to search neighboring houses.

I looked hard at number 1848. It looked like a San Francisco dream house. Cream-colored, with gingerbread trim and a front porch with rocking chairs and a couple of bird feeders hanging from porch beams.

"Brady. C'mon, talk to me, will you?"

Brady said again, "It wouldn't do any good, Boxer. We both need to hear it from Hallows."

"Wait. Wait. You want me to be primary on two new homicides in addition to Jacobi and Robinson?"

"Two days at the most, then Cappy will take over and you'll continue heading up the Jacobi and Robinson task force."

We started walking toward house number 1848. When we reached the cordon, a CSI told us that Hallows was waiting for us inside the front door.

Excellent.

The answer man was on the scene.

CHAPTER 49

WE WERE ESCORTED up the walk to the front door of number 1848. Brady knocked. The door opened and Crime Scene Unit director Eugene Hallows opened it. He looked like he was in pain. He told us to step inside and said, "I don't have to remind you . . . "

We knew what he meant. *Be careful where you walk. Don't touch anything.*

Hallows watched us glove up and pull booties over our shoes. When we were ready, he said, "I'm taking you the long way. Brace yourselves."

The long way took us through the living room, where CSIs were photographing everything: walls, ceilings, windows, carpets, and good-looking furniture from all angles. I saw no blood spatter, no shell casings, no damage to the windows or doors, and no bodies in sight.

Hallows said, "They're upstairs."

I followed Brady and Hallows up a carpeted flight of stairs with a landing at the midpoint. We climbed the rest of the stairs to a hallway on the second floor, where Hallows pushed at the half open bedroom door and stepped aside so that we could see inside.

"Stay right there," he said, reaching around me to flip on the ceiling light.

I looked beyond him. The king-sized bed was soaked in blood. A male body was lying half on the bed. A female body was on the floor beside the bed. Both bodies had been decapitated.

My blood pressure shot up. I looked at Hallows, and he said, "They were both shot before their killer performed surgery. The male got two slugs in the heart. She took a couple of head shots. Both heads are in the bathtub. I'll get you pictures, but no one else goes in until the scene is processed."

Brady asked, "Have the victims been identified?"

"We know who owns the house," Hallows hedged. "We haven't run prints. ID has to be viewed before we know for sure if the victims are the owners and the family is notified."

"Names, please, Gene," I said with my fists balled up behind my back.

"Orlofsky. Martin and Sandra. A judge and his wife."

The judge of the Dario case had been killed like a rabid skunk so that the flash dancer in the dock, probably related to the killer, would get some kind of reprieve.

"When did this happen?" I asked.

"I'm waiting for the ME to say, but their bodies are coming out of rigor. I'd say early this morning."

I had to ask. "Did the killer leave anything behind? A note, for instance."

"No. But a connection occurs to me."

I said, “The decapitated head Dario Garza left on the steps of the Hall.”

“Or a feint so we think the pattern is the same,” Brady said. “Let’s leave CSU to their work.”

I swear he looked as freaked out as I felt. A judge had been killed. A judge on an active murder trial that Brady’s wife was prosecuting.

We turned to leave the way we’d come. I wobbled once on the stairs and reached out for the wall out of reflex. Brady caught me before I landed a paw on it, and a minute later we were outside, walking toward the street.

CHAPTER 50

I WAS BEHIND the wheel of a squad car, but I wasn't going anywhere. My assigned job was to watch, answer questions, and radio Brady if a top-dog decision had to be made or if a person or group tried to breach number 1848.

My eyes were locked on that gingerbread house when I was startled by knocking on the car's roof. I whipped my head around and saw Cappy. I'd never been happier to see him in my life.

I opened the car door as he said, "Boxer, consider yourself relieved of house-sitting duty."

Cappy offered me a hand, and I exited the car. He handed me a paper cup of sweet black coffee, and I slurped it down while telling him between gulps, "Cappy. I don't think I've seen a more horrific crime scene. Ever. Totally sadistic. Total overkill."

"You know the names of the vics?"

"It's Judge Orlofsky," I said. "The bastard who killed him also killed the judge's wife."

"Anything else?"

I told him, "Well, all I've heard is that maximum security is mandatory for the reboot of the Dario trial."

I wish I knew more. When would this new trial happen? Maximum security where? Cappy told me he'd call me if there was any news.

News couldn't come soon enough.

CHAPTER 51

IT WAS MIDDAY and I was at my desk in the squad room, with Alvarez to my right, Conklin to my left, and the remains of lunch spread around our pod. I gave my pickles to Alvarez, and she gave me access to her bag of chips baked in truffle oil. Conklin had nothing to swap but a small bag of M&M's, which he emptied onto a paper plate.

I downloaded Hallows's crime-scene photos to my computer, and Alvarez and Conklin wheeled their chairs closer to mine.

Then I pushed the remains of my sandwich aside, and to the background sounds of ringing phones, cops talking over one another, and twenty-four-hour news coming from the TV hanging on the wall over my head, I clicked the Enter key on my desktop computer and started this nightmare slideshow.

I began with photos from the incident last week, and related to them what I'd heard about that day in court, the first day of Dario Garza's trial, when a box containing a smoke bomb had exploded outside Judge Orlofsky's courtroom, disrupting the trial just as Yuki was finishing her opening statement. The box with the smoke bomb had also held about two dozen colored cards, pictured in the next three photos, all inscribed with the numbers and addresses of the jurors, the judge, and the attorneys for both the prosecution and the defense.

It had been a warning. And now it was a fact.

I continued narrating as I shifted to the carousel of today's crime-scene photos. The first photo on my screen showed the bloody bed and the beheaded body of Judge Martin Orlofsky. On the carpeted floor beside the bed was the headless body of the judge's wife, Sandra Flynn Orlofsky.

I clicked next to shots of the CSIs working the living room, including a door from the yard to the ground level and a close-up of the jimmied lock. And finally, a series of horrific pictures of the severed heads in the bathtub.

Alvarez exhaled a loud, "Oh, my God," and wheeled her chair away, back to behind her desk. Conklin cleared his throat and, after a moment, said, "When I was across the street at MacBain's picking up lunch, I spoke with a depressed patrolman, Joe Greely, sitting at the bar. He said that he'd been one of the officers assigned to watch over the judge after that threat at the trial. And still this had happened."

I nodded. "What'd he tell you?"

"He was slurring a little. Half sliding off the barstool," said Conklin. "But I believed him when he told me that he might have talked to the killer."

"Really? Might have?"

Alvarez said, "Don't stop now, Richie."

"Yeah. So, while I was waiting for our orders to be ready, I took the stool next to Greely," Conklin said. "He told me that early yesterday morning there was a Mexican gardener in work clothes and a banged-up truck parked across the street from the judge's house. Greely went over to check him out, since he was on protection detail. Greely says the gardener didn't seem able to speak much English, but when he asked the guy his business, he got a name, registration, license, and tag numbers. Everything was registered to a Luis Perez."

"Hunh. A pretty common name."

"True," Rich said. "There are a few million Luis Perezes in California, but only one truck with those VIN and tag numbers. And Greely has now learned that that particular Luis Perez has been dead since Alvarez was in grade school."

I sighed. "Suspicious, true. But I can think of a dozen reasons this gardener might use someone else's ID. What makes Greely think this guy was the killer? Did he act suspiciously? Was the guy's truck seen somewhere it shouldn't have been? Did Greely see him enter or leave the house?"

"Nope. It was cop's intuition," said Rich. "But just in case, I'm thinking we check to see if any of the neighbors have security cameras and caught a photo of the gardener. Even if they don't, Greely can describe him to the sketch artist."

"Once he sobers up."

"I'll make that happen," Rich said.

CHAPTER 52

WE DUMPED THE remains of our lunch into the trash, and Conklin, Alvarez, and I changed gears back to trying to get a handhold on the 'I said. You dead' killer.

Cindy's story about the murders had run above the fold on page 1 of the *Chronicle* and now tips were coming in. I was combing through them—hoping for a good lead, praying for one—when Bob Nussbaum called me from the front desk to tell me to pick up line three.

I answered the ringing phone with my name.

Brady said, "Christ, Boxer. I've been trying to reach you for an hour."

"I've been on the tip line, nonstop."

"Find anything?"

"So far just a giant-sized desire to punch the wall, but at least I'm crossing names and bum leads off of the list."

"For instance?"

I sighed. "Okay. A woman calls the tip line and leaves a message. She has a hot lead. I call her back. She says she was at the seafood counter in the grocery store last night. The guy ahead of her in line says to the fish on ice, 'I said. You dead.'"

"Oh, jeez."

"She almost got to me. Instead of yelling, 'Real people died,' and hanging up, I thanked her for calling the tip line."

Brady said, "The way I feel, I would have blasted her and *then* hung up. Good job, Boxer."

The boss told me that he was still at the control center near the Orlofsky murder scene. Gene Hallows was keeping him in the loop, but the CSIs hadn't yet found anything forensically useful.

Brady said, "Boxer, I got a call from Section Chief Craig Steinmetz of the local FBI office on Golden Gate Avenue. You know Steinmetz through Joe, right? He tells me there's a field agent in town from the Boston branch who wants to come in and talk to you. His name is James Walsh, and he says he has a lead into the 'I said. You dead' murders. He's about ten minutes out from the Hall."

Walsh was there even faster than that. I'd barely had time to even tell Conklin and Alvarez about Brady's phone call when Nussbaum called me from the desk to say that a Special Agent Walsh was here to see me. I asked Alvarez and Conklin to stand by, then crossed the floor to the front desk.

James Walsh and I introduced ourselves and shook hands. Walsh was six feet tall, had short grayish-blond hair and big hands and feet, and wore blue trousers and a blue pin-striped jacket. Looked like a former college quarterback now dressed as a white-collar insurance guy.

I brought him directly to the war room. The Jacobi and

Robinson murder books were sitting on the table in there next to a folder of articles and photos about Sadie Witt.

This morning's Orlofsky horror show had not been taped up. There was no evidence that they were connected.

Walsh spent some time looking carefully through the Jacobi and Robinson crime-scene and morgue photos until I said, "Agent Walsh, I'm interested in your thoughts."

He nodded and said, "Call me Jim."

"Lindsay."

"Lindsay, I've read the reports on Jacobi and Robinson, but I'd like you to run the cases for me."

"How much time have you got?"

"Whatever we need."

We sat at the big table and I gave Walsh a short, crisp version of the Jacobi and Robinson murders, which had happened a week ago, within an hour and a few blocks of each other. I told him our current theory, that wealth was part or all of the killer's motive, and cited Jacobi's million-dollar settlement and Robinson's literary and financial success. And I said that a good source had told me that Sadie Witt had inherited a house worth a quarter of a million dollars a few weeks before she was murdered.

He turned down my offer of coffee and said, "Thanks for running the cases for me. But what would really help me is knowing what you think."

I said, "You want me to speculate."

"Right."

"James, I'm at a loss. We all are. I've told you about Frances Robinson, found dead inside the doorway of her apartment. Immediately, two very senior teams canvassed her neighbors and interviewed her friends, relatives, even her ex-husband. They are still digging but so far have only found a great deal of sadness and urgency for the police to find Frances Robinson's killer."

"What was the general opinion of her?"

"People loved her books and loved *her.* There was nothing suspicious or corrupt about her, no known stalkers, or ugly threats, and she didn't know Warren Jacobi. The note on her laptop is the only thing that connects them."

James nodded and asked me for more about Jacobi. "I understand you knew Chief Jacobi for almost fifteen years?"

I said, "I can tell you what I know about Jacobi, but that will take an hour and I still won't be finished."

"Go for it."

CHAPTER 53

"I LOVED JACOBI. We all loved Jacobi. That he was murdered drives us crazy night and day, but we don't have a clue." I picked through my nearly fifteen years of encyclopedic knowledge of Jacobi and told this FBI agent about my friend's integrity and leadership abilities. I told him more about Ted Swanson, the dirtiest of cops whose illegal and lethal activities had caused Jacobi's "retirement."

I said, "Warren Jacobi spent his last hour on Earth bird-watching at dawn in a very nice park when he was shivved from behind by an unknown scumbag. The bird-watching was a surprise to me. It was a new hobby. The killer was a pro or he never could have surprised Jacobi from behind. All that was found at the murder scene was a matchbook hidden in some ferns. No prints on it. No nothing on it except the 'I said. You dead' message and the name of the bar it had come from: Julio's. Dive bar in the Mission."

I opened the Jacobi murder book and flipped through the pages until I reached one with an enlarged photo of the matchbook. I turned it toward Walsh, who focused on the writing inside the cover.

"The block lettering is consistent with the lettering I've seen before."

Did Walsh have something on the killer? I was getting anxious just being with him surrounded by photos of the dead. I wanted to shout, *Just tell me!*

"I understand that there also was a note reading, 'I said. You dead,' in the pocket of Sadie Witt's pants."

"Soaked in her blood." Walsh looked at me. "I worked the case."

Why would an FBI agent from Boston work a murder case in Verne, Nevada? Are there even earlier victims from other states we don't know about? Are we dealing with a serial killer?

"And?" I prompted.

"And nothing. This killer is a ghost. And we haven't been lucky. But I have a semisolid lead that I've vetted and can talk about. It hurts to do it, but I'm ready to share."

Special Agent James Walsh stood up and dragged his chair away from the table, then sat down hard again. He seemed pent-up and anxious. *He* was the one who had come here talking about wanting to share his lead, but now it was as if he wasn't sure he was ready. Or maybe he wasn't sure about talking to *me.*

I didn't yell but spoke in a louder tone than I intended, "So, James, apart from the unsolved cases, can you tell me what's bothering you?"

Walsh ran his hand over the lower half of his face, sighed loudly, and finally said, "I'll tell you, but I'm going to need something from you."

CHAPTER 54

WALSH NEEDED SOMETHING from *me*?

"What do you have in mind?"

He smiled for the first time since entering the war room. Then, with a trace of reluctance, he said, "Okay, Lindsay, here it is. I know your husband. Joe and I were in the BAU together and I always liked him."

My husband had begun his long career in law enforcement as a profiler in the FBI's Behavioral Analysis Unit at Quantico. Was Walsh's case somehow related to Joe?

"What are you saying? What does Joe have to do with—"

"Nothing. Sorry, no, this has nothing to do with Joe. I just mention the connection because I've always trusted Joe, and I'm here to see you because I hope I can trust you, too. I have a working theory on the identity of this son-of-a-bitch note-writing killer. You and I are the top investigators on this case, but if what I say gets out of this room, it could blow up the career of an innocent man. A fellow FBI agent. So if you want to work together on this theory, I need your word that what I tell you stays just between us. For now."

I said, "I'd feel better if you'd tell me what I'm agreeing to."

"Trust me for a few more minutes, will you? If you can't agree, we'll forget this conversation ever happened."

"All right. Tell me or I'm going to beat it out of you."

The G-man laughed, and then he got serious, raked his hair back with his hand, planted his elbows on the table, and said, "There's a guy in the Bureau I've known for about ten years. I worked with him on few cases, say five. We overlapped in Portland for a while. We're not close, but we're friendly."

Walsh grew quiet again. I was trying to read his mind while giving him a full-bore stare, and I was about to slap the table and stand up in frustration when Walsh finally found his voice again.

"I saw this agent checking into a motel in Verne while I was following a lead. More on that in a minute. But this agent, he had no business being there. Verne's major attraction is a slot machine at the town's only gas station. I would have been notified if he was working anything related."

"What did he say when you asked him?"

"He didn't see me," Walsh said. "And I wasn't comfortable asking him, 'What the eff are you doing here?' A murder had been committed. I didn't want to bring this agent into it without first knowing why he was there. But wait. There's more."

I nodded, encouraging him to go on.

Agent Walsh said, "Sadie Witt wasn't the first of the 'I said' victims. There were at least two others. One in Boone, North Carolina, about eighteen months ago. That victim was Alvin

Poole, who died inside his Tesla by a gunshot to the back of his head. He was eighty-one and had no known enemies. His wife was home, and she heard the blast. And they found a note stuck under a windshield wiper."

I took a wild guess. "A note saying, 'I said. You dead.' "

"Correct. It was a little strange but didn't seem meaningful then. There was a write-up about Poole in the local paper. It was short, an obit, and attributed to no one. I learned that Poole's Rollaboard company had bought him out not long before, and his share of the company was worth some money with a lot of zeros at the end.

"I'd say Alvin Poole was victim one."

I was clenching my hands in my lap. *What could Alvin Poole have to do with Jacobi or Robinson?*

Walsh went on.

"Victim two, I believe, is a divorced woman who died under suspicious circumstances. This woman was an acquaintance of mine."

"What kind of acquaintance?"

"Nothing like that. But her ex-husband was actually that other agent I mentioned. They'd divorced after a pretty short marriage, and I'd had a drink with him not long before his ex-wife died. He complained that she was a bitch and a gold digger."

James sighed and apologized. "I'm sorry. This is very painful."

"I understand. Please go on."

"I think I could use some coffee after all."

CHAPTER 55

I TAPPED BRENDA FREGOSI'S number into my phone and asked her to bring two cups of coffee to the war room.

"Brenda, the usual for me. Our visitor takes his coffee with milk and sugar."

Jim Walsh and I went through the clippings in the Sadie Witt folder until Brenda came in with the coffee. Then she left, closing the door behind her.

Walsh cleared his throat and continued. "Okay, I have to back up a bit. The woman I knew was actually the second wife of the unnamed agent—let's just call him 'Mike.' And Mike's first wife died under unusual circumstances. She drowned in the bathtub in the house where they once lived together in Portland, Oregon. Mike was also in Portland at the time, but he had something of an alibi established. He was at his nephew's high school basketball game with family and had the punched ticket stub to prove it."

I shrugged. This was proof of nothing.

Walsh said, "No, you're right. Checking it out, which I did, questioning him, which others did, his alibi was thin, but he'd covered his tracks well enough. He'd been with family and friends in a public setting."

"I'm not really getting this, Jim. In your opinion, did Mike hire a hitter? Was he framed? Or is it a coincidence that he was in the same town when she killed herself? Or do you think he killed her?"

Walsh started to shrug and knocked over his coffee, which spilled and spread across the table. I snatched up the Witt file along with the Jacobi and Robinson murder books, and Walsh found a roll of paper towels and soaked up the mess.

"God, I'm so smooth," Walsh said.

"Don't worry about this. Just get to the point, please. I feel my hair turning gray."

Walsh laughed. And then he said, "Okay, okay. Two things stick out, Lindsay. Mike paid his ex a six-figure divorce settlement. And he married again, only to end in another divorce. His second ex-wife was also killed, and I can't see it as anything less than a murder. This is what eventually brought me to San Francisco and to you."

"I'm ready now, Jim."

"Mike's second ex-wife was found hanged from a beam in the attic of the family home. There was no note, but a message was written on the soles of her shoes in ballpoint pen. In block letters, on the sole of one loafer, were the words 'I said.' And on the sole of the other shoe, the same kind of lettering—"

" 'You dead,' " Lindsay finished. "Damn. Why would he do that?"

"It all may have been a sick setup. As you said. A frame-up. I'd like to prove that. I'd like to exclude Mike. But not if he's a killer. Two ex-wives dead under mysterious circumstances? Both received six-figure divorce settlements. Of course he was questioned. He had another alibi. This time the alibi was substantiated and he was cleared. Still, my suspicions keep mounting."

"Okay. I understand. How do you see me helping you?"

"I'd like us to be silent partners, Lindsay. To share information as we can. To keep the lines open. Help each other and, best case, hunt down this maniac. And I hope to hell it's not my friend."

"Look, Jim. I can't help if you don't trust me enough to tell me his name."

Walsh shook his head, then reluctantly said, "Brett. Brett Palmer. That's his name. He's moving to San Francisco. I'll give you the where and when once I know. But I have to protect Palmer until we have evidence that exonerates him—or nails his ass."

"Got it."

We exchanged contact information and shook hands again. Then I walked FBI special agent James Walsh along the fourth-floor corridor to the bank of elevators. I watched the lights over the elevator go down to the ground floor.

I thought Walsh's gut instincts were probably right. But he didn't like what his gut was telling him.

CHAPTER 56

WHEN YUKI GOT to her desk the next morning, she had an email from Len "Red Dog" Parisi in her inbox, with the subject line: "Esteban Dario Garza Trial, Next Steps."

The message was brief. Her presence was requested at ten o'clock today in the DA's conference room on the second floor.

Yuki, as prosecutor, was on the short list, as was Nick Gaines, and the other invitees were Dario's defense team. Gaines met Yuki in her office, and they walked to the conference room together. It was an imposing space, with windows on the east side and sunlight glinting on the burnished oak table. There was a pad of paper in front of each chair, pens lined up parallel to the pads, as well as a carafe of water, water glasses, and charging stations at intervals along the center of the table.

Yuki and Gaines took seats flanking the chair at the head of the table, and about two minutes later, Red Dog came through the doorway. He was wearing one of his mahogany-colored tweed jackets that brought out the red of his hair. It wasn't just his hair and the jut of his jaw that had given Parisi his nickname. It was because of his reputation as a hardball prosecutor and, later, San Francisco's district attorney. He was fierce, tenacious, and indomitable.

He sat down and gave cursory nods to the others. A few minutes later, Dario's defense lawyers joined them at the table: Jon Credendino plus his second chair, Donna Villanova.

The atmosphere in the room was strained. Those present plugged in their devices, filled their glasses, passed notes, and finally Red Dog tapped the table with the butt of a pencil, which sounded like a gavel.

His opening remarks were stark and, Yuki thought, rightly so.

"You all know that Judge Martin Orlofsky, a fine judge with a great future, was brutally murdered yesterday, along with his wife, Sandra Flynn Orlofsky, a linguist who taught at Berkeley. Their killer decapitated their bodies with a machete to make the point that he had the time and the balls to commit this atrocity."

Parisi swept his gaze across the faces of the rest of the table, then went on. "No doubt that decapitations bring young Dario Garza to mind. We're not stopping until we arrest the killer or killers responsible for this tragedy."

Parisi paused for breath, then: "The Crime Scene Unit has been on the scene nonstop, and although teams of homicide inspectors have been meeting with Judge Orlofsky's friends and associates, no firm leads have come to light."

Parisi asked, "Any questions so far?"

There were none.

"All right, then," he said. "In consultation with the mayor and San Francisco's presiding judge, a new trial judge has been chosen to preside over Dario's trial."

Credendino said, "Mr. Parisi, you'll be relocating the trial to another location, we'll select a new jury, and so on, correct?"

"That's correct, Counselor. The details are to be determined, but maximum security will be required. That's mandatory for everyone here *and* the defendant *and* the new jury. Obviously, all involved will be sequestered for the duration, and the jurors' names will not be revealed."

Questions followed. How long would it take to gather enough people for jury selection? Was there a space large enough for a trial and with enough room to separate the jurors from the attorneys and one another?

Parisi said, "Until the trial is relocated, my office is responsible for the defendant's safety, and police security is available to those who want it. That's round the clock."

"I'd like twenty-four hours to consider your suggestion," Credendino said.

"It's not a suggestion," said Parisi. "The new judge, along with the input of the San Francisco presiding judge, will determine the location and the date. They will discuss moving arrangements with me or Ms. Castellano and confer with defense counsel, but it is their joint decision alone.

"However, Mr. Credendino, you can always resign from representing your client. That's your decision."

Parisi stood. The rest followed, all leaving the room without speaking.

Yuki had many concerns.

Mainly for everyone's safety.

CHAPTER 57

YUKI FOLLOWED HER boss and mentor back to his office, which fit snugly into the southeast corner of the DA's suite on the second floor. That back corner was as far as Parisi could get from the constant chatter coming from the maze of cubicles filling every free inch of space allotted to his department. But to his mind, he still wasn't far enough away.

Parisi reached his desk and, while still standing, grabbed the receiver from his ringing desk phone.

He said into the mouthpiece, "Becky, I'm in a meeting. I'll call them later." To Yuki, Parisi said, "That was the press, of course. In the middle of this tragedy, there's still no escape from the everyday crap."

He logged into his computer, scrolled down, typed a note, and sent it. Then he turned his attention to Yuki.

"So, let's talk. You want to know who, what, where, when, and why."

Yuki set her laptop case down on the carpet beside the leather chair opposite Parisi's desk. Parisi's assistant, Becky, came in, said hi to Yuki, apologized for interrupting, and asked Parisi to step outside for a moment. Parisi threw an exasperated sigh and excused himself, and Yuki leaned back in the chair. She thought about Parisi's "who, what, where, when, and why," and he was exactly right, but she was sure that something within those five little words was going to surprise the hell out of her.

She lifted her eyes to the clock on the wall behind Parisi's desk. It was the round, schoolhouse type, but on the face of the clock was a graphic of a snarling red bulldog.

Len had never told her the story of the clock, but given its prominent placement, he clearly loved it. It was 11:06 bulldog time when the legendary DA reentered his office, settled into his chair, folded his hands on the desktop, and said, "I've got about ten minutes."

Yuki said, "Len. Tell me the plan."

"I can only tell you some of it. The details are still in the works."

"Tell me what you can."

"We don't have a start date on the new trial," said Parisi, "but we have a judge. Robin Walden."

"I've heard of her," Yuki said. "Military, right?"

"Right. Judge Walden served on a military court. She's best known for upholding a death sentence—"

"I remember now," Yuki said. "Kuwait. An army private went nuts and shot up a bunch of tents one night, killing two fellow soldiers and wounding a dozen more."

Parisi said, "Good memory, Yuki."

"His defense was mental illness or defect."

"Keep going. You must've heard about this in law school."

"I haven't thought about it in years. The killer's AA sponsor testified, with the soldier's permission, that he was in a cracked mental state."

Parisi agreed, adding, "Didn't work out for him. He *was* crazy, but not legally. He claimed he was under the influence of both alcohol and an anti-American family member, and he wanted to kill American soldiers. In fact, he couldn't wait. Anyway, the decision was three to two for conviction."

"Wow," Yuki said, getting it. "Robin Walden was on the court that upheld his death sentence. And she's our new judge on the Dario murder trial."

Yuki looked up Walden on her phone, scrolling until she found a photo of a woman in her late fifties, formerly a captain in the US Marine Corps. She held her phone up to show Parisi. "Is this her?"

Parisi said, "Yes. That is her."

"So, Len. That's part of the who and the what. How about the where? Where is this new trial going to be held?"

Red Dog smiled. "Sacramento," he said.

Sacramento? Yuki could only think of one place in Sacramento with maximum security, but could it hold twenty to thirty people in comfort and safety, twenty-four hours a day, for possibly months? Yuki's mind was scrambling with the complex, maybe impossible tasks ahead, but she didn't say so.

"Got it," she said. "And what's the 'when'?"

"When I know, I'll tell you first."

"Thanks, Len."

Yuki knew Red Dog well enough to know that he would not tell her first. She went back to her office fourteen paces away from his, near the interlocking cubicles of ADAs.

She closed her door, opened her laptop, and pulled up a map of Sacramento.

She spent an hour she couldn't spare poring over locations in Sacramento. Schools. Hospitals. Legislative offices. Many of them could, with serious modification, hold officers of the court, a prisoner standing in the dock for a hideous murder, a prominent judge, defense attorneys, witnesses, and the wife of a police lieutenant. That wife being her.

But she saw no way to restructure any of those functioning, many-doored public buildings into the kind of maximum-security stronghold necessary to protect the court from Dario Garza's possible associates.

Yuki knew that the only possible facility in the Sacramento region was the renowned Folsom State Prison.

She homed in on Folsom Prison, and after she looked at photos of it, she found archived blueprints. There was no one she could speak with about this turn of events, but she had a good mind for data and she came to a conclusion quickly.

No sane human being would want to be locked up in that place, packed wall-to-wall with convicted felons.

What was she missing? This time when Yuki dove into government databases, she found real-life shots of the prison from overhead, photos time-stamped the previous month. The focus of the images was activity in the exercise yard just beyond the baseball field. There were trucks. And cement mixers. And workmen carrying equipment. Good-bye ball field, hello—what? A new wing, like a barracks, detached from the main buildings.

This, Yuki deduced, was surely the site Parisi and the mayor were trying to arrange for the Dario trial. Yuki was no architect, but the size and simple rectangular shape of the new wing looked as if it could accommodate sleeping quarters, a courtroom, a cafeteria, and a gym. There were four guard posts overlooking the yard. It wasn't the Palace Hotel, but if the interior of this new building could hold the court and all the players, Yuki saw it was workable.

Any juror or court officer, including herself, who agreed to be sequestered in Folsom's new building, yards away from the prison itself, would more than demonstrate commitment to their civic duty.

If the maximum security could be maintained.

That was a mighty big "if."

CHAPTER 58

JOE MOLINARI AND FBI agent Bao Wong were having lunch at the House of Dim Sum in San Francisco's Chinatown, a casual eatery that was filled with conversation, laughter, and the pungent aroma of hot, flash-cooked Chinese food.

They were expected back at the FBI field office by noon, but Joe sensed that there was something weighing on Bao's mind, so he was using the downtime for some personal talk. Although they hadn't known each other very long, Joe knew he was her closest friend in San Francisco. He poured water into her glass and looked around, making sure no one was watching or listening to them.

Joe had secured one of the small square tables with two barstools in the back of the room. Four men and women, who looked like office coworkers celebrating a birthday, were at the table closest to them and making enough raucous conversation to give them a cover of privacy.

"You all right, Bao?" he asked.

Bao said, "I sure am. And you?"

"Uh-huh."

She cracked a quick grin and said, "I've done nothing but talk about myself. Got any burrs under your saddle?"

"Bao, I'll talk about the burrs under your saddle for as long as you want. If you want to. All that's bothering me is what we don't know."

"Like."

"Like why Steinmetz wants to see us in"—he looked at his phone—"an hour." He snagged the server's attention, and she told him, "It's coming right up."

Joe's educated guess after thirty years psyching out suspects for and with the FBI was that Bao had been spending so much time working as a fill-in with Chief Steinmetz in San Francisco, she had incensed her son and husband back home in DC, who had drawn a line in the sand. Bao was multilingual and experienced in the methods of drug cartels. But she'd likely never expected to juggle a family life on one coast and a working life on another. He guessed that Bao's husband, Brian, was threatening divorce.

Without knowing the guy, Joe considered what Brian might be feeling. And then he turned that thought inward. What if Lindsay wanted to transfer to, say, New York? Even temporarily, like for a year with breaks to travel home? He couldn't leave his job in San Francisco. Their daughter, Julie, was almost six. Would Lindsay even consider disrupting their lives?

Joe turned back to Bao. "Want me to fly to DC and have a talk with Brian?"

Bao laughed. "You're kidding."

"Maybe . . . "

"I can just imagine how that would go."

"So, what are you going to do?"

Bao said, "Joe, I appreciate your support. But I have to handle this . . . "

Joe could also imagine things from Bao's point of view. She was at a make-or-break stage in her career. Despite being a pro with a couple of decades in grade, she'd been consigned to the background in DC. But the SF office was smaller than the one in DC, less populated with senior agents, and she was needed here.

All of this was what Joe had gathered from things Bao didn't say.

The waitress came to their table and set down a tray of bamboo baskets, each filled with the specialty of the house: tasty, steaming little buns stuffed with meats, exotic seafood, spiced vegetables, and other five-star delicacies. In that moment, it was all about the food.

She and Joe unwrapped their chopsticks. Joe had lifted one dim sum halfway to his mouth when Bao's phone rang.

"It's Steinmetz," she said, stabbing the talk button. "Chief? Yes, we'll be there in forty-five . . . Oh. Okay. Twenty is possible. Yes. He's here. We'll see you soon."

CHAPTER 59

SECTION CHIEF CRAIG Steinmetz was overweight and balding, and the creases on his face made him look seventy. But Joe, who'd first partnered with Steinmetz twenty years ago, knew he was closer to sixty, just with a lot of mileage on him.

When Joe and Bao were seated in front of the chief's desk, facing the two US flags flanking the plate-glass window overlooking Golden Gate Avenue, Steinmetz asked, "Can I get you anything? Coffee?"

"We're good," Joe answered for them both.

Bao said, "You said this case was urgent?"

There was a tone in her voice, maybe agitation left over from the interrupted conversation at lunch. Steinmetz caught it and gave Bao a sharp look. He opened a desk drawer, pulled out this morning's edition of the *Chronicle*, and dropped it onto his desk. The headline was in seventy-two-point boldface type: DARIO GARZA JUDGE MURDERED.

An inch-thick folder followed the paper, and when

Steinmetz opened it, Bao and Joe saw that there were enlarged photos inside, along with a packet of documents.

Steinmetz began slapping the photos face up on his desktop in the space between the two agents.

The pictures were gruesome. First, a bedroom with two decapitated bodies. Then a series of close-ups of the bullet holes in the male's chest, the front and back of the female's head, blood soaking the carpeting. And the final scene. The bathtub with the two severed heads, the male's head tipped and leaning against the tub wall.

Steinmetz said, "These are the remains of Judge Martin Orlofsky and his wife, Sandra."

"The FBI is going to get involved?" Joe asked.

Steinmetz said, "There may be a link to a Mexican operation. The only clue we have is this."

He slapped down one more hideous photo; the decapitated head of a young man, Miguel Hernandez, perched on the top step of a flight of stairs.

"When he was alive, this poor guy was some kind of friend to Dario Garza, now on trial for his murder. Does the name Garza mean anything to you, Agent Wong?"

"Only in the sense that the name Garza is pretty common, and I've known of criminals with that surname."

"Molinari?"

Joe knew a lot about the Dario Garza case from Lindsay and Yuki but kept his response neutral. "I've heard about him, yes."

"The Orlofskys were shot before the killer did his surgery. The bullets don't match anything in our database, but this is a fact: Dario Garza's trial has been postponed.

"That's why I called this meeting. I need the two of you to go to Mexico for some undercover work. See what you can learn. Principally, who's behind this."

Steinmetz laid his hand on the photos, then said, "Betty will arrange your airline tickets and will book a car to meet you at Monterrey International Airport. Agents from the Monterrey office will meet you there to give you anything you need, and perhaps some fresh news. Book your rooms today, and when you've worked out a plan, call me. Any questions?"

Joe said, "We can make the first flight tomorrow morning, Craig. Okay?"

"Fine," said Steinmetz. "I'll call your contacts. Good luck. And keep your heads down."

He put the papers and the photos back into his center drawer, slammed it shut, and locked it.

CHAPTER 60

CINDY WAS AT her desk inside her small office at the *Chronicle* with its windowed view of the city room—but she didn't even glance at her colleagues working toward their deadlines. Her mind was split between her office and another small office that was located in the Verne, Nevada, police department.

She and Steven Wilson, the homicide investigator from Verne, had been on the phone for an hour, and this time she was recording it all. Cindy had promised again not to use Wilson's name, to tell the story with fictitious names throughout and the facts as Steve had been able to learn them. And then he told her why he'd called, saying that one of the "I said. You dead" deaths he knew about now appeared to be a homicide.

"Explain 'appeared to be.' How so?"

Wilson said, "She was the second ex-wife of a man in the investigative services. Which one, I can't say. But I saw a photo of the deceased. And I say it was connected to the 'I said. You dead' murder spree."

Cindy asked, "And what about suspects?"

Wilson said, "Nuh-uh. Not saying."

"Steve. I swore not to tell!" *What are we, in kindergarten?* she thought.

"Cindy, you can use what I've said or forget it. What I've told you could be a key to the whole story—or it's nothing. And by the way, you owe me. Big-time."

Cindy agreed. She owed him. She thanked him. And she hoped that one day she could return the favor by giving Steven Wilson some kind of a huge tip with no details and letting *him* research the entire known universe to learn the name of a victim—let alone the killer!

She hung up, telling Wilson, "I'm getting another call," then typed a URL into her browser, calling up the website of a transcription service that would convert her hour-long recording into a perfect transcript in six minutes flat for as many dollars.

Cindy pressed Send and called Lindsay.

When Lindsay picked up, Cindy said, "We need to have a girls' dinner at Susie's. Working dinner. No booze."

CHAPTER 61

WHEN I PULLED open Susie's front door, I saw that the café was packed to the walls with a riotous evening crowd. Rikki's steel-drum band had been moved from the front of the main room to its center, leaving more space at the bar for the after-work regulars and the sleek women from the Financial District who'd come for ladies' night: half price drinks and dancing to the irresistible heat of the Caribbean beat.

Claire, Yuki, and I picked our way through the tipsy dancers, along the kitchen corridor to our usual spot in the room in the back. It's half the size of the front and tonight was jammed with twice the normal number of weekday diners. Cindy was already waiting at "our" booth in the back corner. I read her expression as *What took you so long?*

We hadn't even settled into the banquettes yet when Cindy began talking. "I just learned—"

Claire asked, "Before we start, Cin, okay to order? I skipped lunch today."

She signaled to Lorraine, who held up the flat of her palm. Meaning, *I'll get to you when I can.*

"I can't stay long," I told the others. "Joe's suddenly catching a 5 a.m. flight tomorrow, and we have to shift some plans—"

The girls protested.

"Lindsay, at least give me fifteen minutes," Cindy said.

Lorraine came over with a pitcher of beer, but Yuki said, "We're not drinking tonight. Please bring bread and butter, okay?"

Lorraine said, "Okey dokey," and disappeared into the shifting crowd before Claire could put in an order.

Claire sighed and said, "Okay, Cin. So, what happened?"

"I heard from my contact in Verne . . . "

I was sitting directly across from Cindy and could barely hear her. I said, "Say again?"

Yuki whipped her head around to the left and shouted at three people laughing and talking at the next table, "Will you keep it down, please?"

"Hey," said the man sitting at that table. "Mind your manners."

Yuki turned back to our meeting. "Cindy, you were saying?"

As if cued, Rikki's band launched into a Calypso jazz version of "Down to the Market," making it difficult to form or follow a simple thought.

But Cindy was still on track.

"My cop source in Nevada . . . "

"Wilson," Claire and I said in unison.

"Uh-huh. He called me today. He heard about a cold case in Portland, Oregon—an 'I said. You dead' crime that happened about a year and a half ago."

While twisting her ring, pulling at her curls, and focusing on each of us in turn with her big blue eyes, Cindy told us what she knew about this unsolved case.

"This woman was a divorcée in her mid-thirties. She was found dead. Hanged. But that's not the weird part. The kicker is that when she was found, the words 'I said' were written on the sole of one of her shoes and 'You dead' on the other."

Claire asked, "Her death was a homicide?"

"Undetermined," said Cindy.

"You're saying that the ME called it 'undetermined'?" Claire asked. "This woman's death wasn't ruled a suicide, a homicide, or an accident?"

Cindy said, "Not officially, no. But *someone* knows. So, I'll be digging for leads."

I felt a pang of guilt. Agent Jim Walsh had told me about this same suspicious death in Portland. Now my three best friends were in on this story. Cindy Thomas, a stellar reporter and bestselling true-crime author, was determined to unlock the puzzle and get it out to the world in big black headline news. She was about to turn this cold case nuclear.

I'd promised Walsh that I would be his silent partner. I hadn't broken my promise, but Cindy wanted help. She asked us each in turn: Could Claire speak to her counterpart in Portland? Did Yuki have any strings she could pull with the Portland DA? And did I know any cops who worked in Oregon?

I tried to stop the unstoppable Cindy Thomas.

"Cindy, can you sit on this story until Portland's ME calls it a homicide."

Yuki said, "I agree with Lindsay. I can see a lawsuit if you get it wrong. You really don't want—"

Someone said, "*Excusez-moi.*"

Lorraine was standing at the head of our table, order pad in hand.

"Ladies, these are tonight's specials. We have a jerk chicken wings appetizer, with bones or deboned if you prefer. Also, a very nice grilled sea bass . . . "

This was my cue to leave.

I squeezed my friends' hands, kissed the cheeks of those I could reach, and waded through the crowd toward the door.

The streets were quiet, and the sky was still light when I drove home.

CHAPTER 62

YUKI WAS FINISHING her chicken wings while listening to Cindy's thoughts about the Orlofsky murders when Rikki's steel drums burst into the "Happy Birthday" song. She looked up to see a pink, blue, and yellow cake with flaming candles being carried to a nearby table. Cheers and singing "How oh-old are youuu?" rang throughout the room. But there were no cheers from the booth at the rear.

And that's when Yuki's phone sounded with the muted wail of a police car siren. That ringtone was Brady's inside joke, but now Yuki grabbed the phone and said to her husband, "Hon? Is everything okay?"

Yuki listened to Brady while her friends looked on.

"Great. Thanks. See you soon."

Yuki clicked off, saying, "He's sending a couple of patrol cars for me. He's worried."

"Me too," said Cindy. "The smoke bomb outside the courtroom? The cards inside the box had the names and addresses of the court officers."

"Including mine," Yuki said.

Less than ten minutes later, Lorraine approached. "Yuki, there are police officers at the front door. For you."

"That was quick."

Yuki put two twenties on the table beside Claire, who said, "You'll text me when you're home?"

"You're Claire-voyant, you know that?"

Yuki hugged Claire and Cindy good-bye, then went out to the street, where four uniformed officers were waiting to escort her home.

CHAPTER 63

WHEN I OPENED the door to our apartment, I heard laughter spilling from the kitchen. It was Julie with a severe case of the giggles. And then I heard a dog barking through the giggles. It was our dog. After ten days away, Martha was finally back home!

I locked up my weapon in the bedroom gun safe and then called out, "Mommmmy's heeeeeeere," so that I could hear my daughter's shouts and more woofing from my beloved doggy friend of many years.

I was not disappointed. As I rounded the bend, Julie and Martha reached me. I stooped so I could hold them both at the same time and they bowled me over. There was more laughter and more barking, and then Joe reached his hand down and helped me up from the floor. God, I was glad to be home.

Joe said, "The pasta's ready, sweetie. Come to the table."

I shed my blazer, hung it on the back of a chair, washed my hands, and accepted a bowl of linguine with Joe's chunky homemade red sauce. Joe filled me in on Martha.

"The little nuggets were benign," he said.

I translated "nuggets" into "tumors."

"Joe, is that the end of them? Does she need more treatment?"

"Barbara said no, but she'll watch for any recurrences every three months . . . "

I leaned down and hugged Martha gently so that I wouldn't hurt her, and she gave me a soap-free face washing with her tongue.

After dinner, we had dessert: chocolate ice cream and creamy decaf coffee. Joe loaded up the dishwasher and turned down Julie's bed while I took a hot shower.

I put on Joe's bathrobe, wondering what I could tell him and still keep my promise to James Walsh within the lines of "I swear not to tell." I hadn't yet worked it out when Julie called out to me.

"You go on ahead to bed," I said to my husband. "I'll be back in a minute."

He untied the bathrobe sash with a quick pull and laughed at me, saying, "I'm timing you."

I re-tied the sash and went to Julie's room, kissed her sweet face, tousled her unruly hair, and assured myself that Martha was snuggled in and not whimpering.

"Mommy, I love Martha so much."

"And she loves you. Call me if you need me, Jules. Try not to wake up your dad."

"I know," she said. "He's going to Mexico, but he'll be back soon."

My little girl was comforting me.

I pulled down the blinds, shut off her lights, and went to

our room. Dropping Joe's robe to the floor, I crawled into bed next my husband, and he hugged and kissed me to pieces.

When he took a breath, I asked him. "Joe? What's this assignment in Mexico about?"

"It's about information gathering," he said. "Bao is fluent in Spanish, and you know I'm a pretty good negotiator . . . "

But then he had no words and neither did I. I was supposed to tell Joe something, but I couldn't remember what the hell it was.

CHAPTER 64

YUKI LIVED IN a two-bedroom apartment on Nob Hill. She'd lived there first with her mother after graduating college and now with Brady. At present, two police cars monitored the street. A couple of Yuki's uniformed escorts stayed in one car while the other two walked Yuki into her building, rode the elevator up with her to the fifth floor and cleared all rooms of the apartment, ensuring that her home was secure.

Yuki thanked the cops. One of whom said they would be parked downstairs and for her to call if she needed anything. Yuki bolted the front door, then called Brady to say that she was home.

"I'll be in bed in four minutes," she said. "Maybe five."

"I'll be there soon too," he said.

"Good," said Yuki, adding, "Hurry."

Yuki undressed, slipped into a pale-blue silk nightgown that Brady loved, and got under the bedcovers, where she fell asleep in seconds.

She was awoken by the cracking sounds of gunfire. Five, ten, too many rounds to count. There were screams on the street and the blare of car horns. Yuki crept to the window and, looking out, saw the cops firing back at an old tan Honda Civic. Whoever was firing from the Honda had automatic weapons, and Yuki no longer knew how many guns, how many cops, or where Brady was right now.

She grabbed her phone from the bench at the foot of the bed and took it with her into the closet. She and Brady jokingly called it their safe room, because they kept a safe inside. Yuki closed and locked the closet door, then dialed Brady—but there was no answer on his private line, and his work phone sent her to a recording.

"If this is an emergency, hang up and dial 911." The recording offered options, none of which were *Push 3 and you will be connected with Lieutenant Brady.*

Sweat rolled between her eyes, down her sides, and between her breasts. She heard a mash-up of gunfire and sirens coming from the street below.

Yuki's phone rang as soon as she disconnected the call.

Brady said, "Yuki? Are you okay? Morris and Kuby are on the way up to you."

"I'm fine, but I hear a lot of gunfire—"

"I can see our building," he said. "Keep down. Stay in the closet."

Even with the closet door closed, Yuki heard the gunshots and the squeal of tires on the street. She sat on the carpeted closet floor, clasping her knees with her arms. She thought of calling Lindsay but didn't want to put her friend in the line of fire.

25 Alive

Yuki had no idea how much time passed before she heard Brady's voice.

"It's me, Yuki. I'm coming in."

She stayed behind the door to the safe room and heard Brady bellowing for her. Officers Morris and Kuby began clearing the apartment and then Brady pounded on the closet door.

"Honey. It's safe. Open up."

Brady didn't wait for Yuki to fully open the door. He yanked it open and picked her up. She wrapped her arms around Brady's neck, clasped her legs around his waist, and held on tight.

"It's okay, sweetheart," he said. "We're safe."

CHAPTER 65

IT WAS ALMOST 11:30 p.m., and Cindy was in her office working. But her head was in cyberspace as she searched online through all the daily newspapers posted online in or near Portland, Oregon, over the last eighteen months.

She was hunting and pecking for a possible crime, the details of which had not and would not be released to the press. She was typing in keywords for "female suicide" and "murder victims," and there were too many of those to examine. Because Wilson hadn't given her a *name* or an actual *date* of death or a *street address*!

So, who had died wearing loafers with "I said" and "You dead" written on the soles? She needed a cop in Portland to tell her the victim's name. She texted her husband, Richie, again but got no reply.

Just before she logged off, Cindy found an article in the B section of the *Portland News* dated a year and a half ago. She moved her lips as she skimmed the article on her computer screen.

Angela Kinney Palmer, thirty-nine, of Lake Oswego was found dead in her home on August 15. Her cause of death is still under investigation. Ms. Palmer's funeral will be held on August 23, at the Church of Our Lord, beginning at 9 a.m.

Cindy found a photo of Angela Kinney Palmer. Had she been the woman found hanged to death? She felt for this woman, panicked beyond any fear she'd ever known, fighting to release the rope around her neck before her life was taken. Cindy had once been in a similar situation herself.

She couldn't let herself dwell on those memories. Cindy took her fingers off the keyboard, gave herself a shake, then picked up her cell phone and texted Claire: *Got a second?*

Claire texted back: *Call me.*

Cindy didn't wait for Claire to change her mind. She tapped Claire's contact and her friend answered immediately, saying, "This had better be good."

"Claire. I'm in the office hitting a brick wall. Please. Do you know anyone in the Portland ME's office? Or in a nearby city?"

"Sweetie. It's 11:54. You've already asked me. And now you've woken up Edmund. And no, I don't."

"I have only one question," Cindy said. "We know the Portland woman's manner of death is hanging. But there must be something more. I might not run with it. I might just use it as a clue to get more information. Or save it for a bigger story later. Look. I will protect my sources. I swear. No names will be mentioned."

Claire said, "Wait. You want me to give you the name

of a medical examiner who will give unofficial information to you?"

"Ahhh. Something like that. Claire, it's worth breaking a few rules if it leads to the 'I said. You dead' killer. Don't you think?"

"Cindy, I think this can wait until morning, right? Call Lindsay at the office at 8. Or talk to your husband. Uh-oh. Wait a sec. I know someone who retired from Portland's crime lab at the end of last year. I'll try to find him. Tomorrow. If he's okay with this, I'll text you his name and number. Okay?"

"Thanks, Claire."

"Welcome. Now go home."

CHAPTER 66

CINDY PRINTED OUT a hard copy of the article about Angela Kinney Palmer from the *Portland News* and saved the digital version to her working file. Why hadn't there been any follow-up on this article? Was it because Angela Palmer's ex-husband, Brett Palmer, or some *other* unnamed federal agent, had shut it down?

She wasn't ready to quit tonight. The drive, tenacity, and obsessive personality that had fueled her career as a reporter was pushing her forward now.

She looked up "Palmer" and "Kinney" in the Portland white pages and found dense columns of each. She narrowed her search to an "A. Kinney" living near the church where Angela's funeral had been held. She made notes. But she was still working blind. If the retiree from the Portland crime lab couldn't or wouldn't help her, she'd call Portland's ME and plead.

It was now past midnight. Cindy packed up her laptop and her police scanner and called Richie.

"Sorry, Rich, I'm stuck on this story. I'm closing up now. I should be home in half an hour."

"I'm downstairs listening to music," he said. "I parked in my usual spot. If you don't see me, I'll flash my lights and honk."

Cindy easily found Richie's twenty-year-old Bronco without his having to go to Code 3. She climbed into the passenger seat and gave her husband a good kiss. When they were on Fell Street and the straightaway toward home, she told Rich about Angela Kinney Palmer.

"She may have been a victim of 'I said. You dead,'" Cindy said.

"What makes you think so?"

"Well, my cop friend in Verne got a lead about a federal agent who may have killed not just his second wife but his first wife, too. There's no evidence that either death was a murder.

"But someone, the killer, made it look like his second wife had hanged herself, and wrote his slogan on the bottom of her shoes."

"Come onnn. 'I said. You dead'? And this was even *considered* a suicide?"

"Serials often like to get credit. Wouldn't you say?"

Rich stopped his car at the light on Masonic Avenue. He asked, "You think she wrote it, then hanged herself hoping to frame her husband?"

"I know that sounds far-fetched, but yeah, it's possible. I need help with this, Richie. Who do you know in or near Portland?"

Rich looked at his wife with a straight face, and then he couldn't contain his laughter.

“Geez. Even my husband—” ’

“Listen, love of my life, beat of my heart—”

“All right, all right . . . That’s enough.”

“Cindy. Even if I knew someone, I can’t help.”

“Because the case is unsolved,” Cindy said, “or it’s out of state, or blah, blah, blah. So, never mind. But to me, it looks like Angela Palmer’s ex-husband killed her, and if he didn’t do it, some maniac did and that maniac is still at large—and he’s laughing.”

CHAPTER 67

THE 5 A.M. Aeroméxico flight 33 to Monterrey International Airport had been delayed due to a mechanical problem, unspecified by the flight crew. Joe Molinari and Bao Wong were strapped into their seats in business class when this announcement was made by Captain Fredericks, who promised that the issue was small, that the part was being refitted now, and "Thank you for your patience."

Joe and Bao exchanged glances.

"Let me look," she said.

Bao typed on her phone, scrolled with her thumb, and after a long minute said to Joe, "It's either this flight or the United flight at two this afternoon."

He shook his head no.

The whole operation would fall apart if they weren't in Monterrey on time—three and a half hours from now—when they would meet with FBI agents who had cartel connections. Those connections might lead to the person or persons who had killed the Orlofskys.

Joe texted Chief Steinmetz to give him the flight update, but Steinmetz did not respond. Joe kept his phone on in airplane mode and put it into his shirt's breast pocket. He answered Bao's questioning look, saying, "Let's give it another half hour, and if we're still on the ground, we pull our badges and ditch."

Ten minutes later, the lights dimmed in the cabin and the flight attendant made his announcement. "We'll be taking off shortly. Please return your seat backs to their upright positions and stow your carry-on items . . ."

Through Bao's window over the wing, they watched the airliner roll into position, then coast down the tarmac and lift off into a murky gray sky. Joe checked his phone, then stuffed a pillow behind his neck and fell asleep.

Sometime later, he awoke to the bucking of the aircraft as it bounced onto the runway before coming in for a safe landing.

Soon the aisle was filled with people and their hand luggage. A snarl of carts clogged the exit to the stairway that was slick with rain. Bao and Joe gripped the handrail as they stepped down to the puddled tarmac and entered the crowded terminal.

Joe planned to contact Mick Dougherty and Juan Ruiz. He had worked with them both in the past and trusted them. He also knew that the odds of being identified by the Diablo cartel as they made their way through the luggage retrieval section of the terminal was 100 percent guaranteed. By the time they reached the revolving door, this information would have been sent to cartel leaders, even the head of the entire operation.

Since foreigners were not permitted to bring arms into the country, if anyone was waiting to pick them off, this would be the time.

CHAPTER 68

JOE SAW DOUGHERTY and Ruiz leaning against the outer wall of the terminal building, waiting for them as planned. Ruiz was forty but looked ten years younger in a bright-green LIFE IS GOOD T-shirt, jeans, and high-top sneakers. Dougherty had put on a few pounds and his hair was streaked gray, but he still looked like he lifted weights and took a three-mile run most mornings.

Ruiz shouted to Joe and embraced him. "What'd you do, man? Walk here?"

Joe grinned. "Close enough."

Introductions to Bao were made during the walk to the short-term parking area, where Dougherty exchanged a ticket for a key to a well-used black Mercedes. He opened the doors with a few chirps of the key fob, and all four agents clambered in. Ruiz said of the car, "Don't be put off by her looks. This baby has been retrofitted 007 style."

Joe laughed. Dougherty insisted that he wasn't lying as he adjusted the driver's seat.

"Don't push any random buttons," said Ruiz. "You could launch a grenade or signal a satellite. But here's the exception. When you and Bao get into your vehicle, turn on the radio and leave it on. Mick and I will do the same. With both radios on, we'll be in constant contact."

Dougherty drove the Mercedes out to the service road, changing lanes as traffic merged toward the Federal Highway 40 exit. Ruiz and Dougherty talked to Joe and Bao during this drive and interrupted each other, taking turns describing the upcoming meeting in the town of Cadereyta Jiménez, just outside Monterrey.

"It's a one-stoplight town, and they're lucky to have the stoplight," Dougherty said. "You heard of this place, Bao? Forty miles southeast of Monterrey, a city of 56,000 people, and a history from hell."

Bao and Joe knew and had discussed that history—a massacre that had taken place a dozen years ago on the outskirts of Cadereyta Jiménez. At least sixty-eight people had been beheaded, their bodies dismembered, their heads, extremities, and organs left at the sides of the road.

There was silence in the car as the four agents recalled that tragedy, remembered photos of the horrific scene. Long seconds passed in silence, then Ruiz started afresh.

"We'll be spending twenty minutes or so with a guy named Gustavo, no last name. If he gives up what you need on Judge Orlofsky's killer, we'll make him rich enough to quit his stinking job as a first-class snitch. This should be an in-and-out transaction, Joe. Any delay or nonsense, we get the fuck out of there."

Dougherty told Joe and Bao, "You're going to drive 3.2 miles north on this road. We'll be ahead of you with our coms on. At 3.2, you'll see a church on the corner of the block, right-hand side. Just past the church, there's a no-parking zone. Park there anyway, but stay in the car and talk to us. We'll show up to officiate the meet once Gustavo arrives."

"What do we know about Gustavo No Last Name?" Bao asked.

Dougherty said, "Not very much. He's Mexican. He rarely speaks, but you get the idea that he knows everything. His gang looks up to him. When he does speak, his word is final."

He pulled off the road and parked behind a silver Honda SUV. He said, "There you are. That's your ride."

Ruiz got out of the Mercedes and handed Joe a car key and three weapons: two loaded semi-automatic handguns and an AK-47.

Then Ruiz got back into the black sedan as Joe and Bao settled into the SUV, with Bao at the wheel, Joe riding shotgun. Slipping one gun into his shoulder holster, Joe passed the other handgun to Bao. She placed it on the seat beside her. Joe checked out the AK, then stood it on its butt end between the two front bucket seats.

As Dougherty pulled up slowly, Ruiz shouted out the window: "Turn on your radio!"

Joe did and Ruiz's voice came through, if a bit crackly.

Voices were tested as the Mercedes moved on down the road.

Bao started up the SUV, then followed Ruiz and Dougherty from a distance, watching everything—traffic, pedestrians, and the dashboard—while looking for a church on the right and a no-parking zone just beyond it.

A dog suddenly appeared, limping across the road. Bao jerked the wheel to avoid the dog and hit the AK with her arm, knocking it to the floor.

That's when Bao turned her eyes away from the road.

CHAPTER 69

GUSTAVO SAT IN the passenger seat of a roomy Lexus UX 200 with Manny at the wheel and three Diablo cartel members in the back seat. All were armed and had been watching the two FBI agents from California, one tall white man and one Asian woman. As the two new agents exited the airline terminal, they were greeted by Ruiz and Dougherty, FBI agents based in Monterrey.

Gustavo watched Ruiz hug the one he knew as Molinari, saw the four laughing and walking to short-term parking.

He gave instructions to the driver: "Manny, hang back. Don't attract the traffic cop's attention. Okay, now go. Slow."

Manny slowed the car, backed into an empty parking spot, and watched as the four Feds got into a run-down black Mercedes sedan. He stayed in his parking space until the Mercedes pulled out of the lot. Then Manny followed them to the airport exit road.

It became clear to Gustavo that the Feds were going through Cadereyta Jiménez, the municipality seat. There were parallel roads to the town with intersections crossing Federal Highway 40. As Gustavo and his guys continued on, they would have options to take alternate routes if they were recognized. Gustavo told Manny to let a Chevy truck behind them overtake, and Manny did as he was told.

To prevent the driver of the Mercedes from noticing that they were being tailed, Gustavo told Manny to take a left to the service road running parallel to the highway and cut back to 40 at the first right.

Manny hooked a left at the intersection, then drove a few hundred yards before asking Gustavo, "This right?"

"Yes. And step on it."

Manny again did as he was told.

CHAPTER 70

YUKI CASTELLANO AND her second chair in the Dario Garza trial, Nick Gaines, took seats at Len Parisi's conference table.

Parisi said, "Good news only, please."

Gaines pulled a blueprint from a three-foot-long cardboard tube, unfurled it, and smoothed it out in front of Parisi. Yuki held down one side of the curled paper, Parisi held down the other, and Gaines stood behind Parisi's right arm with a pencil in his hand.

Gaines said, pointing to the blueprint with his pencil, "This is the overview of Folsom Prison's ball field and exercise yard, as well as the main building and several storage buildings."

"And this is for the court?" Parisi was pointing to a rectangular building drawn in a darker blue than other buildings situated in the recreation field.

"That's it, sir. As you know, it was built for prison staff to use for spending nights or weekends with their families. Now it's going to be repurposed for the Dario Garza trial. We're calling it the Judicial Building."

Gaines continued: "These squares at the corners of the yard are elevated guard posts. Guards can see the entirety of the Judicial Building and every part of the yard and the prison as well as the access roads. The exercise yard will be closed until the trial is over and the building empty. The building can only be accessed here. Right off the highway, it's a short drive to the manned gate to the Judicial Building parking lot and then the guarded doors to the ground floor of the building."

Parisi asked, "How will the defense and the prosecution be separated?"

Yuki said, "The building will be split between the jurors' half and the court officers' half. There are two elevator banks on the main floor, two banks of five guards to check IDs."

"And is the construction finished?" DA Parisi asked.

Yuki said, "Yes. We spoke with the architect and the contractors, and they tell us the structure has been completely finished. Electricity and plumbing are completed. They've dry-walled, painted, tiled the bathrooms and kitchen, and are bringing in furnishings today. The elevators have been installed. The judge will have her own suite on the first floor. The courtroom will be on the top floor with doors on the south and the north sides for access to the corresponding elevator banks."

"And the Garza kid? Where will he be held?"

"He'll be in the prison, in solitary, of course, with video cameras in the cell and in the corridors. He'll be escorted to and from the courtroom by armed officers who will also be stationed in the courtroom once the trial begins."

“Any concerns, Yuki?”

“Hah. I always have concerns, Len. My mother was a worrywart who married a wartime soldier—and I married a homicide cop. It’s all good. Makes me hypervigilant.”

Yuki grinned and Len patted her hand. After he had hired her to join the DA’s office years ago, they had gone out to lunch to celebrate. Len had had a massive heart attack at the table. Yuki had gotten paramedics to the restaurant pronto, and while they’d rarely discussed this after he recovered, every time Len had a birthday, he thanked Yuki for saving his life. And when she had a birthday, he always remembered the date with a card signed “With heartfelt thanks, always, Len.”

Now she said, “The Judicial Building is a maximum-security building inside a maximum-security prison. I will feel very safe staying there.”

Gaines said, “Me too.”

“So,” Yuki added, “all of my anxiety monsters are slain. Len, do you have concerns?”

Len Parisi gave her a long, hard look. “No. Good work. Thank you both.”

CHAPTER 71

BAO HAD NARROWLY avoided hitting the dog when her scream collided with a loud, jarring crash that threw Joe sideways against his seat belt and Bao's shoulder.

The car was rocking from the impact, and Joe was dazed. *What is happening?* Bao was yelling his name, asking if he was okay. He saw that she had undone her seat belt and was holding a gun.

Joe tried to get his bearings. Their vehicle had stopped rocking, but he remembered the crash. A car had come from nowhere at full speed and T-boned the passenger's side rear compartment of the SUV.

Bao shouted again, "Joe, are you hurt?"

He couldn't answer. First one bullet, then another, came through the Honda SUV's rear window and lodged in Bao's seat back.

Using the seat back as a shield, Bao fired through the shattered window behind Joe. Joe heard the gun firing again, the sound of more glass shattering, and a man's yelp of pain.

"Joe. Get down on the floor. Grab your gun," Bao instructed him.

Before he got into the footwell, Joe turned his head and saw men carrying automatic rifles scramble out of the car that had crashed into them. Joe unlatched his seat belt and spoke toward the radio, "This is Molinari. We're under fire."

Surely Dougherty and Ruiz had already figured that out from the sounds, but Joe wanted to be explicit.

He spun in his seat and slid into the footwell below the dashboard. It was impossibly tight, but he was able to work his gun arm. He got to his knees and aimed his gun toward the shattered rear compartment window. Both his and Bao's shots landed. Men staggered backward and fell, screaming. Two stood up again. Joe aimed again, this time a few degrees to the right, through the rear window. In broken Spanish, he yelled, "Hands on the trunk. The police are coming."

One of the men broke away from the crash car and the men lying on the street. Bao crouched lower on the driver's side seat, leaning toward the rear passenger area. In a quick move, one of the guys from the crash car started running forward.

Joe saw enough of him to observe that he was young and muscular and fast enough. He was coming up on the driver's side of the Honda. And then he passed it.

Bao said, "Joe, hold on. Hold on!"

She had turned forward again. And then she stepped on the gas.

There was a wrenching sound as the SUV broke free from the crash car. Bao sped past the running man, and when the speed and the distance were just right, she opened her door hard and kicked it. In that same second, she stepped on the brakes.

The runner slammed into the door, a full body blow at twenty miles an hour, then he fell back onto the dirt road, moaning, rolling from side to side.

Dougherty pulled up in the black Mercedes. Joe saw both Ruiz and Dougherty exit the car with guns in hand. And heard police sirens coming toward them from behind.

Bao stepped out onto the road, pulled her handcuffs off her belt, and cuffed the runner. Joe looked at Bao, at the runner rolling on the road. He said, "Bao, that was amazing. I wish I had filmed that for you."

She smiled at him. "Thanks, Joe. Next time."

"I mean it. That was really something."

CHAPTER 72

JOE MOLINARI WAS one of three FBI agents sitting in the front row of an emergency hearing at a local courthouse in Monterrey. He, Ruiz, and Dougherty had been witnesses to the assault. Bao was at the hospital getting checked out for whiplash or a spinal injury, but before the day was over, he and Bao would also face interrogation for their role in the killing of three men whose bodies were cooling in the morgue.

The officers and the FBI agents had described the circumstances of the incident to the magistrate. The three dead men were identified by police chief Nuñez as bandits and killers, members of the Diablo cartel. One man who was alive but not speaking was Gustavo Sandoval, an attorney-at-law and head of the Diablo cartel, currently secured in a separate holding cell.

The fifth and final man was sitting in the witness stand in the dark and windowless courtroom. Emilio Lopez was another member of the Diablo cartel who had been in the car crash. At this moment, he appeared to be in bad pain from the run-in with the car door.

Lopez had volunteered to tell all in exchange for safe relocation for himself and his family and was convincingly appreciative for the opportunity to make his case. He was married with four children. He didn't want to go to jail. He wanted to live in the United States.

The interpreter asked Lopez to listen as she read his statement in Spanish.

"Mr. Lopez, you have stated that you were surprised by the crash with the people in the silver Honda. You say you were sleeping. There was a crash when the car you were in hit the Honda SUV."

"That's correct," Lopez said. "And I speak English."

"In your own words, then," said the interpreter. She switched on her digital recorder.

Lopez repeated his statement, this time in English.

"There was no plan. We were in Manny's car and I fell asleep. I woke up to a loud crash, and I was thrown from my seat. The talk was that the car ahead of us ran through a red light and we were too close to stop."

"The car you were in belonged to Manuel Nuñez?" the interpreter asked.

"Right. After the crash, Manny was yelling. He was very angry that his car was ruined. His idea was to get the driver to pay for the damage or give him the Honda or whatever Manny could get from him."

"At gunpoint."

"Yes. All of the guys I was with got out and rushed the

car we'd hit. There was shooting from both sides. Manny was killed. Eddie and Pedro were also shot dead.

"That's all I know. Big crash. I wake up. There is the sounds of shooting from AKs. I get out, and three of my bros are shot dead. I run. I think the driver of the Honda is going to run me down. She drives past me, fast, then opens her door, and I slam into it. Knocks me out. Next thing I remember, the police come. I talk to the police inside the ambulance that takes me to the hospital. They tape my ribs and release me into the chief's custody. And here I am."

Lopez was holding himself with both arms across his chest. He was jiggling his feet, breathing hard, and running out of air.

The magistrate addressed him. "What kind of gun were you carrying?"

"None. I own a Beretta gun. I lose it in the car crash. I never shot anyone. Only bottles. I shoot bottles and cans."

"Mr. Lopez. Is it true that all five of you in the crashed car were members of a club or association?"

"I don't like to talk for other people."

"I suggest you make an exception to your personal rules so that you aren't detained, tried, and sentenced."

"It was a joke. Our club."

"Feel free to laugh at your joke, sir. What did you call your club?"

"You mean Los Hermanos del Diablo?"

"Mr. Torres," the magistrate asked Joe's advocate. "Do you have a question?"

"Yes, thank you," Torres said. He asked Lopez, "To your knowledge, did the Brothers of the Devil have anything to do with the deaths of Judge Martin Orlofsky and his wife in San Francisco? I remind you, sir, you are under oath."

"Yes, I do understand. I swear, before God, Diablo has nothing to do with that. I heard that cops in San Francisco had something to do with it. I don't know names. I don't know reasons. I only heard 'They were killed by cops.' "

"Who told you that?"

"I didn't hear from one person. It was just talk after someone read about the crime online. I only know it wasn't us. I have never been out of Mexico."

The magistrate asked the assemblage if there were any other questions for Emilio Lopez, after which he thanked Lopez for his testimony and the injured man was escorted to a holding cell while the others discussed next steps. The decision was made that custody of Lopez would be transferred to the FBI as soon as it was convenient for the federal agency.

Paul Robles, FBI section chief in Monterrey, requested a conference with Joe.

The magistrate granted it, and Robles took Joe into a private room.

Robles said, "You're going to have to stay in a cell tonight, as a safety precaution. You'll have the hearing first thing in the morning."

"Can Bao stay in the hospital?"

"I'll work this out with the police chief and the magistrate. Let's say yes. What else do you need to know?"

"That I have the backing of the FBI, that you'll represent us and you'll do whatever is required to keep us out of prison."

"Joe, both the USA and Mexico are delighted to have you

rub out killers for them. Consider it one night in jail. Trust me. You'll be home in time for dinner tomorrow."

Hopeful that Robles could keep Bao safe under security overnight in the hospital, Joe shook Robles's hand, went back into the courtroom, shook hands with Torres, Ruiz, and Dougherty, and followed the guards upstairs to his own holding cell in the jail, where he'd be kept in isolation with 24-7 protection.

It wasn't until the door was shut and locked that he remembered that he'd had to relinquish his phone when he was brought into court. *Oh, God.* He hadn't called Lindsay.

CHAPTER 73

CINDY WAS HAVING dinner at home, alone.

Richie was still at work. Cindy had the TV on, tuned to the news, but was paying more attention to the recording of her latest call with homicide detective Steven Wilson. She sipped her smoothie as she typed up her notes.

She stopped typing for a minute to read them over and see if the transcript made sense to her. Detective Sergeant Wilson thought it was more probable than not that Angela Palmer had been killed by her ex-husband, who turned out to be an FBI agent named Brett Palmer. It was only opinion, not backed by a witness or forensic evidence, but Wilson had added more paint strokes to the picture.

He had said, "I found out that Brett Palmer had a first wife, Roxanne Sands Palmer, who also died before her time. The death certificate says that Roxanne Palmer drowned in the bathtub. The cause of death was 'drowning.' But the means were also 'undetermined.'"

Cindy had then asked Wilson, "The ME couldn't say if

she'd drowned accidentally or on purpose? Was Palmer a suspect? Was he charged?"

Wilson had said, "Palmer was the number one suspect because he was the dead woman's ex-husband, but there were no bruises on the body, and Palmer had an alibi."

"Let's hear it, Steve."

"Well, he was at the high school gym watching his nephew play basketball. It was a playoff for the championship."

"And Palmer stayed in his seat throughout this game?"

"Yup. He came in his car. His sister and brother-in-law came in another, and they all sat together in the gym. Palmer's sister said that Brett was there the whole time. His sister isn't going to say otherwise even if it was possible for him to slip away during this high-tension basketball game and get back to his seat. But I'm thinking, if Palmer drowned his wife *before* the game, the temperature of the bath water would have kept the body warm for quite a while.

"There was no writing on anything, however. No 'I said. You dead' messages. End of story."

"Wait. So, what's your opinion?"

"I'm still thinking. Okay. Off the top of my head. Palmer was married twice. Both of his ex-wives appear to have had died under suspicious circumstances. Could he have gotten away with murder? Maybe he did. Palmer's been professionally trained by the FBI. I don't think it's impossible that Palmer also killed his second ex-wife by hanging her and writing 'I said' on the sole of one of her shoes and 'You dead' on the other. Does that help, Cindy?"

"Sure it does. Steve. Release me from my promise, please. I have to get the SFPD involved."

"Okay. But you have to forget my name."

"Sure thing. Thanks very much."

Cindy turned off the recorder and thought more about Agent Brett Palmer. No inscription reading, "I said. You dead," was found on or near Brett Palmer's first ex-wife. Not on shoes or matchbooks, and not even on a computer screen.

If Roxanne Palmer was Brett Palmer's first killing, he may still have been an amateur. Had Palmer been a serial killer in the making?

If so, by the time he'd killed Jacobi, he would have been a pro.

CHAPTER 74

MY PHONE RANG at half past five in the morning. After fumbling for it in the dark, I pressed the blinking button and said, "Joe? Joe, where are you?"

At first I heard nothing but my own shallow breathing. I said, louder this time, "Joe, are you okay? Joe? *Hello?*"

"Lindsay. It's Cappy. Sorry for the way-too-early call, but I thought you'd want to hear this news right away."

My thoughts spun. Did Cappy know something about Joe?

"There's been another 'I said. You dead' murder."

"Oh, no. Oh, crap. Where are you?"

"There's no need for you to come," Cappy said, anticipating my next move.

I was already picturing waking Mrs. Rose and bringing Julie and Martha over when Cappy said, "No, really, Linds. CSU is here. We'll start a canvass when we've cordoned off the scene."

"Cappy, please. What the hell happened?"

"Oh. Sorry. At around 4 a.m. on Pine Street, a manager was

bringing trash to a dumpster leased by the apartment building where he works. That's where the manager found the vic. The 'I said. You dead' bit was written on her right forearm in lipstick. We're taking her body to the ME's office. Female in her mid-thirties, lying face up. No ID. The manager didn't touch her and didn't recognize her. Says he's never seen her before. Hold a second . . . Lindsay, Ali wants to talk to you."

Alexandra "Ali" Barnhart worked the night shift in the crime lab. I gripped my phone and waited out the shuffling sounds and other background noise until she came on the line.

"Sergeant? I'll know more in a few hours, but I can tell you this: The victim was wearing expensive duds. Like going-out-to-dinner clothes, not party clothes. Her panties were ripped, but her skirt was in place and she wasn't exposed. Her handbag was present but empty. No wallet, no makeup, no phone, no car keys. I didn't see any skin or blood under her nails, which were well manicured. I bagged her hands."

"Cappy's bringing in the building manager for questioning?"

"Yes. His name is Ruben Burnett. He's in the car now."

I heard a grumble of a loud truck motor in the background. It sounded like a garbage truck.

"Is there enough light for good photos in situ?"

"Yes, and I'll get more when she's on the table. Sarge, we have got to get the body out of here right now. That's a flatbed truck you hear, and it's taking the dumpster and its contents to the lab. I'll call you later."

There was a click, then dead air. I had just reconnected my phone to the charger when it rang again. I grabbed at the night table, knocking the phone onto the floor, where it scurried under the bed. I grabbed the charger cord and pulled, begging the universe to show me Joe's name when I looked at the screen.

But no.

"Linds?" It was Cindy.

CHAPTER 75

"LINDSAY. WHERE'S JOE?"

"He's still on a job in Mexico. Monterrey, I think. Do you know what time it is?"

"Almost six. I haven't been to bed yet. I have to tell you about Angela Palmer, the hanged woman. The one I talked about at Susie's. Remember? The one who—"

"Right, right, right. Suicide or murder, no one knows. 'I said,' written on the sole of one shoe with a ballpoint pen, and 'You dead' written on the other."

"You got it. Linds. Listen to me. I have a lead on her ex-husband. Agent Brett Palmer, FBI. I think he could be the 'I said. You dead' killer. Call me back when you're awake. I hate to grovel."

"I promise I'll call you later, but right now I'm waiting on a call from Joe."

After signing off with Cindy, I woke Julie. I called Mrs. Rose and told her I had to leave for work earlier than expected, then I fed my daughter Cheerios and orange juice, filled Martha's bowl with kibble, and despite Julie's protests that it was too soon, I got her dressed and ready for the day.

At 6:45 a.m. Julie, Martha, and I crossed the hall to Mrs. Rose's apartment. She hugged the little ones first and I got a good hug, too. Then I ran down the stairs to the street. I tried Joe's number yet again, letting it ring and ring, but he didn't answer.

Was the satellite connection weak? Had he lost his phone? Had it been stolen? Was it ringing in a drawer at a car rental? Was Joe in the hospital? Or were his circumstances so dire that I couldn't bring myself to think about where he was being kept and in what condition?

I called Craig Steinmetz's office line as I jogged to my car, expecting to leave a message.

To my surprise, he picked up on the fourth ring.

"Craig. Have you heard from Joe?" I asked after identifying myself.

"Not recently. I've called him and his Monterrey contacts. Do you know Mick Dougherty?"

"I know his name."

"Dougherty is working with Joe and Bao, but he told me that they ran into some trouble yesterday. Joe and Bao had to defend themselves, and they shot some armed cartel brutes. Shot and killed. Joe was fine, but Bao needed to go to the hospital and get checked out. Last thing I heard was that Joe had to testify at a hearing. He could be in a cell for his own safety right now, because of the shootings."

"Oh, nooo."

"If that's the case, his phone will have been confiscated."

I swore under my breath. Was Joe in custody? Or was he

dead? I was powerless to get the answer I wanted. Steinmetz had to know. He had to find out. But he gave me no answers, just assurances. He said he was sending people to Monterrey, that he had faith in Joe and Bao.

"Dougherty is a good man. So is his partner, Ruiz. I'm getting more of our people on this. They'll find out where Joe is at and call me. They're smart, and whatever's happening, they know what to do. Keep your phone nearby, Lindsay. Joe will be fine. He will."

I must have said, "Okay," and thanked him. I only know for sure that the line went dead.

CHAPTER 76

CINDY CALLED ME again when I was driving to the Hall. I told her, "You're on speaker. I'm driving in the car."

Cindy said, "Fine," over the staticky crackle. "You haven't heard from Joe? Is everything okay?"

"I can't talk about it, Cindy, even off the record. Talk to me about Brett Palmer."

Cindy said, "He's here. In town. *Brett Palmer is in San Francisco.* I'm having breakfast with him and I want you to join us."

"Cin, you've got this. You don't need me."

"And if Palmer tells me that he killed either of his ex-wives, then what? I can't arrest him. I can't even bring him in for questioning. All I can do is back out of the restaurant and hope he doesn't follow me into an alley, strangle me, and write on my shoes."

I said, loudly, "Cin. Record your conversation with Palmer and call me later."

"Okay. I'll let you out of a free meal with a possible killer and won't guilt-trip you if you tell me why you're waiting on a call from Joe."

"He was supposed to be home last night. He didn't come home, and he didn't call."

"You called Steinmetz?"

"Of course. But I can't talk about that. Will you stop asking me?"

"Lindsay, no. You're saying, 'Off the record'? About Joe?"

"I can't talk about it because I'm scared out of my mind and talking about this will only make me feel worse."

"It sounds like you're saying that Steinmetz hasn't heard from him, either."

God, Cindy was incorrigible. I pulled up to a yellow light and braked. I said to Cindy, "He offered some innocent explanations. He told me that he'd find Joe. Cindy, this whole conversation is off the record. Don't make me have to kill you."

"I hear you, Lindsay. I'm sorry, you know. For being obnoxious."

"Yes, you are, but you know I love you."

"I know. I love you, too."

"I'll call you later. And good luck with Palmer."

The light turned green. A car horn blared behind me. I said, "Gotta go. Talk later, okay?"

Cindy said, "For sure," and I clicked off.

I knew Cindy had never seen this side of me. Closed off. Terrified. And I really hadn't meant to scare and hurt my friend. But I had done it.

CHAPTER 77

NICK GAINES PULLED out a chair for Yuki at the counsel table, which spanned the width of the small, hastily built courtroom. Yuki and Gaines sat at the end of the counsel table closest to the jury box. Defense counsel Jon Credendino and his associates sat at the opposite end, near the outer door.

There was no rail behind them, no banks of chairs, because press, family, and all spectators were barred from entering Folsom Prison and its grounds. This was especially true of the Judicial Building. As Judge Orlofsky's murder had proven, participants in the Dario Garza trial were at risk of death if their names got out.

Yuki took a pill bottle from her computer case and swallowed an Advil with a gulp of water to tamp down a headache that she knew no pill could cure. Her stress level had hit the redline. The urgency of overseeing the completion of the Judicial Building in ten days had drawn Yuki's attention away from the boxes of police reports and court transcripts that had been produced for the prosecution in the original case against Dario Garza. She had been so involved in the completion of this building: the construction, the design, making sure that the living quarters for the principals would be separated by job function and again by gender. If the disparate groups mixed or even spoke together, there would most certainly be a mistrial.

She couldn't let that happen.

Now the twelve jurors and six alternates filed into the makeshift jury box. Yuki knew that there would be no excuse, no way out, if she was unable to convince these people of Dario Garza's guilt in the killing of Miguel Hernandez.

Yuki had mentally rehearsed today's statement again this morning while dressing, but she had not practiced it out loud. She'd rationalized that she knew the case by heart and would be able to deal with whatever Jon Credendino brought to the jurors.

But the moment had arrived.

She looked at Gaines, sitting beside her, his usual cool, calm self. He wrote on his tablet and pushed it toward her: *U OK?*

Fine, she wrote back. *You?*

That's when the bailiff asked the jury to stand. He swore the jurors in and then asked them to remain standing.

A door opened behind and to the right of the judge's bench, and the Honorable Robin Walden swept through the doorway. Everyone in the courtroom got to their feet.

Yuki stared straight ahead, feeling the weight of her responsibility to the people of California and to Leonard

Parisi, who had entrusted her with this case. The judge's entrance felt to Yuki as if the curtain had gone up on the most important trial of her life.

This was her case.

And she had to win it.

CHAPTER 78

THE BAILIFF'S NAME was Noah Stern. He was a large man with a barrel chest and a deep, authoritative voice. He had worked for the Superior Court of California in San Francisco for thirteen years, as a court security officer and now as a bailiff.

He called out to the jurors, "Please be seated."

The jurors and alternates settled into metal folding chairs in the jury box as Judge Robin Walden leaned across the bench to exchange words with the court reporter.

The judge's expression was neutral. She wore a thin dusting of makeup, a lace-collared blouse under her robes, a ring on the third finger of her left hand, and an emblem of the USMC suspended from a thin gold chain around her neck.

Yuki was watching when Judge Walden placed a Kimber handgun on the bench with the barrel facing the room.

This was a first for Yuki. She'd never heard of a judge bringing a gun to court. Was it a threat? A warning? Or did Robin Walden always carry a gun?

The judge sat down in the high-backed chair, and the bailiff called out, "Court is now in session."

Yuki felt the long silence as if it were solid matter that shattered when the judge said to the court officer, "Bring in the defendant."

The officer opened the rear door and Dario Garza, flanked by two armed guards, entered the room.

Today, Garza wore a white dress shirt, pressed chinos, and prison slippers. His dark hair was slicked back, and the chains around his wrists and ankles clanked as he walked. Even so, Dario looked like a billionaire. He smiled as if it was showtime, and as if he was confident he had the judge in his pocket.

His swagger shocked Yuki and reminded her of the street outside the Hall when Dario was first on trial. She remembered the gang of protesters with their red-lettered signs: DARIO INNOCENT. COPS GUILTY.

As Dario and his guards crossed the well toward the witness stand, Yuki gripped the arms of her chair. Gaines had just put his hand on her wrist when a male voice roared, "Noooooo!"

The howl, a protest in the key of rage, came from juror number 5, who yelled at the defendant, "YOU!"

Then he vaulted over the side of the jury box and ran toward Dario with a knife glinting in his hand.

Three guards and the bailiff charged the juror and brought him to the floor, piling on him. While he was emitting his loud, wordless scream, they cuffed him and dragged him from the courtroom.

Judge Walden's expression hadn't changed.

She spoke loudly over the commotion. "Bailiff, take the jurors back to their room. Court is in recess until further notice."

CHAPTER 79

WHEN CINDY HAD emailed Brett Palmer to arrange this meeting, she knew he was flying that night from Portland, Oregon, to San Francisco. She'd written to him requesting a meeting and gotten his reply after midnight.

I can meet you for breakfast at the Ritz, he'd written. *By the way, I enjoyed your book* Fish's Girl.

Thanks very much, Mr. Palmer.

Sure. And if you don't mind me asking, how did you know my travel plans?

Lucky guess.

I don't believe you.

Cindy had shot back, *Okay, you got me. But, you know, reporters never reveal their sources, Mr. Palmer. Anyway, it's just breakfast.*

He'd sent a string of laughing emojis, then, *Why do you want to see me, anyway?*

I just need some background, she wrote. *I'll tell you when we get together tomorrow.*

He'd written, *Sure,* then, *Breakfast at 8 a.m. at Ritz-Carlton's restaurant. Does that work for you?*

Cindy arrived at the hotel's restaurant a little early and found the maître d' podium unmanned. She scanned the dining room and saw a man in a business suit at a table by the windows overlooking the city skyline.

She started across the room but didn't get far before she heard a voice behind her calling, "Miss? Excuse me, miss?"

Cindy turned to see the maître d' attempting to get her attention.

"Oh, hi. I'm meeting Mr. Palmer here. He's sitting over there."

"Sorry, miss. That's not Mr. Palmer. He just called and said he was running a little late. Would you like to be seated at a table? Or would you be more comfortable in the waiting area?"

"A table will be fine," Cindy said.

"Very good."

The maître d' walked ahead of Cindy as they crossed the sand-colored carpeting to an empty table, where he pulled out a chair for her and asked her if she would like coffee or tea.

"Coffee, thank you."

Cindy took her phone from her bag and started checking her messages as a waiter arrived with coffee and cream.

For the next fifteen minutes Cindy downed her coffee and answered messages on her phone. She sent an email to Richie. She also read the front page of the *Examiner* and then answered more emails before checking the time.

The waiter stopped by to refill her coffee, then asked, "Would you like to order now?"

Cindy looked up from her phone and said, "Could you ask the maître d' . . . "

"Ma'am?"

"Would you ask him if he has received another message for me from Mr. Palmer?"

The waiter slipped his order pad into his jacket pocket and, after speaking to the maître d', returned to Cindy's table.

"No, ma'am. There is no further word from Mr. Palmer."

Cindy looked around the room and saw that it was filling up.

"I'm going to wait a little longer. Thank you."

She started to text Palmer but stopped without sending. Had Palmer decided to make her wait until she got the none-too-subtle message that he'd stood her up?

Well, Cindy thought, *I'll be returning the message. I won't be leaving. At least not yet.*

CHAPTER 80

CINDY TAPPED AN icon on her phone and opened the notes she'd made about FBI agent Brett Palmer. The maître d', whose name was Maurice, and whom she'd pretended not to recognize, was her source. Maurice was a fan of her column in the *Chronicle* and had confided to her that Brett Palmer came to San Francisco about once a month and stayed at the Ritz.

According to Maurice, Palmer frequented the lounge here and was known to pick up women who were also staying in the hotel. This had been going on, Maurice guessed, for about three years, which meant that Palmer already had a habit of picking up women while he was still married to Angela Kinney Palmer, wife number two.

A shadow fell across the table and Cindy looked up at a fortyish man dressed in a snappy suit. "Cindy?" he asked, smiling nicely. "I'm Brett. I'm sorry I'm late."

As he took the chair facing hers, he said, "I'm in the import business. I had to take a call from my client in Singapore, and he was speaking through a translator. I just couldn't get off the call. Have you ordered?"

"No, Mr. Palmer. I was waiting for you."

"Well, wait no more. I'm famished. Are you? The banana pancakes here are just tremendous. And it's Brett. Please call me Brett."

The waiter brought menus, and Cindy used the time to gather her impressions of the man with thinning brown hair and blue eyes sitting across from her. He was smooth and unthreatening, but she knew he was at least a cheater, and very possibly a serial killer. She didn't know what to make of the fact that he'd introduced himself as an importer, not an FBI agent.

He signaled for the waiter, and when the waiter returned, Palmer said, "My usual, please," while Cindy asked for scrambled eggs and toast.

Palmer smiled at her.

"I'm glad to meet you, Cindy. You're a terrific writer. So, let me give you the story that you clearly want to write. I didn't kill my wife. Either one of them. I loved Roxanne and I never hurt her. I never would. In fact, one time she turned over in bed and broke *my* nose. In her sleep. With her arm. That's a true story. In case you're interested in the truth. Are there any other truths I can share with you?"

CHAPTER 81

I HAD BEEN anxious before, but when FBI section chief Craig Steinmetz said he didn't know where Joe was, my fear struck like lightning. I tried to picture Joe. Was he hurt? Had he been captured? I didn't know what to do.

All I could do was wait, and that was just not how I handled fear.

And now I was worried about Cindy. She was meeting a person of interest in a homicide, and she was alone. Cindy Thomas was smart and cagey enough to avoid trouble. At least most of the time. On the other hand, she sometimes forgot that she wasn't a cop.

I texted Cindy to check in.

How's it going?

She texted back: *SOS Ritz dining room.*

I was five minutes away from the Ritz, and I wanted to be there with Cindy. I also wanted to see Palmer. Both excellent reasons to turn left on California, take another left on

Stockton Street, both of which I did, and bang, there I was, pulling up to the Ritz-Carlton.

I left my ride with the valet and entered the five-star hotel. I followed my nose to the restaurant, told the maître d' that Cindy Thomas was expecting me. A waiter walked me over to the table where Cindy was eating breakfast with a fortysomething man in a suit.

I said, "Hi, Cindy. Sorry to interrupt. I heard that this was a great place to have breakfast and I'm starving."

Cindy's companion said, "You heard right."

And my angelic-looking friend said, "Oh, great, Lindsay. Glad you made it."

The waiter brought over another chair, and I asked for a coffee. Cindy told her breakfast companion, "Brett, meet my good friend Lindsay Boxer. She happens to be a cop, but don't let that bother you. She's off duty. Lindsay, this is Brett Palmer, just in from Portland. He's in the import business, and he's here to verify that the banana pancakes at the Ritz are awesome."

I reached out and shook Brett's hand. I couldn't even remember if I'd brushed my hair or my teeth this morning, but I did remember to say, "Nice to meet you."

Brett said, "Please sit down, Lindsay. What kind of cop are you?"

I thought of saying, *Meter maid,* then thought better of lying to a person of interest.

"I'm a homicide inspector."

"Interesting," Palmer said. "Now I understand why you and Cindy are friends."

I said to Palmer, "Cindy and I met at a crime scene quite a long time ago. We bonded. I think Cindy solved that crime."

Cindy put her fork down and grinned. She said, "You think?" She shook her head and laughed. Then, "Brett, tell Lindsay what you told me."

"If you tell me why I agreed to have breakfast with you."

"You know why, Brett. You like my writing."

He rolled his eyes in a joking matter and said to me, "My first ex-wife, Roxanne, drowned over five years ago. There was an investigation, of course." Palmer continued, "I wasn't the guy they were looking for. And I have no clue why my second ex-wife, Angela, hanged herself. We hadn't lived together or seen much of each other since our divorce, and I have a solid alibi for when she was killed."

Palmer went on: "I read Cindy's column, and I know there've been some recent murders in San Francisco, so I can see why Cindy may have linked them with Angela's improbable death, because there were a few similarities. But in my opinion, they were not even close. And just so you know, I was nowhere near San Francisco when those other murders happened here. I've told Cindy that I can prove this, but not over breakfast. And I have another appointment. So, nice meeting you ladies. Fun, actually, but I've got to go."

Good point, I thought—if there hadn't been another "I said. You dead" murder just last night, with Brett in town and the victim tossed into a dumpster. I made a mental note to follow up on Palmer's date of arrival in San Francisco while Cindy told Palmer that the *Chronicle* would pick up the breakfast tab.

Palmer said, "I wouldn't dream of it. Lindsay, please order breakfast. It's all on me."

The mild-looking gent put a hand on Cindy's shoulder after he rose from his chair and said, "Thanks for getting in touch, honey. So long."

Cindy's normally bright expression wilted once Palmer was out of sight, and she asked me for my thoughts.

I said, "On the surface, he seems credible. But serial killers, as you know, tend to be careful. They don't leave prints or DNA, or accidentally confess to a cop. What do you think?"

"If he hadn't spent years picking up women in this hotel, if he hadn't called me 'honey,' I'd be more inclined to cross him off my list."

"So, you still view him as a person of interest."

"He hasn't changed my mind. I'm going to have to pry into his life a little bit. Or a lot."

"Virtually?"

"No. I'm going to hunt him to his lair."

I nodded and slid Palmer's fork off his plate and wrapped it gently in a cloth napkin.

Cindy gave me a smile, revealing her totally charming two front teeth that crossed over a teeny bit.

When the waiter came to the table, I went ahead and ordered myself the banana pancakes all the way.

CHAPTER 82

BAO WAS STARTLED awake. What was happening? It was her nurse, Ana, shaking her by the shoulder.

"What's wrong?" Bao asked in Spanish.

Ana replied in English. "Everything all good, Mrs. Wong. You are to leave hospital now." Switching to Spanish, she quietly added, "Four FBI agents are here and have showed IDs to the fourth-floor head nurse and me."

Ana was a small, efficient woman of fifty, and she moved quickly, following orders.

Bao had a sick feeling about her abrupt eviction from the hospital. She had been parked here for safety. There were cops in the corridors, at the intersections between departments, at the heads of stairs, at turns leading to the elevators. It was far more dangerous outside, where, given a clear shot, the Diablo cartel could take her out in seconds.

"Ana? What time is it?" she asked in English.

"Eight and fifteen."

"I have to stay longer. Did the doctor say it's okay to release me?"

"*Sí.* Dr. Rodriguez say, Mrs. Wong all good.'"

Ana fussed around her, but Bao was thinking about the four men who had come to take her from the hospital. They may have been vetted as FBI, but they could easily be fakes. Imposters. Maybe the cartel had found her. But they didn't have their hands on her yet.

Ana was tugging and pulling Bao into a standing position beside the bed. When she was on her feet, she let Ana disrobe her and re-dress her in the same dusty, soiled clothes she'd been wearing during the gunfight.

"You be home soon," Ana said in English.

She leaned toward Bao as she buttoned her shirt and said softly in Spanish, "Mrs. Wong, it is not safe for you here anymore. These men are your people. They will answer your questions and take you to airplane."

Then, in a louder voice, Ana switched back to English again and said, "Sit down, please, Mrs. Wong. I put shoes on now."

Bao asked the nurse, "Will you hand me my purse, Ana?"

The nurse opened the closet and handed Bao her brown leather shoulder bag she'd brought to a gun fight. Bao felt around inside the bag. Wallet. Makeup kit. But her gun was gone. Of course.

Bao opened, then shut, her mouth. She had used her gun. It was either being kept as evidence or lying on the roadside.

She looked up as Ana opened the door for a tall, clean-shaven man in a dark gray suit who walked into the room. He had a hard look in his eyes and, in his hand, a shiny FBI badge.

CHAPTER 83

"AGENT WONG. I'M Robert O'Rourke, FBI, San Diego office. A car is waiting to take you to the airport." Having shown his badge to Bao, O'Rourke reached into his breast pocket, withdrew a folded paper, and handed it to her.

Bao read the letter.

It introduced Special Agent Robert O'Rourke, and his instructions to take her to Monterrey Airport and escort her onto the FBI's private jet to San Francisco. The last line in the letter: "Please come to see me when you're rested."

It was signed by Craig Steinmetz.

Bao put the letter into her handbag and asked O'Rourke, "Where's Joseph Molinari?"

"In jail, awaiting a hearing."

"Damn it! We have to get him out."

"Our guys are on it," said O'Rourke. "FBI. Ambassador to Mexico. Others from the administration. I know the circumstances of the shooting, but you and Agent Molinari have been charged with killing three citizens. So, we're getting you out of the country before you're jailed, too, Agent Wong."

Bao felt dizzy, as if her blood had dropped from her head to her feet. She interpreted O'Rourke's warning as confirmation of her fears that the cartel might gain access to Joe and kill him in his cell. That if she was caught, she, too, would be jailed pending trial—or worse.

Tears came. Ana handed Bao a wad of tissues and said, "I will pray."

Bao nodded, at the same time wondering if the nurse was leading her to a slaughterhouse.

CHAPTER 84

TWENTY MINUTES AFTER leaving the Ritz, I was parking my Explorer in my preferred parking space on Harriet Street, perpendicular to Bryant, and a hundred yards from the medical examiner's office. I had questions for Claire, and I hoped she had time for me.

I blew through the ME's main entrance, bypassed the vacant reception desk, and buzzed myself into the office and autopsy suite. I found Claire in scrubs and mask standing over a half-draped body on an autopsy table.

She took one look at me, put down her scalpel, ripped off her gloves and mask, and gave me a big hug that nearly knocked me off my feet.

I grabbed both of Claire's shoulders until I was steady, and by then Claire was asking, "You haven't heard yet from Joe, have you? Lindsay. Talk to me. Tell me what I can do."

I told her the truth, there was nothing she could do, and spelled out where things stood without saying my worst fears: that Joe could be dead, and I wouldn't even know it. But Claire could read my eyes.

"Claire, I'm just going to be a wreck until I hear from Joe. Once I do, I'm calling you first!"

And then I asked, "What can you tell me about the woman found dead in a dumpster?"

She said, "I gave Cappy the death certificate, but come with me."

I followed Claire to the cool room, where she pulled out one of the drawers and cranked a lever. And then I was standing beside a drape-covered female body.

Claire drew down the sheet, saying, "Her family was looking for her, so we have her name. This is Caroline Ford of Chicago. She's single, thirty-five, an account executive or something like that. She was here in town on a business trip. Cause of death: asphyxiation. She was strangled to death. Manner of death: homicide. Her underwear was torn, but she hasn't been sexually penetrated. There's no semen, no bruising. Maybe her killer tried and couldn't manage it. On another note, she was about two months pregnant. 'I said. You dead' was written in lipstick on her right forearm. It was smudged all to hell, but we have pictures from before the Forensics folk moved her. The lipstick on her mouth was also smeared. Maybe her killer kissed her."

"So, maybe DNA?"

"Maybe. This is all I have for now."

I thought of the breakfast fork I had wrapped in a napkin, in my purse. "I have something for Hallows to test against, too." I expelled a bottomless sigh. "You have photos of her from when she was found?"

"Yes, I have them, and I'll send them to your phone. Right now."

I thanked my dear friend, hugged her again, and then left the premises. I walked briskly up the breezeway to the Hall's back door, handed my gun to the security guard so that the metal detector didn't freak out, took it back, and climbed the stairs to the Homicide bullpen.

CHAPTER 85

CRAIG STEINMETZ WAS at his desk, waiting for Bao in his plain, government-furnished office. Bao took the chair across from him. She finally felt safe.

Steinmetz asked, "Bao? How are you doing?"

"I'm sorting it out, Craig. I've changed."

"How so?"

She shook her head and thought, *I'm a wife, mother, FBI agent, and now? Call it, Bao. You're a killer.*

"That gunfight," she said. "It was . . . bad."

"Of course," Steinmetz said. "If you hadn't taken action—"

"Joe and I would both be dead." Bao added, "I don't need to tell you, Craig. We can't leave Joe in a Mexican jail. The cartel will pay off the cops and he'll be murdered if he isn't released today."

Steinmetz sat back hard in his chair, which squeaked once before returning him to an upright position.

"Bao, I understand your concern."

"Concern? If he isn't released with protection, we'll never see Joe again."

"No, no. Listen," Steinmetz said. "My counterpart from DC is in Mexico City with an appointment to speak with the *presidente.* Joe should be exonerated and released in a day or two."

Bao leaned in toward Steinmetz and shouted, "That's too long! It will be *too damned late.*"

Steinmetz ignored her outburst and said evenly, "Bao, government agents, heavy hitters from the White House, are having talks with Monterrey and Mexico City. Don't doubt me. Keep your phone on your person, and the second I hear that Joe is free and clear, I'll call his wife. And I'll call you."

Bao noted that Steinmetz hadn't added *I promise.* But she heard the subtext. He was doing what he could.

"Understood," Bao said.

She thanked the chief and left his office.

Bao's assigned driver, Lennie DeRosa, was waiting in a black car at the curb. He drove her home and stayed with her when she opened the door to her apartment.

There was a wire crate, three-quarters sheathed in cardboard, in the center of her living room. Written on the cardboard was the note "To be delivered to Bao Wong," and her address. She pulled the cardboard away from the crate and saw what was inside. It was a brown, medium-sized, mixed-breed dog.

"I call him Pete," said DeRosa. "He likes the name. There's dog food in the kitchen to get you started. I have dogs, so if you have any questions, call me. Anytime."

"Oh, my God."

Bao stooped, opened the crate door, and "Pete" padded over to her. He pressed his forehead against her chest, and she reached her arms around him in a hug.

For the second time that day, Bao cried.

CHAPTER 86

CINDY WAS WORKING at her usual spot at the dining table in her apartment with only one thing in mind. She was going to find out whatever there was to know about Brett Palmer. However long it took.

She had access to criminal databases; the Portland, Oregon, police database; and Oregon DMV records. And she had access to numerous newspapers archived on the internet. She had made notes of some intriguing leads. For one, she had the address of the home Brett Palmer had owned and shared with his second ex-wife, Angela Kinney Palmer, who had died by hanging. The main thing that tipped this hanging from suicide to homicide was the writing on the soles of the victim's shoes.

Cindy thought that if the "I said. You dead" killer had written this catchphrase, he was either very arrogant or very cagey. Both traits were characteristics of sociopathic killers. Too bad block letters matched a hundred handwriting samples in any forensics database.

But Cindy had found more useful data: Brett Palmer's

parents lived in Portland. So did the parents of Brett's first wife, Roxanne Sands Palmer, who'd suspiciously drowned in the bathtub. But Palmer's second wife, Angela Kinney Palmer, had parents living in Vallejo, California.

Vallejo was about a half hour drive from San Francisco.

The Kinneys' phone number was listed online, and Cindy was feeling lucky. She punched the number into her phone, turned on her call recorder, and listened to the phone ring.

Two rings. Three rings. Cindy was gearing up to leave a message that would actually encourage the Kinneys to return her call when a woman picked up the line.

"Yesss?"

"Hello, is this Mrs. Kinney?"

"Who is this and what are you selling?"

"Hi, Mrs. Kinney. This is Cindy Thomas from the *San Francisco Chronicle.* I'm a reporter."

"Oh? Do you write your own stories? Or do you gather information and pass them on to a writer?"

Cindy laughed. "Wow. Are *you* a reporter?"

"Was. A long time ago. So, what can I do for you?"

"I'd like to talk to you about your daughter Angela's ex-husband, Brett Palmer."

"Hold on, Cindy. I'm looking you up. Hmmm. Okay. Okay. You're a crime writer, and you want to know about Brett and Angela?"

"That's right, Mrs. Kinney. Can you help me?"

"Are you going after Brett?"

"I want to find out what happened to your daughter. With your help, maybe I can get a handle on why she died and what Brett may have done or didn't do to cause her death."

"Where are you?"

"San Francisco."

"If you'll come here, I'll talk to you. Lord knows, I'm not doing this over the phone."

"I can be there in an hour or so, traffic depending."

"My name is Joann, by the way. You need my address?"

Cindy confirmed the address she'd found online.

"Well then, giddyap," said Joann Kinney.

"See you soon," Cindy said.

She washed her face, fluffed her hair, put on a baby-blue cardigan over a white turtleneck and khakis. She called Richie and left him a message. Then she gathered her things, locked up the apartment, and went out to her car. She turned on the ignition and put the Kinney family's address into her GPS.

Then she put the car in gear and headed north.

CHAPTER 87

THERE WAS A nine-by-twelve-inch manila envelope in the pile of mail on Steinmetz's desk. He pulled it out of the stack and opened it, extracted the contents, and reviewed it all again. Then he buzzed his assistant.

"Rogers? I need you."

"Yes, Chief."

Brooks Rogers, a tidy forty-year-old man in shirtsleeves, had been assistant to the section chief for the last five years. He entered Steinmetz's office and asked, "What can I do for you, sir?"

"I want you to phone Lieutenant Jackson Brady at the SFPD, Southern Division. Identify yourself to whoever answers his phone. Your name and mine and that this call is urgent. If there's any kind of bull crap, stress that it's a matter of life and death and they're to get Brady on the phone."

"Yes, sir. Or die trying."

"Exactly, Rogers."

Steinmetz smiled at his assistant, who smiled back.

“Anything else?”

“Yes. After I speak to Brady, I need you to deliver a package to him and get a signed receipt.”

“Got it, sir. I’m calling him now.”

A minute later, the chief’s desk phone rang.

CHAPTER 88

YUKI SAT AT the counsel table inside the courtroom, a far cry from the courtrooms in the Hall of Justice.

The entire room was paneled with rough-hewn pine boards, floored with concrete that had been covered with gray linoleum, furnished with metal folding chairs, and lit with standing halogen lights. Now, once again, the room was populated with highly consequential people.

Judge Walden had called the court to order. The jurors, excepting number 5, who'd been replaced by alternate number 3, were in the box. The defendant, Dario Garza, sat at the counsel table between his attorney, Jon Credendino, and Donna Villanova, the lawyer's second chair.

Yuki noticed that Dario's right arm was in a cast and a sling. He also had a black eye and a large, angry bruise on his cheek, the result of being piled on by 750 pounds of law enforcement officers.

Judge Walden asked Yuki if she was ready to give her opening statement, and Yuki said that she was. When she rose to her feet, the jury turned their heads thirty degrees to face her. She had only brought a few things with her to the Judicial Building and among them was a jet-black suit, white silk blouse, and four-inch black high heels. Gaines had told her that she looked like a seasoned prosecutor who took no prisoners. Even so, Dario Garza grinned at her—or, rather, leered. He was sitting at the far end of the defense table, and Yuki didn't look at him, but she knew he was still smirking as she began her opening argument.

"Your Honor and ladies and gentlemen of the jury. The defendant, Esteban Dario Garza, is a self-described party-goer. He regularly attended dance clubs and was often the center of attention. Singing, dancing, and frequenting dance clubs are not crimes—but murder is. And the murder committed by Mr. Garza was horrific and unforgettable, and we will prove that he deserves the maximum penalty the law allows."

Yuki stepped around the end of the counsel table and, with her head slightly bowed, walked to a spot between the judge and the jury.

When she looked up, all the eyes in the courtroom were on her.

"The State's primary witness," she began, "will not appear in this courtroom in person because his life is in danger. That's a fact. But he will appear before you live on a video monitor. He will put his hand on a Bible and swear to tell the whole truth and nothing but. And he will testify as to what happened the night Mr. Dario Garza murdered their friend Miguel Hernandez. And yes, he will be cross-examined by Mr. Garza's defense attorney."

Yuki said, "Here's what happened on a pleasant summer night last June. Mr. Garza was driving his car through southern San Francisco with two passengers. The three of them were old college friends from UC Berkeley. One young man sat in the front seat, passenger side. That was Miguel Hernandez. The other passenger sat in the back seat, by himself.

"The back-seat passenger we will refer to as El Gato, 'The Cat,' since using his real name could make him the subject of a hit, given what the young man witnessed that evening. First, El Gato heard Dario Garza lure Miguel outside to look at something under the car's hood. Then he witnessed Mr. Garza shoot Miguel Hernandez through the back of his head.

"El Gato saw a chance to run. And he took it.

"Mr. Garza couldn't chase him. He had to dispose of his former friend Miguel's bleeding body. El Gato hid across the street, watched the defendant's car, and between its stops and starts, he managed to follow that car on foot.

"Mr. Garza had an idea. He drove to a construction site close by, which had an unlatched gate. El Gato watched Mr. Garza pull Miguel's body from the car, lay him out on the ground, and decapitate his dead former friend with an electric saw. El Gato videoed some of what he was seeing from where he was hiding behind heavy equipment. He saw Dario Garza roll the body into a hole on the site. And finally, he watched as Garza left the construction site with Miguel Hernandez's severed head in his car.

"According to other witnesses, Mr. Garza then took Miguel's head and left it precisely in the middle of the top steps at the Hall of Justice.

"We have a few ideas as to why Mr. Garza did this. Perhaps he meant it to be seen as a trophy. Or as a threat. Maybe a challenge. Or possibly all of the above. And we have other witnesses to Mr. Garza's crimes against his murdered friend. The shooting, the abuse of the corpse, the unceremonious burial, and the ta-da placement of the severed head—a sight that will live in many nightmares for years to come.

"Miguel was twenty-three and just starting out in life. But his life was snuffed out too soon, and with it, everything he might have been.

"Dario Garza denies it all."

CHAPTER 89

YUKI SAW THE stunned looks on the faces of the jurors and was glad for it. She'd only just gotten started.

But before she could continue, Dario jumped to his feet and, releasing a full breath, screamed at Yuki.

"Everything you just said was a lie! You don't know any of that! You can't prove any of it, and you won't get away with this, this, slander! Go ahead and try and I will sue you. And I will reveal your masked witness's name. Right, El Gato?"

The judge's expression was the picture of pure, undiluted fury. Using the butt of her handgun, she rapped the bench with several sets of ringing blows and called for silence. "Mr. Garza. Sit down and shut up. Mr. Credendino. Take charge of your client. If there's another outburst from him, he will be watching his trial on CCTV from a cell in Folsom Prison."

CHAPTER 90

AFTER JUDGE WALDEN had shut down the shouts and murmurs, she asked Yuki if she was ready to go on.

"Yes, Your Honor."

Yuki again turned to the jury, making eye contact with each of them as she asked, "Why would the defendant kill his friend? What was his motive? The witness, El Gato, was sitting in the back seat of the car behind the driver. Miguel was talking to him. And he will tell you about that conversation. Miguel was telling El Gato, bragging actually on behalf of his friend, about Dario's many sexual exploits—and he named some of the women. Seven of these women have disappeared, and a few have been found dead."

"Objection, Your Honor," Credendino called out as he got to his feet. "The prosecution has no basis for this implication that Mr. Garza knew these women or that he had any part in killing them. This is hearsay, pure and simple. It's also an outrage and should be struck from the record."

"Objection sustained," Judge Walden said emphatically, and she instructed the court reporter to strike the contested section of the prosecutor's statement.

"I'll rephrase," Yuki said, not showing any sign that under different circumstances the defense could have demanded a mistrial. And she was thrilled with her deft implantation of that bad seed in the jurors' minds.

"Be careful, Ms. Castellano," the judge said.

"Yes, Your Honor."

Yuki went on. "The defendant's friend who survived that night will be speaking to you by secure video link. He will tell you what triggered the defendant's murderous anger and what went down after that. Additionally, as we said, we will introduce other witnesses regarding the decapitation of Miguel Hernandez and his hasty burial. You will also hear from two women who went out with Mr. Garza, and they will describe events of their dates.

"By the end of this trial, we will ask you to find the defendant guilty of the murder of Miguel Hernandez, who was unarmed and unthreatening but did not understand that the defendant had a limit to his self-aggrandizement . . . Unsatisfied with Miguel's murder, the defendant also committed abuse of a corpse by severing the deceased's head and putting it on display out of petty conceit." Yuki took a deep breath, and thanked the jury in advance for their attention, then walked over to the prosecution table.

The judge said, "Mr. Credendino. Does the defense wish to respond?"

"Yes, Your Honor," said the accused's imposing defense

attorney. As Yuki took her seat next to Gaines, Jon Credendino put his note cards down on the table and walked into the small well between the counsel tables and the jury box. And under the laser-focused eyes of the judge, Dario Garza's lawyer began to speak.

CHAPTER 91

CINDY SAT ACROSS from Joann Kinney at her dining table, a platter of walnut-raisin muffins between them and fresh coffee in their mugs.

Cindy said, "I'm writing about a number of murders by an unknown person who is being called the 'I said. You dead' killer. This could be a book or a newspaper series. I am hoping that I can identify him and turn the information over to the police."

"I'd be happy to help," Joann said. "I think you called me because you think I know who this killer might be."

"But can't prove it, right?"

"Totally right," Joann said. "I think I've been waiting for you to call me since my daughter was killed by her monster of a husband."

"Maybe I can help you now. Do you have any evidence against the monster, Joann?"

"I don't know for sure. But I loved Angela so much. She would never, never . . . " And then she pushed her glasses up into her hair, snatched a paper napkin from the table, and pressed it to her eyes.

Cindy reached over and took Joann's hand.

Joann squeezed Cindy's hand in return and apologized, excused herself, got up from the table, and walked down a narrow hallway.

Cindy looked around the plain white-painted room. There was a wall of bookshelves, a brown velvet-covered sofa and a matching reclining chair, a coffee table with two or three photo albums and a shallow bowl holding wrapped candies. At the far end of the room were sliding doors opening onto a balcony with a view of trees and blue sky. Centered over the sofa was a lovely portrait of a young woman in her thirties. She had a soft gaze and a shy smile. She looked like a good person. A sweet girl.

Although Angela Palmer had died a year and a half ago, Cindy knew that her call today had cracked her mother's grief wide open.

Joann had told Cindy that she and her husband, Victor, Angela's father, had lived in this condo for only a few years. Then shortly after Angela died, her husband had a fatal heart attack. So she now lived here alone.

Joann came back into the living room and sat down at the table. She pulled her thick auburn hair back into a ponytail and reset her eyeglasses. Cindy thought that Joann's eyes looked permanently reddened from crying.

"So, where were we?" Joann said, giving Cindy a wistful smile.

"Um. You were saying that Angela would 'never' but didn't finish . . . "

Joann leaned back in her chair, let out a short scream for effect, and then straightened up and said, "As I was saying, Ange would never have married that rage-a-holic if she had known about his temper and his absence of actual feelings."

"For example?"

"Too many to list," Joann said, "but they'd fight. He'd say ugly things to her, insults, threats, curses, and he'd never apologize. Never. And Angela would blame herself. But what Brett Palmer had was charm. He could be funny. Socially, he wasn't aggressive. Privately, with my daughter, he was unfeeling and cruel. From what Angela told me, the man was a sociopath."

Cindy pictured the mild-looking man she and Lindsay had met with. Was he a sociopath? She'd known a few. They were excellent at masking. She looked toward the painting on the wall over the sofa and asked, "Is that painting of Angela?"

Joann nodded yes and passed her phone over to Cindy with the screensaver face up. It was a photo of Angela and Joann at the beach, their arms around each other, both smiling, relaxed, happy.

"When my husband took this picture, Ange was five days away from getting married," Joann said. "I took this one of Ange with Vic."

Cindy looked at the photos of happy times before the unthinkable tragedy. She asked, "None of the three of you had any sense then that Brett was dangerous?"

"Not then," Joann said. "Like I said, he had a nice way about him. Vic and I thought Angela had made this decision too soon, but she was in love." Joann took back her phone and smiled sadly at the photo. "And maybe Brett *didn't* kill

Angela. There was no physical evidence that he did. No witnesses. No drunken confession."

"Joann, did you see writing on the bottoms of Angela's shoes?"

"Yes. 'I said. You dead.' Why would Angela write something like that on her own shoes? Makes no sense. It's not written from the point of view of a suicide, is it?

"But I wonder if we would have even suspected Brett if it wasn't for what happened to his first wife, Roxanne. You heard how she drowned in the bathtub? Yet there was no evidence of 'foul play.' No drugs in her system, no suicide note, no sign of a struggle. The police thought Roxanne may have drowned herself on purpose. Or did Brett kill her? In my opinion, yes, he did. I've talked to Roxanne's mother a couple times. Donna Sands. It was hard to be with her. Even though her daughter died longer ago, this pain doesn't really go away. We were both so raw."

"Did Donna think Brett killed her daughter Roxanne?"

"Donna never accused Brett. But I think she holds Brett responsible. She definitely thinks he seduced her daughter, emotionally abused her, then divorced her—and that Roxanne then killed herself out of shame, depression, and heartbreak. Donna doesn't say so, but I'm sure she thinks my daughter killed herself, too. But *I'm* sure that she didn't. I never ever thought that Angela killed herself, Cindy. She would never write something as dumb as 'I said. You dead' on her shoes. Not suicide. Not Angela.

"Brett Palmer killed my daughter. And I also blame Brett for breaking her dad's heart and killing Victor, too."

CHAPTER 92

CINDY TOLD JOANN how sorry she was, and the grieving woman shook off some of her sadness and brought a printed photo album back to the table. Cindy noted the happy faces and playfulness of this family—including a photo of Brett and Victor playing a paddleball game on the beach.

Cindy said, "Can we talk a little more about Brett? When did you start to feel suspicious of him?"

Joann sighed. "The first time Angela called me after a fight, she was sobbing hard. I thought, *Well, that happens with newlyweds.* I was rationalizing. But I felt there was something sick going on when Brett brought his stepbrother, Nate Miller, to have dinner with us. Nate didn't converse. He made cracks. We were all uncomfortable.

"After Nate left that night, Brett told us a lot of awful stuff about his stepbrother. He said that Nate was perpetually angry. That he killed small animals for fun when he was a boy. That he had been in the military, and after that, his anger could get out of control. Brett said than Nate could be violent. A trait that I think Brett and Nate shared.

"After Angela died . . . I blamed Brett. I didn't see how Nate could have gotten close enough to Angela to do that to her. I even thought that Brett had told us about Nate to throw suspicion onto the violent brother. But my gut still believed it was Brett. Both of them had alibis, and that left me with ambivalence and doubt."

Then Joann said, "I have something for you. Hang on."

She got up from the table, went to the kitchen, opened a drawer, and when she returned, she was holding a small, handheld digital recorder.

Joann sat down again and passed the recorder to Cindy.

She said, "Picture this. A week or so after Angie's funeral, Brett came to the house to see us. He had a lot of bags and cases with him. He was going to London to see a client. He sat in Victor's chair and unloaded his briefcase and computer case and carry-on bag. After his visit, maybe six hours later, he called from the airport, to ask if he'd left his voice recorder here. I looked around and said, 'No.' Months later, when I was doing a real clean, I found it way under Victor's lounge chair. I didn't call Brett.

"I thought about listening to the recording, but then I didn't want to hear his voice. I thought maybe some other time, when I felt stronger. I kept it in the junk drawer. And then, when I was tidying up ahead of your visit, I thought about that mini recorder. Here. You take this. Just . . . tell me what you find on it, okay?"

"Really? Great. Thank you."

"And if you don't mind, Cindy, may I see you out? I'm all stirred up and I need to take a nap."

"Of course, Joann. I'll call you after I do some research."

"That's fine. Oh, Cindy, one more thing. Nate Miller lives in San Francisco."

Cindy's mind put on the brakes. Nate lived in San Francisco? Joann said he was abusive and a trained fighter and maybe he was crazy. Brett or Nate could have killed Angela. But one thing really bothered Cindy about that theory.

How could either stepbrother have had a murderous hate on for Warren Jacobi?

CHAPTER 93

I WAS AWAKE and staring at the ceiling at 4 something a.m.

Chamomile tea and Tylenol PM could only do so much. I stayed in bed, thinking about Joe, hoping for a phone call from him, furious that my husband was gone and the only information I'd been given was "We're working on it."

Dr. Sidney Greene once told me that if I couldn't sleep, I should get out of bed, sit in a chair, and read. When the book or magazine fell out of my hands, go back to bed, and I would fall back asleep.

I had one of Joe's magazines on my nightstand, and I had dog-eared an article about "chair yoga." It didn't sound exciting. I positioned the bedside clock so that it threw light on the pages. I don't know when the magazine fell out of my hands, but it was Julie who woke me up for good. She got into the bed and bounced until I opened my eyes.

"What are you doing, Jules?"

"I'm going to miss the bus and you're going to be late and Daddy's still not home."

"Oh, Jules, he's still away in Mexico on his business trip," I told her, hoping to God that I was right.

"Where is he? Is he going to call?"

"If he can, Jules."

"Why can't he?"

"I told you," I said. "He's in a foreign country. His phone might not work there. He'll call as soon as he can."

I had lied to my daughter without even crossing my fingers. I checked the time. It was 7:45 a.m., and Brady had called a task force meeting for 9.

"Let's get ready, Julie-bug. Go brush your teeth."

I moved fast. I got Julie into a new outfit that I'd been saving for a special occasion.

"Thank you, Mommy. I guess."

She'd put on the new black tights and big pink shirt I'd bought, but she didn't like the look. I would come up with something she'd like better. There was time.

Meanwhile, I fed the two of us plus Martha and sprinkled fish flakes into the goldfish bowl. Julie chatted with Martha and even had a couple of things to say to the TV hosts of *Good Morning, San Francisco.*

I sat on my bed to pull on my shoes and lost track of time until Martha came into the room and woofed.

"Boo? Want to go for a walk?"

She woofed again, danced a circle, then rounded up Julie. After I'd leashed my old border collie, she shepherded me and Julie down the stairs and up the street to the bus stop. We arrived just as the school bus pulled up to the curb. I kissed my kiddo good-bye, then waved as the bus drove away.

CHAPTER 94

CINDY WAS RACING to discover the truth about Brett Palmer. Brett's voice on his lost-and-found recorder had been chilling. As Cindy had listened to his complaints and declarations to his brother, Nate, she got a sick feeling that she was in real danger.

She hadn't felt this way when she and Brett were chowing down on their breakfast at the Ritz. Now she felt as if Brett were standing behind her with a coiled rope in his hands.

Cindy went back to the beginning and prepared herself to listen again to the whole damned hour and a half of Brett's "Notes for file."

Twenty minutes in, Brett said to Nate, "I couldn't stand it anymore. When Ange and I got divorced, I gave her the house, the car, even the damned plants. Plus 300K in cash."

Nate said, "No respect—that's what she gave you."

"I gave her what I had. I said, 'You dead.' "

Cindy was still rocked by Brett's admission. He'd all but admitted to killing his ex-wife, Angela Kinney Palmer—and how many others might there have been? He had to be stopped. A recorded conversation pertaining to a crime was legal as evidence. But she also knew that in a trial setting there were a dozen ways the defense could undercut it.

But if Brett's confession was confirmed by Nate Miller, Cindy would be handing the prosecution an almost certain win. And maybe, maybe, she'd write another true-crime bestseller.

Cindy fast-forwarded past Brett Palmer's appointment schedule, meeting notes, and list of expenses. Then she slowed to catch the last of Brett's "I said, 'You dead'" declaration. She was obsessing, but she had to follow this lead. Yes, she was dogged. Yes, she was tenacious. But doggedness and tenacity were necessary if she was going to find the truth.

She wasn't at the truth, yet, but she felt close.

Cindy was outlining her story to date when the front door opened.

"Hon?"

"In here, Richie."

Rich Conklin stuck his head into the small room Cindy used as her home office.

"You're busy. Call me when you take a break."

"Rich. I need you to listen to something."

"Okay. What's up?"

"It's a recording of Brett Palmer, talking to his stepbrother, Nate Miller. Brace yourself."

Rich dragged a chair over to the table Cindy used as a desk and sat down. "Hit me," he said.

"The first voice. That's Brett, talking to Nate."

Cindy pressed Play.

Brett's voice came from the recorder's small speaker accompanied by the clanking of cutlery. He said, "It still makes me furious. Angela kept calling. Texting. She sent me a pair of her panties. I told her no in every way imaginable. I told her, 'All I've got left is the sweat on my balls.' She still wouldn't quit. So. You know. I said, 'You dead.' "

"Good job, bro. I never liked that bitch."

Cindy hit Stop. She was shaking at the coldness and brutality.

She looked up at Richie, who said, "Oh, my God, Cindy. Palmer is cooked. Well done."

Cindy handed her phone to her husband. She didn't have to explain.

"It's the right thing to do," said Conklin. He tapped in a number.

"Lieutenant. It's Conklin. Cindy turned up great evidence on the 'I said. You dead' psycho. Yep. That's the one. Here's Cindy."

He handed Cindy the phone.

CHAPTER 95

I LOOKED AT the clock as I neared my desk in the Hall of Justice. Good news: I was going to be on time for the "I said. You dead" task-force meeting. Just then, of course, my cell phone rang.

Cindy calling.

"Cin, I'm going into a meeting. Can we talk later? I'll call you."

"It's up to you," she said. "But I have something regarding Brett Palmer. And trust me, I think it's something you really want to know."

I shouted into my phone, "Cindy! I don't want to be late."

Cindy fought back with increasing intensity. "You *won't* be late. Listen. Listen to me. Just *listen,* will ya? Look up. I'm sitting next to Richie, two feet from your desk."

I gave in to the indomitable Cindy Thomas, who was grinning at me from the next desk over. She showed me a small digital recorder, saying, "This is Brett Palmer's. He used it as a daily journal, mostly for reminders, and notes about his work. And he recorded phone calls. He lost this gizmo in the home of his ex-in-laws," she said. "Listen."

She pushed Play. I listened to the sound of someone telling Brett Palmer that his ex-wife, Angela Palmer, had been found dead. It was painful to hear. But I felt sure that the exchange was real, not acted out. The recording ended before Brett reacted.

I suggested to Cindy that she make an appointment to meet with Brady and that if I could, I'd join them. Then I thanked my friend the pit bull, who was looking more and more like she had a Pulitzer Prize in her future. Richie kissed her and they both beamed. Then Rich Conklin and I walked to the war room.

Conklin switched on the lights, I yanked up the shades, and Brenda wheeled in a mail cart that held a coffee urn, paper cups, and a tray of quartered bagels with a cream cheese spread on the side. Brenda placed a cup of black coffee and a pile of sugar packets next to me along with a sheet of copy paper, folded in half.

She said, "Linds. This's from the boss."

I opened the note and read, "Lindsay, Bao Wong is temporarily on our task force and will be partnering with you. She'll be in the meeting. Before you ask, she has no news of Joe."

CHAPTER 96

RICHIE CONKLIN, SONIA Alvarez, Cappy McNeil, and Paul Chi were seated on one side of the long conference table. I sat across from them with an empty seat on either side of me. I was trying to pay attention, but my head was pounding with the contents of Brady's note: that there was no news about Joe.

Psychologically speaking, I was spiraling. Thoughts of Joe circled my brain in an endless loop: the sound of his laugh, his way with Julie, his support for how hard I worked, and the last thing he'd said to me: *I'll call you tonight.*

What was happening to Joe right now? I wanted to know how he was, where he was, how to get him back. And while I waited for word of him, I wanted to find, interrogate, and lock up Jacobi's killer.

All of us, everyone in this room, were united in our desperate desire to solve this case. Our unity was our strength, and it gave us the resolve to push forward.

A tired-looking Asian woman in her thirties came through

the door. I'd met Bao Wong after she and Joe started working together, and I liked her. I guessed now the two of us were going to partner up for a while. She looked depressed. I'm sure I looked the same or worse.

Bao waggled her fingers at me and took the empty seat to my right. She whispered, "The lieutenant wants me to work with you on this case. Okay with you?"

I nodded in agreement. "Absolutely."

She asked, "Lunch later, after the meeting?"

"Sure. Good idea."

Brady swung down into the chair at the head of the table. Seeing that we were all present and had coffee and fatty snacks beside us, he said, "Awright. We have news.

"Please say hello to FBI agent Bao Wong, who is joining us for a while. She will be working with Boxer on this assignment for now. She has information gathered by and sent to us by the FBI. Bao, you know Lindsay, of course."

And then he introduced her to the others seated at the long, scarred table. There was a welcoming murmur and hands stretched across the table to shake hers.

CHAPTER 97

BAO WONG SAT between Lieutenant Jackson Brady and Lindsay Boxer at the war room conference table. She placed a padded manila envelope on the table, and the group leaned in for a better look.

Bao hoped that the material Chief Steinmetz had passed to her through Brady would give the task force what they needed to solve the unfathomable murders that had no apparent motive and often a bizarre catchphrase written on or near the victims.

Bao addressed the group, saying, "Good morning, everyone. It's good to be here. Graig Steinmetz, FBI section chief of the San Francisco field office, has sent me what may be evidence of a suspect in the murders of Judge Martin Orlofsky and his wife, Sandra Orlofsky.

"I understand that several of you in this meeting were at the Orlofsky crime scene and possibly saw the suspect—but he's a blue-ribbon chameleon. If you didn't recognize him as a seasoned killer, that's his superpower and why he's still free. Also, I've been told that two former inspectors from this department, now retired, may have been involved with this suspect. I have some photographic evidence that may prove or disprove that theory."

Bao reached into the open envelope and extracted a half dozen eight-by-ten photos and a small hard drive. She spread the photos out on the table, saying, "I'll tape these photos to the wall in a few minutes. This one," she said, holding it up, "shows the killer in profile. He is sitting behind the wheel of his gardener's truck, which is part of his disguise. The photo was taken by a security camera wired to the next door neighbor's home and was recorded at 6:45 a.m. three days ago. That's the Orlofsky house. In the next photos, the truck's driver had moved the truck out of camera range.

"This hard drive," Bao said, holding it up, "was part of the same security system, and that system recorded the same truck at the same time and same day. The truck comes into the frame from down the street, pulls into position where the driver is in range to watch police activity.

"This photo was taken by the still camera five minutes after this one in my hand. And here is a uniformed officer telling the driver of the gardener's truck to move along. He obeyed.

"Change of scene," Bao said to the task force. "Here's the same truck awaiting its turn to go through the border checkpoint from Tijuana deeper into Mexico. We have video of this truck, and of this man getting out of the truck to show his passport to the border police, returning to the truck, then driving on.

"There are no stills or video of this man doing actual murder or entering or leaving the Orlofsky house. He left no DNA and no prints. He is an accomplished killer, and his name is Santiago Garza, known as Tiago. He's the former boss of the drug cartel Los Hermanos del Diablo. The last I heard, Tiago Garza is now an assassin for hire."

Bao paused and looked at the people at the table, making sure they were all with her. Then she said, "Tiago's son, Dario Garza, is on trial for murder, here in California, and is currently confined to a cell in a maximum-security location.

"Back to Tiago Garza. Here's a mug shot of him taken fourteen years ago when he was arrested for the theft of a half dozen catalytic converters that had been ripped out of high-end vehicles, then found in his nondescript junker. He denied any knowledge of the thefts but had no explanation for how they ended up in his car. He was booked and charged, and we have this information: He is five eleven, U.S. born, with dual U.S.-Mexico citizenship.

"His prints are on file, but nothing has yet shown as a match. Most probably Garza knew how to prevent house security cameras from getting clear shots of his face.

"Bottom line, Tiago Garza is at large."

CHAPTER 98

YUKI SAT BACK in her chair and listened to Dario's defense counsel, Jon Credendino, begin speaking. Credendino was impressive in style and tone, but the story he laid out for the jury was total garbage.

Credendino said, "Ladies and gentlemen of the jury, you've heard an incendiary version of events from the prosecution. It's a terrible story they've laid out—but it's not what happened. Esteban Dario Garza—Dario, as he is called—is accused of a horrific murder that he did not commit. This is what *actually* happened on that tragic night last June: On the night in question, Dario was taking his two friends to a place called Club Hvar. Dario was a star at that club. The promoters always begged him to come, since other customers enjoyed watching Dario dance and would tell their friends about this handsome premed student who could sing and dance and do party tricks.

"It was a Saturday evening. Dario was driving his second-hand BMW, and he invited two friends to go along for the ride. All three young men had graduated from UC Berkeley and were starting their independent lives. Murder was not part of the plan.

"Dario was behind the wheel, his friend Miguel Hernandez was in the front passenger seat, and their friend—the one who the prosecution calls 'El Gato'—was in the back seat, when Miguel said he felt nauseous.

"Miguel asked Dario to pull over so that he could throw up in the street.

"Dario said a few words like 'Do not throw up in my car' and attempted to pull the car over. But he was at a traffic light that had just turned green, and the cars behind him were backed up and blowing their horns."

Yuki looked over at Dario Garza, who was nodding his head in agreement, like *Right. Right.*

Credendino walked to the jury box rail, put his hands on the rail, and went on with the defense's opening statement, picking up his narrative at the green light. He added to the picture by saying, "A big bruiser of a truck driver got out of his sixteen-wheeler and started toward Dario with a wrench in his hand."

"At that time, Dario told his friend El Gato, the prosecution's star protected witness, to get out of the car and stay with Miguel. El Gato and Miguel exited the car, fast, slammed the doors shut, and Dario pulled ahead, avoiding the truck driver and going through the green light, which was about to turn yellow. Dario circled the block and was stopped by another light. He estimates that ten minutes had passed since he'd let his friends out of his car.

"When Dario returned to the spot where he'd last seen his

friends, he couldn't find them. He honked, called out, then drove around for a half hour, looking for Miguel and El Gato, calling their cell phones—and neither one answered. Dario figured that they must've gotten a lift and either went to the club or somewhere else for drinks. He kept his phone on, but no one called. So he went to Hvar, alone.

"A few hours later, after an evening of dancing, Dario went home from the club with a girl he knew, and she will testify that he spent the rest of the night with her at her place. Then, when he got home to his own apartment the next day, Dario made more phone calls, trying to find his friends.

"Little did he know that the police were out looking for him. Miguel's body had been found in a pit at a construction site. Someone had called the police with Dario's partial license plate number, and Dario was arrested on suspicion of murder without *any* evidence—except for a self-serving report from El Gato, the prosecution's star witness, who also directed the police to Miguel's body."

Credendino said, "I'll be introducing other witnesses from Club Hvar who will establish Dario's presence there that night, and they will tell you that he had no blood on his clothes. In fact, his hair was combed and he was in a calm, unagitated mood.

"So, what did happen?" Credendino asked the jury rhetorically. "Was Miguel mugged? Killed by a stranger on the street? Did El Gato himself dispatch Miguel Hernandez and put the blame on Dario? We only know that Dario never touched Miguel. Dario had no reason to kill anyone."

Not a bad argument, Yuki thought.

But she knew things that Dario Garza's lawyer didn't know.

CHAPTER 99

"AND THERE'S MORE," Bao Wong continued, pulling out more photos. "Too bad the angle on these shots is off-center and unfocused, but maybe someone in the room can identify the police officers in these photos."

Cappy McNeil and Paul Chi both leaned forward to examine the FBI's set of photo enlargements. They had spent the most time in the SFPD's Southern Division, and while Cappy knew all the cops at 850 Bryant and on the street, Chi had an encyclopedic mind for cases and events.

Cappy said, "I recognize a couple of them. But I can think of a dozen reasons why cops talking to criminals is job one. I don't concede that these cops are dirty based on photos of them speaking with Tiago Garza. But anyway. I knew them for about a year a long while ago." Cappy stabbed one of the photos with his forefinger. "This guy in the Giants windbreaker, that's Mike Randall. He's maybe about fifty now. He worked in Drugs and Organized Crime with the Chicago PD. Jacobi hired him when he first moved here.

"At about the same time, Jacobi hired a patrolman from West Boondocks, New Jersey. Doug Bernardi. The Doug I remember was smart, had good instincts, kind of intense, and he was a seriously good cop. He followed the rules. Right, Paul?"

Chi said, "A hundred percent. I partnered with Bernardi on patrol for about a year. He was a straight arrow. Didn't make or even really get jokes. He was promoted from uniform to investigator just like that."

Cappy asked his partner, "You got anything else?"

I stared at Chi, kept looking at him. Unblinking. He said, "Boxer. I have a cat that stares at me like that. Cut it out. I'm thinking."

I laughed and closed my eyes.

Chi said, "Here's the thing. Both Randall and Bernardi ended up transferred to what was eventually called 'Swanson's criminal enterprise.' But Ted Swanson flunked them both at their performance reviews. He called them insubordinate, pushed for their dismissal. Jacobi was new as chief and he took Swanson's word. He let them go."

Cappy said, "I remember now. Those two must've been on to Swanson before anyone. Point is, they were both good cops on the way up. Then they were disgraced. Just saying, Boxer, I wouldn't hold it against them, them getting transferred to work for Swanson."

Bao asked, "Where can we find them now?"

Chi said, "I'll get their last known addresses for you."

Bao picked up one of the enlarged photos in both hands and said, "The guy these officers are talking to . . . Can we get these images even more enlarged?"

"Sure," I said. "I'll be right back."

I walked to the far end of the war room, where Swanson's desk had been pushed against the wall, drawers facing into the room. I opened a drawer, rummaged around in a litter of pens and bulldog clips and whatnot, and found what I was looking for. I marched back to the conference table and positioned the magnifying glass over the photo, moved it in and out for a couple of seconds. Then I ID'd the person talking to Randall and Bernardi.

"That's Warren Jacobi."

CHAPTER 100

ONCE THE MEETING broke up, I said to Bao, "Follow me. They make good lunch across the street."

MacBain's is a homey bar and grill, a favorite of cops and other workers at the Hall of Justice, and named after a police captain from back when my father was on the job. Bao and I were shown to a table for two, the only table in the niche under the sweeping staircase to the second floor. When my favorite waitress, Sydney, came to take our order, we kept it simple. Tomato soup. Grilled cheese. Iced tea for two.

I asked Bao how she was holding up, and she said, "I used to smoke three packs of cigs a day. I quit ten years ago, when I was pregnant with my son, Cameron. Since Mexico, I've hungered for the smell and taste of tobacco. But that's not what you want to know . . . "

"What's your brand? There's a newsstand on the corner."

"Thanks, but no. I know better than to play chicken with an addiction."

I smiled at Bao's comeback, but she looked glum, and I was

right there with her. She said, "I'm glad to spend time with you, Lindsay. How are you?"

My thoughts were still spinning, and I told her so. I was afraid for Joe. I missed him terribly and had no assurances from anyone that he was okay now or that I would ever see him again.

"I want to know everything, Bao. I want to know about what's being called the 'big shoot-out.' Was Joe injured? What was your sense of the overall situation? Where do you think Joe is now?"

Our lunch came, and when we were alone again, Bao told me about the attack on their car.

Bao said, "I was freaking terrified. 'Shoot-out' doesn't begin to describe five minutes that felt like opening the doors to hell." She looked at me. "It was totally unexpected. I was driving. We were armed, of course, and this gang T-boned our car on the passenger side, rear compartment. We didn't see them until it happened."

Bao continued: "After the crash I told Joe to get under the dash. He could fire to the rear and be protected by the seat back. I was in a better position to return fire on the driver's side, so I kept firing until three of the shooters were dead. The fourth started running up the road, and I drove past him and then braked hard and kicked open my car door. He slammed into it. He's got broken ribs, but he's alive. He's talking.

"Joe was standing with me," Bao said, "after I knocked down the fourth guy with the car door and again when the cops put me in an ambulance. He wasn't injured. Maybe dazed, but I think he was fine."

Bao stopped talking, sniffled into a handkerchief. And that got me going, too. I grabbed a table napkin and buried my face in it.

I heard Bao saying, "Oh God, oh God, oh God."

I took the napkin off my face and put my hand on her arm. I said, "Bao, we don't have to talk about this."

"I want to," she said.

I kept my hand on Bao's arm. She hadn't been home to see her son and her husband. She was waiting here for news, orders, perhaps a warrant to appear in a Mexican court.

She said, "Joe got me sent to a hospital for my protection and then he went to jail to await a hearing on the gangsters I killed."

Her face sagged. "I feel heartsick for him. And for you. I don't know if the police are guarding him or are being paid off to take long dinner breaks. That's all I know, Lindsay. I'm so, so sorry."

"Bao. You were heroic."

She said, "To what end? I don't have words to express how I feel, Lindsay. Joe is a great colleague and a great friend. And now he's in a jail cell, totally vulnerable. Steinmetz says he's working on it, but he won't let me bring a battalion of troops to go get Joe back."

I said, "Call Steinmetz and demand that he tells you whatever news he has."

Bao made the call, and we pressed our heads together. The phone was between our ears when Steinmetz got on the line.

"Bao. We're working on getting Joe out of there. There are terms. We're trying to meet them. Don't ask me anything else. Do you want to go back home to DC? If so, go. You can be excused from the task force. Take some time off. I'll call you when I have news. That's my advice. Trust me. And take care of yourself."

And then all we heard was a dial tone. Steinmetz had gone.

CHAPTER 101

BRADY CALLED WHILE Bao and I were leaving MacBain's.

"Boxer, I need you now in Observation One."

"Bao and I will be right there," I said. "What's this about?"

"We have Doug Bernardi in the box with Chi and Cappy. Mike Randall has already been interviewed. I'll fill you in when you get here."

I hurried Bao out onto the street, telling her what Brady had told me as we crossed Bryant. Once we were in the Hall on the fourth floor, I led Bao to the observation room closest to Interview One, where Brady and Conklin just about filled the small anteroom to the walls. Brady stepped outside and told Bao and me how the Randall interview had ended.

"We're holding Randall as a material witness so we may get to keep him for forty-eight hours. He said that he had seen Warren Jacobi a couple dozen times in the last decade and had had a few drinks with him at Julio's."

"Julio's. The matchbook."

"Yes, a definite maybe," Brady said. "But either of them could have picked it up at the bar already inscribed—"

"'I said. You dead.'"

Brady cracked a smile, then said, "Let's go observe Interview Two. Chi and Cappy are just starting with Bernardi."

Observation outside Interview Two was a mess: paper napkins on the table, empty paper cups on the floor near the trash can, pads and broken writing implements lying where they had fallen or were flicked. But it was empty, and Brady, Bao, and I had room to breathe. We could easily see through the one-way glass. The mic was on and the cameras were rolling.

Cappy and Chi were interviewing Doug Bernardi, Chi's former patrol partner. Chi was sitting in a folding chair next to Bernardi, Cappy sat across from him, and there was a beat-up metal table between them. I faintly remembered Doug Bernardi. He had a stern look, a slight build, and a nervous tic. He was tapping the table between himself and Chi in rhythm. *One. One, two, three. One. One, two, three.*

Chi said, "Doug, we've known each other for too long for me to lie to you. I know you and Jacobi had your issues, and honestly, I thought what he did was wrong, dismissing you like that. I told him so. But I couldn't move him."

"I know all that, Paul. I know it was Swanson who pushed us out. I was pissed at Jacobi for a while, but life did not stop and I got way over it. I read in the paper about Jacobi being killed, and I sent flowers to the church. So did Mike. Neither one of us ever touched him, crossed swords with him, or killed him. We had no cause. He was like someone you used to know in school. Not an enemy. Not a feature in your life."

"Doug, I've got a couple of questions. Bear with me."

"Let me guess. Where was I Monday morning a week ago?"

Chi smiled. "Okay. Right. Where were you?"

"What time in the morning?"

"Say, six o'clock."

"What do you think? I was in bed, asleep next to my wife."

"Did you go to work that morning?"

"Yes, Paul, I went to work. I own a security firm. I don't clock in. But I was there at eight. Going through paperwork. Greeting the staff as they came it. Reading headlines in the news that Jacobi had been killed. And now I have a question for you."

"Sure. Go ahead."

"Why the hell are you talking to me?"

Cappy said, "Several people have reported that a couple of cops killed Jacobi. We have photographic evidence of you and Randall talking to Jacobi."

"That's bull. Cappy. We were seen talking to him? *Talking.* That's evidence?"

"It's enough to hold you as a material witness while we check it out."

"Now, hear me. I have seen Jacobi casually a couple dozen times in the last twelve or thirteen years. We'd have to look up when I left the job to be sure of the approximate date. Go ahead and ask your questions. But I'm telling you the truth," said Bernardi. "I didn't kill him. And I'd swear on my family Bible that Mike Randall didn't touch the guy, either. Let me see this photograph,"

"It's evidence, and I don't have it to show it to you. But it does exist."

"Am I under arrest?"

"As of this moment, no, but I'm putting you under pre-charge detention. You know how it goes. You have the right to an attorney, you have the right to remain silent . . . "

Bernardi's hand was flat on the table, and he used his arm as leverage to sharply get to his feet. "I want my lawyer."

"Fine," Cappy said. "Paul and I will take you upstairs to holding and you'll get your phone call."

Doors opened. Conklin and Alvarez left the observation room, ready to escort Bernardi up to the jail on the sixth floor.

Sonia Alvarez said, "Mr. Bernardi, please come with us."

Bernardi ignored her completely.

Cappy stepped in. "Do what Alvarez says, Bernardi. Don't make this whole thing worse."

Chi said, "I'll go upstairs with you, Doug. I'll call your lawyer myself if you want. Save your one phone call to call your wife."

I'm a pretty good judge of character, and I thought Bernardi was telling the truth. But hell. He was a cop once, and he knew the drill.

CHAPTER 102

BAO, BRADY, ALVAREZ, Conklin, and I piled back into the war room for the post-interview wrap-up of Cappy and Chi's interviews with Bernardi and Randall.

Some of us got comfortable. I hung my jacket on the back of my chair. Chi kicked off his shoes. Cappy took off his cap and fanned himself. I got up and turned on the air conditioner.

Alvarez typed on her phone, and Conklin asked Brady, "We have them, for what . . . another two days?"

"More or less. We want to use those hours well, so if we have to kick them, we'll feel that we gave them the third degree without the rubber hose. Understand?"

Brady straddled his chair, facing us, and crossed his impressive arms over the chair back, saying, "Who wants to go first?

Cappy said, "Me, of course. Look. I'm not attached to Bernardi or Randall, but I am still loyal to Jacobi. We've now interviewed two likely candidates for his murder, but we can't charge them. Holding them for a couple of days isn't enough."

Brady thanked him, saying, "Right, Cappy. Most important

is to have the right guys, and these two strike me as unmotivated to kill a sixty-year-old man who lost the fight to keep them on staff."

Cappy agreed, saying, "We'll keep talking to them."

Brady turned his head toward me. "Boxer. You've still got those external drives with Jacobi's digital media?"

"I do."

"So, go over them again and screen for anything useful. More pictures of Bernardi and/or Randall would be especially helpful."

"Will do, Brady."

Brady gave out more assignments. Alvarez and Conklin were to go back to Julio's as they'd done before.

"Wear your badges outside your jackets. And take copies of the FBI photos of Bernardi and Randall. Chi, Cappy, if you hook a whopper, call me."

My phone rang.

I looked down at the screen, but for a long moment I couldn't see it. It was the stark, crazy fear of learning something that would change my life forever. I pressed the talk button.

"Chief Steinmetz?"

"Yes. Sergeant Boxer? Are you with Lieutenant Brady?"

"He's right here."

"Put him on, please."

I mouthed "Steinmetz" and handed my phone over to Brady.

He said, "Chief?"

I heard Steinmetz's voice say, "You and Boxer can go into a private room, right?"

Brady excused the two of us from the group, saying he'd be available later. I couldn't read his look. But once we'd entered Interview One and closed the door, Brady put my phone on speaker so we both could listen and talk.

Steinmetz sounded subdued when he addressed Brady.

"Lieutenant, I've gotten word that the Diablo cartel have learned the location of Dario's trial. That's the end of anonymity for legal counsel, the judge, the jury, court officers, and the defendant. I can't explain how this got out."

I raised my voice so that Steinmetz could hear me. "What are we doing about this?"

"In a word, security. The warden has put their prison guards, all shifts, on high alert," Steinmetz said. "He's assured me that all the access points are under heavy watch, that there's no way to sneak over the walls, onto the grounds, get into the Judicial Building without being shot. If this is a rumor, the trial will be secure. If there's a breach, it's going to get loud."

"Craig. Any word on Joe?"

"I haven't heard anything. We're being stalled, sidetracked, and lied to. We're working on it, Lindsay. I'm not going to say, 'thoughts and prayers,' but understand that I am doing everything I can. I care a great deal about Joe.

"I'll call you if I hear anything. Brady, your office has my number."

I had questions, but typical of Steinmetz, he didn't say good-bye, God bless, take care, or big hug. He just hung up.

CHAPTER 103

I HAD A nightmare-filled night, and in the morning, as I rushed to do chores, take care of our dog and the kiddo, get out of the house and on the way to work, I forgot what I'd dreamed.

My phone rang at eight thirty while I was still driving to the Hall. The caller ID read: *RC.*

"Rich?"

"Yeah, Lindsay, I've got some pretty big news. When will you be in the squad room?"

"Ten minutes, depending."

"Don't stop for coffee. We're meeting with Brady. And Cindy."

"What?"

"Here's a clue. 'I said. You dead.' More later."

"I can't hear you, Richie. Static on the line."

He laughed at me.

"I'm counting on coffee," I said.

I arrived in eleven minutes and spent an extra three going from my car to the entrance of the great granite cube of a building with carved letters over the main door reading, HALL OF JUSTICE.

After taking an elevator to our floor, I shoved open the squad room door and did the same to the hip-high wooden gate just inside.

Bobby Nussbaum was at his station at the front desk.

He said, "Morning, Sarge. They're waiting for you."

I looked down the center aisle and saw that Brady's office was full. I waved at Nussbaum and kept walking down the aisle. Conklin opened Brady's door for me and gave me his chair. Before I could even wonder why Cindy was in Brady's office, I was in the chair beside her, and she was glowing.

I said, "Morning, Lieu, everyone."

I propped my feet up on the edge of Brady's desk. I wasn't trying to look nonchalant, but I was getting an average of three hours of sleep a night. My smartwatch told me so.

Brady passed me a cup of coffee across his desk, asked me how I was, and I said, "Fine. Considering."

He nodded sympathetically, then said, "Cindy is bucking for our jobs."

"I cannot wait to hear this," I said. I meant it.

I sipped my coffee, looking up at Richie, who could not hide the glee lighting him up.

Brady said, "Boxer. Cindy met with Angela Palmer's mother, Joann Kinney. Cindy, if I get this wrong, say something."

"You know I will, Lieutenant."

More laughter, this time from all of us. We knew Cindy well.

Brady said, "Girl Reporter, you have the floor."

Cindy looked damned pleased.

She said, "Thank you, all. She leaned forward and put a small digital recorder on the surface of Brady's desk.

Cindy said. "Joann Kinney, Angela's mother, thinks Brett Palmer killed her daughter. It's just her opinion. I was about to leave her house after our interview, and as an afterthought, she gave me this recorder.

"This gadget belonged to Brett Palmer, who was at the Kinneys' condo after Angela's death. Apparently, he stopped there en route to a 'business' trip, and he was packing and repacking assorted bags and cases. Later, Joann Kinney told me, Palmer called her from the airport saying he'd misplaced his digital diary and asked if she had found it. She looked for it but didn't find it, and texted Brett that she didn't have it—then.

"She eventually found the device a year or more later and kept it, but she didn't listen to it. So, she gave it to me. I played it for Richie and he called Brady. Lindsay. Here comes the message. The first voice is Brett. The other voice is his stepbrother, Nate."

Cindy turned on the recorder and I recognized Brett's voice from our meeting at the Ritz with Cindy a couple of days ago. Brett was saying, "It still makes me furious. Angela kept calling. Texting. She sent me a pair of her panties. I had told her no in every way imaginable. I told her, 'All I've got left is the sweat on my balls.' She still wouldn't quit. So. You know. I said, 'You dead.' "

Cindy said to me, "Next. This is Nate speaking."

"Good job, bro. I never liked that bitch."

Cindy turned off the recorder and looked at me.

I was in shock, but I took my feet down from the edge

of the desk. Was I getting this right? Had Brett Palmer just admitted to wanting to kill his ex-wife? Had he gone further than that and actually killer her . . . and others? Was he the "I said. You dead" killer?

Brady said, "Thanks, Cindy. I'll log the recorder in evidence. Conklin. Boxer. Find Brett Palmer and bring him in."

CHAPTER 104

RICH CONKLIN AND I parked our squad car across from the Ritz-Carlton Hotel, then walked through the lobby to the dining room. Maurice the maître d'—Cindy's source—wasn't at his post. Someone else was running restaurant traffic. He was thirtysomething, a genuine redhead whose name tag read RYAN MCCALL.

I badged him, introduced Conklin, and asked, "Is Maurice around?"

Ryan told us that Maurice was off today and asked if he could help.

Conklin told Ryan, "We're actually waiting for Mr. Brett Palmer."

"Oh, he was just here," Ryan said. "Was he expecting you?"

I said, "Oh, boy. I must have gotten the time wrong."

Ryan seemed eager to have a conversation that didn't involve seating and menus.

"Maybe I can help you," he said. "I've been working here for a year and I see Mr. Palmer a lot."

I said, “Do you have a couple of minutes? We’ve got some questions.”

Ryan offered us seating in the little waiting area ten feet from his post, and I said fine to that and set my phone down on the end table. I asked, “Ryan. May I call you Ryan?”

“Of course.”

“Okay. Ryan, by chance did Mr. Palmer say where he was going?”

“No, but after breakfast usually he’s in a hurry to get to a meeting somewhere, and then I don’t see him until late afternoon, or after dinner in the lounge. Let me call his room for you.”

A few seconds later, Ryan shrugged and said, “No answer. If you don’t mind me asking, is Mr. Palmer in some kind of trouble?”

Conklin said, “No, no. To be clear, we think Mr. Palmer may be able to help us with one of our open investigations.”

Ryan said, “Good to hear. Would you like me to give him a message if I see him later?”

I gave Ryan my card and Richie’s.

“If you see Mr. Palmer, give him our contact information, and if he asks what this is about, just say that you don’t know. Then call me or Inspector Conklin and one of us will take it from there.”

“Mmmm-hmmm,” said McCall. “You know, I might have something for you.”

My head snapped around. I said, “And that would be what?”

Just then a group of four hotel guests arrived at the maître d’s station asking to be seated. McCall led them to a table that suited them, and when he returned, he stood with his back to incoming guests.

He said, "I wonder. Just between us, would you be interested in knowing about the woman Mr. Palmer was seeing earlier this week?"

Conklin said, "Well, yes, we would. What can you tell us?"

"All I know is what I see," Ryan said. "The lady has been staying with us since last Tuesday. I overheard her and Mr. Palmer talking . . . "

I saw another party of four heading our way. Ryan did a one-eighty away from them.

He said, "I don't know if she's checked out of the hotel, but I haven't seen her in a couple or three days."

A thought cut through my brand-new splitting headache. I picked up my phone and scrolled through the photo library.

"I want you to look at a picture, Ryan. If you recognize this person, you'll be helping us a lot."

I stood up and showed him an image of the "dumpster victim" prior to her autopsy at the morgue two days ago. Her body was draped in a blue sheet from her shoulders down and over her feet, but her face was exposed and mostly unbruised.

"Ryan? Do you recognize her?"

He staggered back a bit, reached out for something to grab on to and, failing that, regained his balance.

"That's, that's her. Caroline Ford."

CHAPTER 105

TIACO CARZA SAT in the copilot's seat aboard the multi-million-dollar Sikorsky UH-60 Black Hawk helicopter. Below them was the Pacific coastline. The pilot followed that beautiful, divided pathway of sand and sea, along the edge of San Diego, passing over the cities of Encinitas, Carlsbad, and San Clemente, which were so far below, they looked like handfuls of small wooden blocks tossed along the coastline.

Garza was not mechanically minded, but the pilot, his childhood friend Enrique Santos, had been trained by the US Marine Corps. He handled the collective, the throttle, and the pedals that controlled the blades and rear rotors. In short, Enrique knew what he was doing, and Garza liked to hear him talk about the bird itself.

Garza had learned that this particular Black Hawk was able to fly a long distance, about 1,600 miles, without having to refuel. This was excellent, since the Black Hawk was stolen, and stopping for fuel could end their mission.

However, if they used their fuel wisely, they could travel

far. As Enrique had told him, the chopper had special auxiliary fuel tanks mounted to external stores support system wings. This bird was loaded.

But as Enrique also had explained to Garza, all helicopters by their nature were somewhat unstable. So, extreme care had to be taken when lifting off and landing.

Now Enrique was jabbing a finger at him and then touching his headset, indicating that Garza should put his ear gear on so that he could listen to and communicate with him, cutting out the aircraft's racket. Garza clapped on the headset.

Enrique said, "Good man." And then he pointed out land features, asked after Garza's comfort, and told him that there were sandwiches and a thermos of cold water between their seats. The soft, choppy sound of the blades and the sunny view of the Pacific gave Garza great pleasure, and then his eyes closed and he caught up on some missed sleep.

Sometime later, when Garza had lost his sense of time, he felt a hand on his shoulder and came out of a deep dream. Paco, who was Enrique's nephew, was in the seat behind him.

He said, "Sorry, Señor Garza. We are almost there."

Garza saw it. The meandering route of the American River. And beyond that, a collection of buildings enclosed by a stone fence all the way around. They were only minutes away. Just minutes.

Garza opened the thermos, slugged down some water. Offered it to Paco, who drank deeply and handed the thermos back.

Enrique was too busy. He pulled up on a lever, and the chopper's altitude dropped.

"Tiago," he said, "look down and see what God made."

Garza pulled his phone from his pullover's pocket and snapped off some shots of the magnificent waterway and then spotted the walled cluster of buildings where they would be landing soon.

"Paco," he shouted out to the boy behind him. "Cue the music."

As the opening bars of Johnny Cash's greatest hit filled the cabin, the chuffing of the rotor and the blades sounded more like the chugging of a train rolling 'round the bend.

CHAPTER 106

YUKI FELT SURE that once El Gato testified today, the jurors would decide if Dario Garza was guilty or not before they even heard other witnesses, and before she or Credendino summarized their case.

El Gato was that important.

Not only was he an eyewitness to the murder of Miguel Hernandez, but he also had taken several photos and a few seconds of video of Dario aiming a gun at Miguel Hernandez's head.

Yuki had entered that material into evidence.

El Gato was young, unsophisticated, and he felt inferior to the slick killer on trial. Still, the jury had to believe him. That required him to have confidence and a good memory, and he had to be honest.

Days ago, El Gato had told Yuki that he had the shakes because of this responsibility. He said that he was afraid of public speaking even if he couldn't see the audience. And he was afraid of what Dario would do to him if he was found not guilty and set free.

After their talk, Yuki spent hours speaking with her witness over a secure Wi-Fi connection. She outlined the key points of his testimony so he would have notes if he got confused or overwhelmed. And she assured him that he knew what he'd seen and what was said.

Days after Yuki had begun the coaching sessions, El Gato thanked her for standing by him. It was important to him knowing that he was doing the right thing, that he was doing his part to put away the man who had killed his friend.

Nick Gaines had also worked to protect El Gato. He'd collaborated with computer techs to make sure that the network was secure, and that the voice modulation would fully alter El Gato's voice, that the facial mask would truly disguise him, that the shades and curtains would be drawn so as not to give away his location.

All of these preparations came down to now.

Court was in session. Judge Walden asked Yuki, "Are the People ready to introduce their first witness?"

"Yes, Your Honor."

The multiscreen computer was on and visible to the jurors and the legal counsel. The link had been sent, and Gaines initialized the connection so that El Gato was now seen sitting in an ordinary reclining chair against an eggshell-white backdrop. His mask was made of black latex, and his voice was clear and unaccented.

The bailiff swore in the witness and it was on.

"Mr. El Gato, you've recently told me you prefer just to be called 'Gato,' no 'El.' Is that correct?

"Yes, if that's okay."

"It's fine. Gato, please tell the court what you know about

the events of June 15th when you were a passenger inside Mr. Garza's car."

"Yes. Okay. Well, I want people to know that I am not a so-called popular kid like Mr. Garza and Miguel Hernandez, may he rest in peace. So, I was very excited to be going out with them. I knew Miguel much better, and he was in the front seat next to Dario, and he was, like, Dario's public relations guy."

"Can you expand on that, please?" Yuki asked her witness.

"Yeah, sure. Miguel was telling me that Dario was a sex magnet. That he had slept with a lot of girls and women, no strings attached, and Miguel said, like, 'Have you ever heard of snuff films? Well Dario does them without the cameras. It's the real thing.' "

Gato went on, saying, "Dario got very mad at Miguel for talking about him like that and to me. So, he pulled the car off the road and took a gun out of the glove box and told Miguel to get out of the car."

Yuki said, "Please go on," but this story had changed since Gato had told her about that June 15th. Wherever he was going, she couldn't stop him now.

"Dario was aiming his gun at Miguel," said Gato. "I got out of the car and I had my phone out. So, I took pictures of the gun in Dario's hand, and Miguel was in the frame, and I was getting scared, so I said, 'Dario, don't do it.' And he told me to shut up, so I said, 'Miguel, run,' and he did. And then Dario shot Miguel, and he turned his gun on me, so I jumped behind a parked car."

This was the first time Yuki had heard about a threat on Gato's life. She felt as if she were walking on a high wire between two skyscrapers without a net. There was no way to talk to Gato privately, even if she could pause his testimony now. Everything he said was being broadcast into the Judicial Building on the Folsom Prison grounds.

"And then what did you do?" Yuki asked.

"I watched him," said Gato. "He muscled Miguel's body into the trunk of the car and took off."

Yuki was absorbed in Gato's narrative and didn't see Dario rise from his seat. He yelled, "*He's lying! Nothing but lies!*" He shot Gato a threatening look, saying, "He did it. *I demand to testify!*"

Dario's outburst so derailed Gato's testimony that Yuki barely noticed Judge Walden banging her gun butt on the bench. Attorney Jon Credendino grabbed Dario by the arm and tried to pull him back into his seat. But Dario shook him off, insisting, "Don't I have rights? I want to speak to the jury."

A new sound filtered into the courtroom. It was a muffled rumble like that of an old car engine, and for a moment Yuki conflated the engine sound with the roar of Dario's car, which was in her imagination.

But this new engine sound was coming from the south and outside of the building, and it was not imaginary.

The jurors grabbed at and talked to one another, and even Gaines was shouting, "What the hell?" By then, everyone in the courtroom knew that something was going very wrong.

CHAPTER 107

YUKI WAS CONFUSED by the roaring sound. She knew everything about this building and couldn't figure out what the rumbling could be. Credendino was on his feet, with his briefcase in hand.

He yelled at her over the noise. "Yuki! You and Gaines get the hell out of here!"

"What's happening?" Yuki called back. But no one was listening to her.

Judge Walden shouted, "Court is adjourned. Everyone take the stairs and vacate the building!"

A guard came toward the counsel table, on his way to detain Dario Garza.

Panic erupted as something enormously heavy thumped onto the roof. Yuki looked up and saw the plywood ceiling start to splinter. The sounds were unmistakable now. A helicopter had landed on the roof of the Judicial Building, which had not been built to bear the weight of an aircraft.

Yuki crossed her arms over her head, and Nick Gaines

guided her toward the courtroom's side door, which was blocked by terrified jurors trying to get out.

Just as the logjam at the door began moving, the chopper broke through the ceiling of the makeshift courthouse, the body of the helicopter crashing to the floor, shattering the titanium blades and causing the floor to shimmy and buckle underfoot. And now the walls were vibrating.

Gaines was doing his best to hold on to Yuki as the motion toward the side door propelled them forward, causing her to stumble in her high-heeled shoes. Gaines put his arms around Yuki's waist and lifted her until she was wobbling on her feet.

"Hold on to me, Yuki. No. Leave the shoes."

Now gunfire came from the helicopter. Guards and court officers returned fire.

Nick had gotten her to her feet when the helicopter's engine finally cut out. The silence lasted for only a second, before being filled by the sounds of gunfire and the warbling shrieks of sirens coming through the gates.

Inside the courtroom, agonized wails could be heard from a man who was lying across a young man's body, crying out in Spanish.

"Son, son! Speak to me! Please. Damn it, boy. Speak!"

CHAPTER 108

YUKI LOOKED AROUND the courtroom, which was littered with helicopter parts and debris lying on the gray linoleum floor. The wounded cried out and begged for help.

Judge Walden stood in the corner, speaking with a Sacramento police lieutenant. A few yards away from her, Jon Credendino stared at Dario Garza's face-down, handcuffed body. He stepped aside as two guards lifted the dead man onto a stretcher and made for an exit.

Tiago Garza strained against his own handcuffs and the guards holding him, asking, "Where are you taking my son? Where?"

He asked this again and again until he was removed from the courtroom by the sheriff, who'd had more than enough.

"We're driving you both back to San Francisco. Now shut the fuck up."

Tiago Garza gave up the fight. As he was taken outside, he wept, apologizing in English and in Spanish to his dead son, to his wife, and because he was sobbing so loudly, there was no way of understanding him at all.

CHAPTER 109

LORRAINE O'DEA STOOD by our table at Susie's and commented that we all looked like hell. "Except you, Claire."

Claire laughed and Cindy joined in.

The bottomless pitcher of beer was on the table, along with the frosted mugs and corn chips. Yuki, Cindy, and Claire ordered. I was too preoccupied and just told Lorraine, "I'll have whatever Claire's having."

"Are you sure?" she asked me.

"Not quite. Claire, what did you order?"

"Chicken gizzards in jalapeño sauce."

Yuki said, "Lorraine, in your own words, what did Dr. Washburn order for her main course? Remember, you're under oath."

Lorraine looked at her order pad, flipped over one page, and said, "Dr. Washburn ordered steak fajitas. What now, Sergeant Boxer?"

"I'll have what she's having."

There was more welcome laughter. None of us had laughed in a while.

Cindy said, "Lindsay. The table is yours. We all want to know. Correction, we all *need* to know."

"I wish I could tell you. I've been told that no one knows where or how Joe is, or when or if he's coming home. He hasn't called, and of course he doesn't have a phone. I'm not giving up on Joe, nor is the FBI."

"Ohhh, Lindsay." Claire put her arm around my shoulders and squeezed me tight. I leaned into her hug while looking into Cindy's and Yuki's sad eyes.

More questions came at me, all caring but unanswerable. I cut it short by taking a nice long swallow of beer, and then I said, "Let's hear from Yuki."

As if she were jumping into the deep end of a cold pool, Yuki told us how just when the trial got going, a helicopter had landed on the roof, and caved it in.

The story had been dominating the news, and still, Yuki detailing for us her eyewitness impressions terrified me. To what extent had this bloody mayhem traumatized her and what effect might that have over time? At least, she said, they were lucky there were so few people in the makeshift courtroom—the body count was limited to the cartel members, including Esteban Dario Garza, and two prison guards. Yuki admitted to having been grazed by a bullet to the right thigh, Nick Gaines had then gotten her out of the "shooting gallery," and the mark of the bullet looked like a comet trail. Or a locomotive.

"I may get my first tattoo to embellish whatever scar it leaves."

Cindy asked, "Why a locomotive?"

"It's weird, Cindy. After the helicopter crashed through

the roof, I heard this song, coming from the wreckage. It was about a train and being stuck in Folsom Prison . . . I can't shake it out of my head."

Claire asked, "You mean that old Johnny Cash song, 'Folsom Prison Blues'? What, they were playing that in the cockpit like they thought they were in *Apocalypse Now* or something?" She shook her head and muttered, "Sick freaks."

Yuki said, "Dario's father, Santiago Garza, was one of the guys who came in the chopper. When I looked around, I saw him holding on to his dead son, absolutely stricken with grief." She continued: "Speaking of Tiago Garza, that bastard, he spoke to Brady once he was booked. And he wanted to talk about making a deal!

"No surprise. Although he's one of the worst of the worst—I have to tell you—he confessed. He's the one who stabbed Jacobi in the back. Yes—him! Why? Garza says Jacobi was shadowing him, so he returned the favor. Garza had heard about 'I said. You dead,' and had written that on the matchbook to throw the cops off. But he wasn't done yet."

Yuki stopped talking for a moment. Long enough to swallow down some beer and take a breath, and then she picked up where she'd left off. She told us how Garza had also confessed to killing Frances Robinson, the all-star romance writer, for no reason at all. And how he'd also killed the Orlofskys.

Yuki said, "But he had a reason for killing the judge, even though it was sick and twisted. It was to help his son. He told all of this to Brady, and he didn't want a lawyer. Said he just wants to die. That life is meaningless without his boy. And he told Brady, 'Dario was a great kid.' "

We all groaned, and Yuki said, "Your turn, Cindy."

Cindy was still chasing the "I said. You dead" story. She twiddled her fork and said, "Let's hear from Claire. Claire?"

"What? Why, Cindy? We all know you have a story to tell."

"It's not wrapped up yet," Cindy said. "I don't want to blow this true-crime drama before its time."

Claire booed and hissed and laughed at Cindy, who was laughing, too. Then Claire said, "All righty. I'm not afraid to blow the punch line." And then she sighed. "Gene Hallows called me today, seeing as I was the only person around. He said that you sent a table fork to the lab for testing, Lindsay. Brett Palmer's fork."

"True. I wrapped it in a cloth napkin and filched it while Cindy and I were having breakfast with him. What came back?"

"Well, Hallows said there was a match between Palmer's DNA on the fork and DNA found on Caroline Ford, our dumpster victim. Palmer's DNA was all around her mouth and on some of her clothes. It's a match to Brett Palmer, no doubt about it."

It was another link in the chain, but I was done. I hailed Lorraine and asked for my check. I leaned in and kissed all the ladies' cheeks—and surprised the hell out of Lorraine when I kissed hers, too.

I half hoped that my husband would be waiting to surprise me outside the café, but there was no Joe. It was a starless night, and when I remembered where I'd parked my car, rain was coming down.

CHAPTER 110

FBI SPECIAL AGENT James Walsh drove the armored black Escalade. I was in the passenger seat. We were both armed. There was a steel mesh divider between the front and back seats, and in the back seat was another FBI agent, a hefty one. His name was Brian "Buddy" Houghton of the San Francisco field office of the FBI. Today Buddy's assignment was to be a human restraint on our forthcoming passenger.

Walsh pulled the black Caddy to the curb in front of the Ritz-Carlton Hotel. James tipped the valet to leave the car right there, told him we'd be back shortly. Then we entered the hotel through its gilded doors.

I had spoken with maître d' Ryan McCall at eight fifteen this morning, and he had told me that Brett Palmer had a breakfast reservation for nine.

I hoped to hell Palmer hadn't changed or cancelled that reservation. I wanted to put this scum away.

Walsh said, "You okay, Lindsay?"

"Sure. Just hoping Brett Palmer is in the dining room."

I unhooked my badge from the chain around my neck and pinned it to my breast pocket. My gun was in its holster, and if all went to plan, Walsh and I would be out of this place and back in the Caddy with a serial killer in five to ten minutes.

Ryan McCall was at the maître d's podium. He smiled when he saw me, and I introduced him to Walsh and asked him to point out Palmer's table.

Ryan said, "He's at the small table in the far southeast corner. Blue jacket."

I looked across the floor to the southeast corner. The room was spacious, and the tables were nearly full. I didn't see Palmer. And then I saw him.

"He's half hidden by the pillar over there."

Palmer was alone, facing away from us, using his phone. Keeping in mind that if he suspected anything, Palmer might panic the moment he saw Agent Walsh—and not knowing if he, too, was armed—we made a simple plan.

We would approach Palmer's table from behind, me to the right, Walsh to the left. It wasn't a long walk to that table, but the dining room was an obstacle course. I was aware of Walsh as we crossed the room from different angles, and then we were both within five paces from the man in the blue jacket.

Palmer was reading his phone and had a plate of pancakes in front of him.

Walsh called out, "Brett. Hey, Brett. It's me, Jimmy Walsh."

Palmer turned around in his seat. He was clearly happy to see Walsh. He put the phone down, tossed his napkin to the table, got to his feet, and opened his arms to his old friend. Then he saw me coming toward him, too. And he recognized me.

"Wait," he said, looking from Walsh to me and back to Walsh as we closed in on his table. "You two know each other?"

"Yes, Brett, we do," Walsh said. "We're both armed, and neither of us wants this to get ugly. So just put your hands behind your back. Sergeant Boxer is going to cuff you, and we're going to walk out of the hotel together without a fuss."

Palmer looked around for an escape route, knowing that the only way out was through us.

He turned back to Walsh, saying, "What is this? What's going on here?"

I said, "Brett Palmer, you're under arrest. We can talk about the details in the car and at the station. Now. Hands behind your back."

Around us, people got up from their tables and moved away. Brett Palmer looked me in the eyes, his expression a mix of fear, anger, and then resignation. I had a feeling he'd seen similar expressions on the faces of the women he'd killed.

"Brett. Don't make us ask again."

"Why not? This is as good a time and place to die as any. Better than most."

Walsh closed the distance between himself and Brett Palmer in two steps. He was bigger than Palmer, taller and stronger. He grabbed Palmer's left arm and easily twisted it behind the man's back. I moved in and did the same from Palmer's right side, and then I cuffed him. James and I turned our prisoner around and marched him between the tables and out of the restaurant, right to the car.

CHAPTER 111

THE NARROW STREET in Monterrey, Mexico, was lined with colorful stucco housing and small businesses with large signs. Walking away from the police station, Joe Molinari, wearing his own clothes, looked around for FBI agents Dougherty and Ruiz.

If they weren't there to pick him up, he was screwed. He had no money, a phone with no service, no friends in Monterrey.

A car honked behind him and Joe turned his head. That dusty gray Buick from the 1960s might be them. He stood with his back to a wall as a man on a scooter blew past him. Then he picked out the car again. Was it them . . . ?

Yes. Dougherty was driving. Ruiz was in the passenger seat. Dougherty waved and Ruiz called out to him.

"Hey, jailbird. Get in the car."

Joe called out, "Hang on. Can I borrow a phone? I've got to make a call."

Ruiz called back, "Asshole. Get in the car."

*

I was home in bed when the phone rang.

I didn't recognize the number or the area code. It seemed like it was international. Maybe it was Mexico.

I answered with one tentative word and a question mark.

"Joe?"

"Hi, sweetie. How are you, my dear wife?"

I was flooded with emotion, love, anger, relief.

But I said, "Much better now."

Joe said, "My ride is here. Dougherty has lent me his phone. They're taking me to the airport."

I started asking him questions. Was he all right? When would he be arriving in San Francisco? Then I heard a shot.

Then another.

I was yelling, "*JOE!? JOE!?*"

He didn't answer. I heard a car and street noises and that was all. Then—thank you, God—Joe's voice came over my phone again.

"Lindsay, my partners put down some bad guys. We have to get out of here fast . . . "

Another voice came over the phone.

"Lindsay, this is Agent Ruiz. I'm one of the good guys. Stand by for a happy ending. Here ya' go, Joe."

Joe said to the quivering mess of me: "I'm here, Blondie. I'm good. I love you very much. And I'm coming home."

ACKNOWLEDGMENTS

WE WISH TO thank our advisors, researchers, spouses, and friends, who were with us, in fact and indeed, during the writing of this thriller. Phillip Birney, retired judge and chief trial attorney for his Sacramento law firm WFGH&B, has practiced law for more than fifty years. As always, we are grateful to the real-life Richard J. Conklin, assistant chief of police, in charge of investigations at the Stanford, Connecticut, PD. We are indebted to our good friend Michael Cizmar, special agent (retired) FBI and former private military/civilian contractor, Afghanistan. We also want to thank Robert Adkins. He is an aspiring writer, former Marine, aviation buff, and serial entrepreneur. And happy dances for our friend and doctor of Veterinary Medicine, Barbara Clayton, for saving Martha's life, one of fiction's longest-living canines. Dr. Clayton's practice includes dogs, cats, horses, cows, squirrels, and all varieties of birds.

We are lucky to have found Ingrid Taylar, a wildlife rescuer and stellar photographer who has worked with us as our researcher and guide around San Francisco for fifteen years. Thanks, too, to Heather Malcom Parsons, research scientist at the Cary Institute, and to Mary Jordan, who organizes and manages the flow of information with a cool head and steady hand on the controls and to whom we are grateful.

ABOUT THE AUTHORS

JAMES PATTERSON is one of the best-known and biggest-selling writers of all time. Among his creations are some of the world's most popular series, including Alex Cross, the Women's Murder Club, Michael Bennett and the Private novels. He has written many other number one bestsellers including collaborations with President Bill Clinton, Dolly Parton and Michael Crichton, stand-alone thrillers and non-fiction. James has donated millions in grants to independent bookshops and has been the most borrowed adult author in UK libraries for the past fourteen years in a row. He lives in Florida with his family.

MAXINE PAETRO is a novelist who has collaborated with James Patterson on the bestselling Women's Murder Club, Private and Confessions series, *Woman of God*, and other stand-alone novels. She lives with her husband, John, in New York.

Read on for a sneak peek
at an intriguing
New York City detective case . . .

THEN

CHAPTER ONE

Log 10/18/2018 18:58 EDT

Transcript: Audio recording

[Detective Declan Shaw] Maggie Marshall?

[Voice unidentified] Yeah. Fourteen years old. Student at Barrett's Academy. She went—

[Shaw] I know who she is. We've all had eyes out for her since the Amber Alert. Transcriber, for the record, Maggie Marshall was reported missing two and a half days ago by her mother. Last seen leaving school, and she never made it home. She's been all over the news. The whole city's looking.

Has she been touched or moved in any way?

[Voice unidentified] No. That's exactly how she was found.

[Shaw] Electrical repair team found her?

[Voice unidentified] Yeah.

[Shaw] Where are they?

[Voice unidentified] We're holding them at Eighty-Sixth Street.

[Shaw] Central Park Precinct?

[Voice unidentified] Yeah.

[Shaw] Okay, give me a little space. [*Clears throat.*] We've had rain the last three nights. She's lying in the mud about a foot off the northeast exterior wall of Blockhouse in Central Park. Severely bloated and discolored from exposure. Same shoulder-length brown hair as in the photo circulated. Do you have positive ID?

[Voice unidentified] We found her backpack in the bushes over there. Student ID card inside, and her name is written in a few of the textbooks. It's her.

[Shaw] We'll confirm ID back at the ME office, but high probability this is Maggie Marshall. Aside from her left sock, she is naked from the waist down. I have eyes on her jeans, other sock, and shoes, all discarded randomly about four feet from her body. Left sock is still in place. Her underwear is twisted around the base of her left foot. The ground immediately around her has been severely disturbed. Even with the standing water, maybe because of it, I can see deep indents on either side of her where it's clear he stood over her. There are also trenches approximately six to eight inches in width both on her sides and between her legs. They appear to be marks left by our unsub's knees. There are obvious signs of struggle—kick marks and gouges in the mud and dirt around her feet and hands, almost like... almost like she tried to dig out from under him.

[*Twelve seconds of silence.*]

I can see clear bruising around her neck consistent with a single hand—right—about the same size as mine. Thumbprint begins about one and a half inches to the left of the hyoid bone with the other four fingers rounding the right side. He used a single-hand grip. There is another large bruise directly above her navel, giving the impression he held her down with his knee. Additional bruising visible on the undersides of her wrists. If he strangled her with his right hand, he most likely pinned both her hands above her head with his left hand as he did it. It's clear from the surrounding ground she put up a struggle, but she didn't stand much of a chance. Both eyes are bloodshot. Petechiae in the right supports strangulation. This is an isolated spot, but why the hell didn't anyone hear her screaming? She must have screamed. [*Sniffle.*] Upon closer examination of her hands, her fingernails are caked with dirt from clawing at the ground. It's possible she scratched her attacker, but retrieval of trace may prove to be problematic. We've got a mess of footprints. We'll get elimination prints from all first responders and the crew that found her; maybe we'll get lucky.

[*Nine seconds of silence.*]

Where's that backpack?

[Voice unidentified] Over here.

[*Shuffling.*]

[Shaw] Transcriber, confirming for the record we've got a student ID in the front flap of the backpack for Barrett's Academy reading "Margaret Marshall." Three textbooks inside, got some math homework, and a paperback copy of *Little Women* by Louisa May Alcott. Library card being used as a bookmark at page ninety-seven also reads "Margaret Marshall."

[Voice unidentified] Detective, you'll want to see this!

[*Shuffling. Eighteen seconds of silence.*]

[Shaw] [*Shouted but muffled.*] Hey, get a few pictures of this before we move it. Up close and at a distance to establish proximity. Get these tracks around it too… [*Unintelligible, then muttered.*] Goddamn rain. We've got a Citizen watch. Old. Tan face with a tachymeter bezel. Brown leather stitched band. Looks like the top pin broke. Fell off the owner's wrist. It's a windup and still ticking, which means it was lost recently. Surrounding tracks appear similar, possibly the same as the ones around Maggie. Fresher, though. With the rain, less than twenty-four hours old.

[Voice unidentified] You think your guy came back?

[Shaw] Maybe he came back to move her or something. Could be he just wanted to revisit. They do that. Based on the tracks, looks like he stood here and…ah, there it is. Cigarette butt. Bag that.

[Voice unidentified] Fucker stood here and smoked?

[Shaw] Looks like it. There's an inscription on the back of the watch. It says "Lucky."

[Second voice unidentified] I think I know who that belongs to.

[Shaw] You do?

[Second voice unidentified] Robert Morter. Head of park services.

[Shaw] You recognize this watch?

[Morter] Not the watch, the name. *Lucky*. We've got a guy on grounds crew who goes by Lucky.

[*End of recording.*]

/MG/GTS

NOW

CHAPTER TWO

DECLAN SHAW WAS a good cop.

Is a good cop, he tells himself.

Because until he actually jumps, he is still living in the present tense. And that's the rub, right? Anyone can find a deserted subway station; anyone can inch up to the edge of the platform and wait for the next train. But how many can actually work up the balls to launch themselves from the platform to the tracks? There is a science to it. Jump too early, and you'll end up under the train. Too late, and you're bouncing off the side. The key is to be in the air, meet the metal head-on. No pain, just lights-out.

The Eighty-First Street station is a dirty little secret known to New York's Finest. It's directly under the Museum of Natural

History on the A/B/C lines, and once the museum closes for the night, the platform becomes a ghost town. Also a suicide hot spot. Few trains stop. Most speed up as they shoot through because there is a tacit understanding among engineers: If you're going to hit a jumper (and odds of that are high at the Eighty-First), you want to do it quick.

The faint rumble of a train in the tunnel, maybe a minute out.

"Do it, you pussy. You're bleeding all over the nice white paint." Declan's voice sounds foreign to him, and the second the words leave his mouth, he gets all self-conscious about it, like talking to himself is the craziest thing in his life at the moment, like *that* is where all concerned observers should be pointing their fingers.

The blood is coming from a cut on his hand. Nothing too serious, just a scrape. But enough to make a mess of the metal pipe above his head. The one he's been holding for the better part of an hour. Without letting go, he inches closer to the edge of the pavement and stops when his shoes are half on, half off the concrete.

Declan tests the angle.

The balance.

Tenses his leg muscles.

Relaxes.

Tenses again.

Draws an oily, humid breath, lets it coat his throat when he swallows.

The train grows louder.

In his fourteen years with NYPD, Declan knows of four other cops who died in this very spot. Probably holding the same damn pipe. There's no plaque or commemorative photo on the wall, but when he closes his eyes, he can feel them standing right there with him. He can hear them quietly counting down the seconds until that train emerges from the tunnel. He can feel their hands on him, ready to give him a little shove. A little encouragement.

Ain't no thing, one of them mutters. *We got you.*

Bend your knees. Makes it easier to push off, says another.

It was the next one that got him. The next one struck him like a gut punch, because it sounded like his father.

You best be sure. 'Cause there's no coming back.

"There's no coming back from what I've done either," he tells him. His voice carries a faint echo with all the tile.

The train grows louder. The pipe, the concrete, the air—all come alive with the vibration of it.

Maybe twenty seconds out now.

Declan has very few memories of his father. He was only seven when he died in a construction accident over on Forty-First. One that wouldn't have happened if the foreman hadn't been pushing everyone to put in double hours to hit some ridiculous deadline nobody gave two shits about all these years later. His father lost his footing—that's what they told him and his mother. Would he have slipped if he hadn't been on fifteen straight hours? Not his father. No fucking way. Declan can barely picture the man's face anymore, but his voice... his father's voice, that thick Irish brogue—it's as clear today as it was when Declan was a kid.

You don't run from your problems, boy. You grab 'em by the fucking throat.

"Pops, you don't know."

A drop of blood falls from his hand, hits Declan's cheek. He wipes it away and catches a glimpse of the small tattoo on the skin between his thumb and forefinger: *MM*.

"Sometimes you dig a hole and there's no climbing back out."

Lights visible now.

The train just beyond the tunnel bend.

Ten seconds.

Every muscle in Declan's body goes tense. His fingertips are electric. Every sound, smell, and color are amplified.

Seven.

When the train rounds the corner, it's moving so fast it has no business staying on the tracks, but somehow it does. Sparks fly. There's a harsh screech. Declan's eyes find the engineer and a moment later the engineer spots him, and for that quick instant, their gazes lock. Declan tells himself he looks stoic, hard. Resolved. But in truth, he can't hide his fear any more than the engineer can.

Three.

The world slows.

The engineer reaches for the emergency brake. His fingers curl around it. But he doesn't pull. They both know it's too late for that.

Two.

Declan closes his eyes.

"Sorry, Pops."

One.

Why everyone loves James Patterson and the Women's Murder Club

'It's no mystery why James Patterson is the world's most popular thriller writer. Simply put: **nobody does it better**.'
Jeffery Deaver

'**Smart characters, shocking twists . . .** you count down to the very last page to discover what will happen next.'
Lisa Gardner

'No one gets this big without **amazing natural storytelling** talent – which is what Jim has, in spades.'
Lee Child

'**Boxer steals the show** as the tough cop with a good heart.'
Mirror

'**Great plot, fantastic storytelling** and characters that spring off the page.'
Heidi Perks

'Patterson boils a scene down to the single, telling detail, the element that **defines a character** or moves a plot along. It's what fires off the movie projector in the reader's mind.'
Michael Connelly

'James Patterson is **The Boss**. End of.'
Ian Rankin

Have You Read Them All?

1ST TO DIE

Four friends come together to form the Women's Murder Club. Their job? To find a killer who is brutally slaughtering newly-wed couples on their wedding night.

2ND CHANCE
(with Andrew Gross)

The Women's Murder Club tracks a mystifying serial killer, but things get dangerous when he turns his pursuers into prey.

3RD DEGREE
(with Andrew Gross)

A wave of violence sweeps the city, and whoever is behind it is intent on killing someone every three days. Now he has targeted one of the Women's Murder Club . . .

4TH OF JULY
(with Maxine Paetro)

In a deadly shoot-out, Detective Lindsay Boxer makes a split-second decision that threatens everything she's ever worked for.

THE 5TH HORSEMAN
(with Maxine Paetro)

Recovering patients are dying inexplicably in hospital. Nobody is claiming responsibility. Could these deaths be tragic coincidences, or something more sinister?

THE 6TH TARGET
(with Maxine Paetro)

Children from rich families are being abducted off the streets – but the kidnappers aren't demanding a ransom. Can Lindsay Boxer find the children before it's too late?

7TH HEAVEN
(with Maxine Paetro)

The hunt for a deranged murderer with a taste for fire and the disappearance of the governor's son have pushed Lindsay to the limit. The trails have gone cold. But a raging fire is getting ever closer, and somebody will get burned.

8TH CONFESSION
(with Maxine Paetro)

Four celebrities are found killed and there are no clues: the perfect crime. Few people are as interested when a lowly preacher is murdered. But could he have been hiding a dark secret?

9TH JUDGEMENT
(with Maxine Paetro)

A psychopathic killer targets San Francisco's most innocent and vulnerable, while a burglary gone horribly wrong leads to a high-profile murder.

10TH ANNIVERSARY
(with Maxine Paetro)

A badly injured teenage girl is left for dead, and her newborn baby is nowhere to be found. But is the victim keeping secrets?

11TH HOUR
(with Maxine Paetro)

Is one of Detective Lindsay Boxer's colleagues a vicious killer? She won't know until the 11th hour.

12TH OF NEVER
(with Maxine Paetro)

A convicted serial killer wakes from a two-year coma. He says he's ready to tell where the bodies are buried, but what does he want in return?

UNLUCKY 13
(with Maxine Paetro)

Someone returns to San Francisco to pay a visit to some old friends. But a cheerful reunion is not on the cards.

14TH DEADLY SIN
(with Maxine Paetro)

A new terror is sweeping the streets of San Francisco, and the killers are dressed in police uniform. Lindsay treads a dangerous line as she investigates whether the criminals are brilliant imposters or police officers gone rogue.

15TH AFFAIR
(with Maxine Paetro)

Four bodies are found in a luxury hotel. Lindsay is sent in to investigate and hunt down an elusive and dangerous suspect. But when her husband Joe goes missing, she begins to fear that the suspect she is searching for could be him.

16TH SEDUCTION
(with Maxine Paetro)

At the trial of a bomber Lindsay and Joe worked together to capture, his defence raises damning questions about Lindsay and Joe's investigation.

17TH SUSPECT

(with Maxine Paetro)

A series of shootings brings terror to the streets of San Francisco, and Lindsay must confront a killer determined to undermine everything she has worked for.

18TH ABDUCTION

(with Maxine Paetro)

As Lindsay investigates the disappearance of three teachers, Joe is drawn into the search for an international war criminal everyone thought was dead.

19TH CHRISTMAS

(with Maxine Paetro)

Lindsay's plans for a quiet festive break are undone when she receives a tip-off that the biggest heist ever to hit San Francisco is being planned for Christmas Day.

20TH VICTIM

(with Maxine Paetro)

When simultaneous murders hit LA, Chicago and San Francisco, SFPD Sergeant Lindsay Boxer is tasked with uncovering what links these precise and calculated killings.

21ST BIRTHDAY

(with Maxine Paetro)

When a young mother and her baby daughter are reported missing, Lindsay takes up the investigation to find them.

22 SECONDS

(with Maxine Paetro)

Lindsay investigates an illegal shipment of drugs and weapons crossing the Mexican border, risking both her badge and her life.

23RD MIDNIGHT

(with Maxine Paetro)

Detective Lindsay Boxer must stop a copy-cat killer who's after fellow WMC member Cindy Thomas before it's too late.

THE 24TH HOUR

(with Maxine Paetro)

The Women's Murder Club must track down a high society killer before one of their own is targeted.

Also By James Patterson

ALEX CROSS NOVELS

Along Came a Spider • Kiss the Girls • Jack and Jill • Cat and Mouse • Pop Goes the Weasel • Roses are Red • Violets are Blue • Four Blind Mice • The Big Bad Wolf • London Bridges • Mary, Mary • Cross • Double Cross • Cross Country • Alex Cross's Trial (*with Richard DiLallo*) • I, Alex Cross • Cross Fire • Kill Alex Cross • Merry Christmas, Alex Cross • Alex Cross, Run • Cross My Heart • Hope to Die • Cross Justice • Cross the Line • The People vs. Alex Cross • Target: Alex Cross • Criss Cross • Deadly Cross • Fear No Evil • Triple Cross • Alex Cross Must Die • The House of Cross

THE WOMEN'S MURDER CLUB SERIES

1st to Die (*with Andrew Gross*) • 2nd Chance (*with Andrew Gross*) • 3rd Degree (*with Andrew Gross*) • 4th of July (*with Maxine Paetro*) • The 5th Horseman (*with Maxine Paetro*) • The 6th Target (*with Maxine Paetro*) • 7th Heaven (*with Maxine Paetro*) • 8th Confession (*with Maxine Paetro*) • 9th Judgement (*with Maxine Paetro*) • 10th Anniversary (*with Maxine Paetro*) • 11th Hour (*with Maxine Paetro*) • 12th of Never (*with Maxine Paetro*) • Unlucky 13 (*with Maxine Paetro*) • 14th Deadly Sin (*with Maxine Paetro*) • 15th Affair (*with Maxine Paetro*) • 16th Seduction (*with Maxine Paetro*) • 17th Suspect (*with Maxine Paetro*) • 18th Abduction (*with Maxine Paetro*) • 19th Christmas (*with Maxine Paetro*) • 20th Victim (*with Maxine Paetro*) • 21st Birthday (*with Maxine Paetro*) • 22 Seconds (*with Maxine Paetro*) • 23rd Midnight (*with Maxine Paetro*) • The 24th Hour (*with Maxine Paetro*)

DETECTIVE MICHAEL BENNETT SERIES

Step on a Crack (*with Michael Ledwidge*) • Run for Your Life (*with Michael Ledwidge*) • Worst Case (*with Michael Ledwidge*) • Tick Tock (*with Michael Ledwidge*) • I, Michael Bennett (*with Michael Ledwidge*) • Gone (*with Michael Ledwidge*) • Burn (*with Michael Ledwidge*) • Alert (*with Michael Ledwidge*) • Bullseye (*with Michael Ledwidge*) • Haunted (*with James O. Born*) • Ambush (*with James O. Born*) • Blindside (*with James O. Born*) •

The Russian (*with James O. Born*) • Shattered (*with James O. Born*) • Obsessed (*with James O. Born*) • Crosshairs (*with James O. Born*)

PRIVATE NOVELS

Private (*with Maxine Paetro*) • Private London (*with Mark Pearson*) • Private Games (*with Mark Sullivan*) • Private: No. 1 Suspect (*with Maxine Paetro*) • Private Berlin (*with Mark Sullivan*) • Private Down Under (*with Michael White*) • Private L.A. (*with Mark Sullivan*) • Private India (*with Ashwin Sanghi*) • Private Vegas (*with Maxine Paetro*) • Private Sydney (*with Kathryn Fox*) • Private Paris (*with Mark Sullivan*) • The Games (*with Mark Sullivan*) • Private Delhi (*with Ashwin Sanghi*) • Private Princess (*with Rees Jones*) • Private Moscow (*with Adam Hamdy*) • Private Rogue (*with Adam Hamdy*) • Private Beijing (*with Adam Hamdy*) • Private Rome (*with Adam Hamdy*) • Private Monaco (*with Adam Hamdy*)

NYPD RED SERIES

NYPD Red (*with Marshall Karp*) • NYPD Red 2 (*with Marshall Karp*) • NYPD Red 3 (*with Marshall Karp*) • NYPD Red 4 (*with Marshall Karp*) • NYPD Red 5 (*with Marshall Karp*) • NYPD Red 6 (*with Marshall Karp*)

DETECTIVE HARRIET BLUE SERIES

Never Never (*with Candice Fox*) • Fifty Fifty (*with Candice Fox*) • Liar Liar (*with Candice Fox*) • Hush Hush (*with Candice Fox*)

INSTINCT SERIES

Instinct (*with Howard Roughan, previously published as* Murder Games) • Killer Instinct (*with Howard Roughan*) • Steal (*with Howard Roughan*)

THE BLACK BOOK SERIES

The Black Book (*with David Ellis*) • The Red Book (*with David Ellis*) • Escape (*with David Ellis*)

TEXAS RANGER SERIES

Texas Ranger (*with Andrew Bourelle*) • Texas Outlaw (*with Andrew Bourelle*) • The Texas Murders (*with Andrew Bourelle*)

STAND-ALONE THRILLERS

The Thomas Berryman Number • Hide and Seek • Black Market • The Midnight Club • Sail (*with Howard Roughan*) • Swimsuit (*with Maxine Paetro*) • Don't Blink (*with Howard Roughan*) • Postcard Killers (*with Liza Marklund*) • Toys (*with Neil McMahon*) • Now You See Her (*with Michael Ledwidge*) • Kill Me If You Can (*with Marshall Karp*) • Guilty Wives (*with David Ellis*) • Zoo (*with Michael Ledwidge*) • Second Honeymoon (*with Howard Roughan*) • Mistress (*with David Ellis*) • Invisible (*with David Ellis*) • Truth or Die (*with Howard Roughan*) • Murder House (*with David Ellis*) • The Store (*with Richard DiLallo*) • The President is Missing (*with Bill Clinton*) • Revenge (*with Andrew Holmes*) • Juror No. 3 (*with Nancy Allen*) • The First Lady (*with Brendan DuBois*) • The Chef (*with Max DiLallo*) • Out of Sight (*with Brendan DuBois*) • Unsolved (*with David Ellis*) • The Inn (*with Candice Fox*) • Lost (*with James O. Born*) • The Summer House (*with Brendan DuBois*) • 1st Case (*with Chris Tebbetts*) • Cajun Justice (*with Tucker Axum*)• The Midwife Murders (*with Richard DiLallo*) • The Coast-to-Coast Murders (*with J.D. Barker*) • Three Women Disappear (*with Shan Serafin*) • The President's Daughter (*with Bill Clinton*) • The Shadow (*with Brian Sitts*) • The Noise (*with J.D. Barker*) • 2 Sisters Detective Agency (*with Candice Fox*) • Jailhouse Lawyer (*with Nancy Allen*) • The Horsewoman (*with Mike Lupica*) • Run Rose Run (*with Dolly Parton*) • Death of the Black Widow (*with J.D. Barker*) • The Ninth Month (*with Richard DiLallo*) • The Girl in the Castle (*with Emily Raymond*) • Blowback (*with Brendan DuBois*) • The Twelve Topsy-Turvy, Very Messy Days of Christmas (*with Tad Safran*) • The Perfect Assassin (*with Brian Sitts*) • House of Wolves (*with Mike Lupica*) • Countdown (*with Brendan DuBois*) • Cross Down (*with Brendan DuBois*) • Circle of Death (*with Brian Sitts*) • Lion & Lamb (with *Duane Swierczynski*) • 12 Months to Live (*with Mike Lupica*) • Holmes, Margaret and Poe (*with Brian Sitts*) • The No. 1 Lawyer (*with Nancy Allen*) • Eruption (*with Michael Crichton*) • The Murder Inn (*with Candice Fox*) • Confessions of the Dead (*with J.D. Barker*) • 8 Months Left (*with Mike Lupica*) • Lies He Told Me (*with David Ellis*) • Murder Island (*with Brian Sitts*) • Raised By Wolves (*with Emily Raymond*) • Holmes is Missing (*with Brian Sitts*)

NON-FICTION

Torn Apart (*with Hal and Cory Friedman*) • The Murder of King Tut (*with Martin Dugard*) • All-American Murder (*with Alex Abramovich and Mike Harvkey)* • The Kennedy Curse *(with Cynthia Fagen)* • The Last Days of John Lennon *(with Casey Sherman and Dave Wedge)* • Walk in My Combat Boots *(with Matt Eversmann and Chris Mooney)* • ER Nurses *(with Matt Eversmann)* • James Patterson by James Patterson: The Stories of My Life • Diana, William and Harry *(with Chris Mooney)* • American Cops *(with Matt Eversmann)* • What Really Happens in Vegas *(with Mark Seal)* • The Secret Lives of Booksellers and Librarians *(with Matt Eversmann)* • Tiger, Tiger *(with Peter de Jonge)*

MURDER IS FOREVER TRUE CRIME

Murder, Interrupted *(with Alex Abramovich and Christopher Charles)* • Home Sweet Murder *(with Andrew Bourelle and Scott Slaven)* • Murder Beyond the Grave *(with Andrew Bourelle and Christopher Charles)* • Murder Thy Neighbour *(with Andrew Bourelle and Max DiLallo)* • Murder of Innocence *(with Max DiLallo and Andrew Bourelle)* • Till Murder Do Us Part *(with Andrew Bourelle and Max DiLallo)*

COLLECTIONS

Triple Threat *(with Max DiLallo and Andrew Bourelle)* • Kill or Be Killed *(with Maxine Paetro, Rees Jones, Shan Serafin and Emily Raymond)* • The Moores are Missing *(with Loren D. Estleman, Sam Hawken and Ed Chatterton)* • The Family Lawyer *(with Robert Rotstein, Christopher Charles and Rachel Howzell Hall)* • Murder in Paradise *(with Doug Allyn, Connor Hyde and Duane Swierczynski)* • The House Next Door *(with Susan DiLallo, Max DiLallo and Brendan DuBois)* • 13-Minute Murder *(with Shan Serafin, Christopher Farnsworth and Scott Slaven)* • The River Murders *(with James O. Born)* • The Palm Beach Murders *(with James O. Born, Duane Swierczynski and Tim Arnold)* • Paris Detective • 3 Days to Live • 23 ½ Lies *(with Maxine Paetro)*